Anonymous

The Talk of the Town

A novel - In three volumes - Vol. 2

Anonymous

The Talk of the Town
A novel - In three volumes - Vol. 2

ISBN/EAN: 9783337348175

Printed in Europe, USA, Canada, Australia, Japan

Cover: Foto ©Andreas Hilbeck / pixelio.de

More available books at **www.hansebooks.com**

THE TALK OF THE TOWN.

A NOVEL.

IN THREE VOLUMES.

VOL. II.

London:

T. CAUTLEY NEWBY, PUBLISHER,
30, WELBECK STREET, CAVENDISH SQUARE,
1868.

THE TALK OF THE TOWN.

CHAPTER I.

It was the end of September then, and a warm time that year. When George returned from his walk next morning, there was nobody in the breakfast room. The windows were thrown back to let in the sweet air, which he, standing still, gathered on to his face. By and bye the butler brought an urn, and plates and toast. And then Mr. Tresham came, holding some letters. "Despatches for everybody," said he.

Helen entered, shook hands with George, and began making tea. He still kept away from them, with head bent, swaying the window case to and fro. Mr. Tresham looked at him amused.

'What a quaint chap that is,' thought he.— "Well, sir," he said, waiting, with a comical expression upon his face, "Are we to shake hands—or do you prefer to fight to the death?"

George gave a woeful smile and held out his cold hand. When he felt Mr. Tresham's honest squeeze, he shuddered a little, and was glad to turn away and stare out of the window again.

"Walk over to Shottisham with me, George?" said his host, while they were drinking their tea. "I promised to give Ramsay some hints about ventilating his new schoolhouse; the mistress will drive over and bring us back, I daresay."

George hesitated—on the point of telling them that he had made up his mind to say good-bye that day. But he had no courage at this time. What a fool he would look to those who could not allow for his alarms and fancies. He said, therefore, "Yes; I'd like a walk very much." And so the weight of deciding instantly, was off his mind; he must stay that day and await a better excuse for leaving.

They had a brisk walk together, and Mr. Tresham chatted away most of the time. George was very absent; he used, he believed, to set his tongue going and then leave it, while he returned in fancy to Helen. He wondered what was she doing

while they walked? Could he recall every word
she had said? She did not look angry that morning, he was sure of that.

He hardly knew how the next few days passed.
He used to go about with Mr. Tresham and hear
him talking about all sorts of things. In church,
when Sunday came, George and Helen held the
hymn books together. Then he was watchful not
to think about her, but with hazy eyes he used to
perceive her pink nails come out and settle on
the page of the book—like bees on flowers. And
this, in spite of himself. One Sunday evening
Helen left their pew while Mr. Tresham was put-
ing on his surplice, and quietly went into the
pulpit and put the candles in their sockets. It
was strange to see her there, and she blushed as
she did this, though there was only Farmer Birt
and his wife; the miller's family, and a few
cottagers, for a congregation. The clerk was ill
that evening, she told George later, and she feared
Mr. Tresham would be nervous if he found no
candles lighted when he came to read his Sermon.
How reverent she looked up in that place!
When service was over, George lingered in the
vestry.

"I make a good clerk, do I not?" she said.
And he inclined his head. "I believe you've

never half seen the Church. I ought to show you our lions. Have you ever seen this brass?"—

A portion of the chancel had been boarded off long ago, to make a vestry. By lifting up a piece of carpet laid on the tiles there, a very perfect brass was to be seen.

George, kneeling, read the inscription upon it:—

"Orate pro anima Nicola Tresham de Norton Armiger, qui obiit vii⁰ die Marco, Anᵒ. Dom., MCCCCLXXXVI."

She attended him while he read. "I can read it, too," she said. "There were always Treshams here, you know. It is a shame to cover it over, but Charles says it is preserved that way. The slab you are kneeling on is where that man's son is buried."

On it was written, "Underneath lieth buried the body of Sir Claudius Charles Tresham, Knight, of Norton Constantine," and when he died. 'These were, no doubt, brave and honourable men in their day,' thought George. 'It is something to bear this name. One would guard it from reproach, I am sure.' He was silent for a while and then he asked absently, "Will you be buried here?"—

She was not startled much. "Will you be buried at Sawtry, George? Sometime I t ink that is my home. I was very happy there. You were happy too when you were little?" she asked.

"Yes, very happy," said he. "And once unhappy." And then they walked back to the house. It was easy to talk. And also easy to stop talking. For they both thought of the same things.

In those days, when he was confused and wretched, he used often to say to himself, "It would be pleasant to die here. At the last I would beg that she might come. And I would tell her how I loved her. I might say that— were I quite sure of dying. I wonder would she come? Any one would forgive me—when I could not live again."

Meanwhile he prided himself on keeping his secret well. Sometimes he had a day's shooting and then he forgot Helen for a little. Mr. Tresham did not preserve; but General Rumbold had plenty of birds on his land—and, as he was not coming down till October—had sent a message begging Mr. Tresham or his friends to thin off his partridges as they liked. So George occasionally went with the general's keeper over the outlying fields. After a brisk morning's walk he would reason himself into a better humour. ' Will I never have sense,' he used to say tramp-

ing through the swedes, the pointers ranging
eagerly before him. 'Can't I conquer this
sickly folly of mine? One might be happy. How
beautiful these woods are and this clear air! I
have health and hope for my own, and I nourish
a blind and cruel tyrant—sure to slay me later.'
And yet it all came back when he remembered
this beloved face. Helen generally went out to
meet him returning. She liked to hear the account what he had shot and she was not afraid
to handle the birds when they were warm. One
day when he had been only an hour away, she
saw him strolling back with his gun on his
shoulder. He told her the pointers were lame or
something, and Foster's, the keeper's, child was
ill.

"Are you sorry to come back?" asked
Helen.

"No," he said, very gravely.   .

"And you have lost your sport.   Poor boy!"

He was in a cynical humour. "You are fond
of sport, too, Mrs. Tresham?"

"Why do you call me 'Mrs. Tresham?' I
think it's when you are in a bad humour. I call
you George. And you have not that confidence
in me. Perhaps I've done something wrong, and
so am not to be spoken to."

He walked along thoughtfully.—"You have all Æsop's fables in the library," said he.

"I suppose we have. It is a pretty book. Do not shoot me please. Turn your gun the other way. I dislike being shot!"

—"Do you remember about the boy and the frogs? What a nice story, Mrs. Tresham. Yes," he went on, in a low tone, "said the frog, 'what is sport to you, O boy with brown eyes! is death to us.' But Æsop knew nothing of human nature or he would have made it girls and frogs."

She smiled.

"So that is your verdict on Æsop?"

"Yes. And the girls would have said—'we're not throwing stones, we're only going to wash these pretty pebbles of ours quickly in the pond' —and gone on throwing them faster than ever."

"You are far too clever for me. How sad it is to be a stupid woman."

"Sad to be like you, Mrs. Tresham."—He murmured that, intending it to be for himself only. But she heard him.

"Perhaps it is," she said, wearily.

George felt as if his senses were leaving him. He walked on past the hall door and round the house with her. When they stood on the lawn at the back, "Where shall we walk, Mr. New-

march?" she said, raising her soft and beautiful
eyes towards his face.

"I don't know; I must put this gun away,"
he answered, dreamily, and turned towards his
room.

—"Are you in a good temper, now?" said she,
meekly, when the tether had drawn him back
to her again. "Will you row me in your boat
if I ask you, I wonder. I daresay not?"

They had not been on the water since that moon-
light night. At once he knew 'Now I ought
not to go. Now ought I to pause.' But could
he refuse her? She looked so strangely lovely.
And for the first time, a little anxious. And
imploring. He might reason aptly, but could he
leave her there alone—when she asked with be-
seeching eyes and an unusual flush upon her
cheeks? "Where shall I row you to?" he said,
out loud, while he was still undecided if it were
right or not.

"Oh! where there is shade. What a good
and gentle boy you have become now. Dear me,
I have forgotten to bring any work! So I shall
be obliged to talk to this boy all the time that
we are out."

They spent the next hour on the river, chatting away about everything; and gradually

George got back his confidence, and ceased to hear the reproaches spoken to him in the morning.

"It is time for me to go back and see if my child has had its sleep," whimpered Helen. "Suppose it were crying for me all this time, George? I should hate you, then."

So they returned, and he walked to and fro on the lawn till she came back from seeing the child. But she was tired of the river. "I shall go in and rest," said she; "where is my husband?"

But he was not to be found in the drawing-room. And then they recollected that he would not be back till dinner time. "You must amuse me all day, now," she said, as soon as she had fetched her work. And then Helen ordered him to tell her stories. But he knew none.

"I think we had a most sensible talk this afternoon," said George.

"Yes, but you are so cross now a days. I shall be afraid of you—always. Do you know, I used to think you a boy once; but now you call me by official names—"

"What are you working?" said he, evasively.
—"You call Lucy Felton, 'Lucy,' do you not?"

"Who is Lucy Felton?" asked he. "Oh! yes; I did forget, really. I call her 'Lucy,' to be sure;

but then one would as soon call her 'Tommy' or 'Bobby.' She must have some name."

"Oh! you would like to call me Tommy and Bobby, perhaps."

"No; but I mean first cousins, you know, are like household every-day words. And there's nothing—no meaning in the names one gives them."

"There! pick up my thread again, please."

He had to stoop down to do that, for it rolled on the floor. Helen meantime sat in a low arm-chair, looking steadily upon her work.

"You are making muslin curtains, are you not?" asked George.

"Muslin curtains! It's a collar."

"How stupid l am; but I mean it would be like muslin curtains, if you made enough of it."

"What a complete boy you are!"

"What a lot of rings you have!"

"Yes," said she, and stopped to look at them. One caught George's eye. She had often looked at it. And then they both were silent.

"Let us talk sense, now," said he, after he had paused a while to collect his strength, and indeed his ideas, as is said.

"Tell me—will you have more of those horrid examinations to pass now, George?"

" I don't know—yes. I have been very idle. I shall begin to read soon. How long have I been here ?"

" You mean you have been very much bored. You will tell Lucy Felton that I bored you fearfully, will you not ?"

She looked at him wistfully, and he returned her glance with dim and feverish eyes. He only shook his head. Bored ! Thinking of the rack on which he had been all these last weeks, he could have laughed at that distorted word.

" Read some of that book to me, since you will not talk," said Helen.

George took up a volume of Beattie, and commenced reading aloud. His voice was low and trembling, and he could hardly distinguish the words ; she, too, was thinking of something else besides the book. " There ! my thread has fallen again," Helen said, plaintively, " And my dear little knife, too."

George sought about for them. To do this he had to kneel before her chair. Her dress touched him.

" What a baby's knife," he stammered, opening a blade when he had found the thing, and coming close to her.

But Helen still kept her eyes fixed upon her

work. In it the thread twitched, and her
scissors she could scarcely hold.

"What tiny hands you have to work with,
Mrs. Tresham."—His voice was hardly audible,
and they, alas! could clearly hear each other's
breathing. "I would like—" he said, and touched
her finger with the point of the blade. As Helen
felt it cold and sharp, she gave a start, and thereby lightly pricked her skin. "Look what you
have done," she complained, languidly.

And George beheld with fear a little speck of
shining blood, growing slowly larger. Then he
no more remembered the things he had so often
resolved, being aware only of a despotic throbbing
in his forehead. And—wrestling not—took her
weak white hand and lifted it in his. There,
enamelled across his own brown fingers, it lay,
the hand soft, smooth, and mystical, sending
from each point of contact living threads, which
shook his arm through. "Have I hurt you and
cut you, dear," he said, harshly; for he raved.
"Oh! let me kiss your precious blood away."
He did indeed kiss it. "My darling!—my own
darling!"

Helen did not move again; her work dropped
down. The hand, instead of drawing back,
abode where he had taken it, and her foolish

head dropped back to avoid the sight of him, during all which he twice touched her little bloody fingers with his lips.

That done, George staggered up from his knees. Their culprit eyes met, and he looked like a man who sees some crime—hidden a long time ago—flaunted out again. His lips were white, barring that drop of wet blood, which she still saw glittering. Helen—who had no force of anger ready—through gazing on his face, by degrees acquired the horror of his own look. "Oh! wretched," she was able to say, slowly. "Now I know what you are. False! and false to him!"

Then she buried her wounded face in her hands, shutting out all trace of his presence.

Thus he was left standing before her, convicted by her words and accursed. His life, therefore, was over. He repeated stupidly what she had said. His thoughts came painfully and slowly. Not one drop would have flowed, had his thoughts been blood in arteries.

He had long known that he was a coward and a traitor. Now she knew it too.

" You are quite right," he repeated humbly, and then he shuffled away from the miserable room. He was a coward and he now fled away like one. A choir of cruel noises performed in his ears, as he went between the pretty rooms. Until he stopped in the hall, he hardly saw the way under his feet. Muttering, 'I shall never come here any more,' he took his straw hat and went out into the soft sweet air. As he left Norton gates far behind him, and tired himself with walking, that which had happened gradually unfolded itself more plainly to his mind. He now recollected, bit by bit, the shameful and dishonourable thing he had done. He hoped at first by the bitterest self reproach to atone for a thing which he knew was sweet; and this satisfied him for a while. But when he had allowed this remorse to have its way, he found that he was cheating himself. What right had his conscience to put in its say—when he well knew that he loved her, in reality, more than he did life? He could choose. He would choose this. She knew it now; there was triumph in that, and besides a conviction kept haunting him, that her hand had rested wilfully in his, and that, even as he had looked at her, so she had looked at him. Scarcely daring to think of it, he still remembered how— half fondly—she had spoken in the morning. Yet he had none the less cut himself off from her. She must now certainly abhor him. Could he expect her to be a Criminal, as he was—lost to all sense of honour? No, she would surely never speak to him again, and *he*, too, would learn how his guest had repaid his hospitality. This was the pleasant course of lofty and helpful friendship which he had once mapped out. The only guide and friend he had ever wished for was lost to him utterly, and cursing himself and his fate, he tramped on and on. The road, when he looked about him at last, led over a bleak common; he was in the centre of a flat stretch of gorse and heather—towards the horizon, finished by a black frame of fir trees. Unable to remember where he was, he wandered on for a mile farther, till by and bye from weariness he stopped to lean against a gate. He had left, meaning to see Norton Constantine no more; no matter whether his absence would seem wild and rash or not. She had told him *what* he was. Long he stood shaking this gate on its fastenings, and sighing fit to break his heart. At last he looked back. There were the well-known gravel pits and this was the Farwell Abbas Road. So then he knew where Norton lay; not very far away, and she was his darling still. Could he go elsewhere and lose her, when he loved her alone. And then grow old, and still longing for her to be his love, never grow any better. To be henceforth without Helen—and yet none the more clear with God after all! Since she repelled him, the decision was not all in his hands. Had it been possible for her to sin he would not have had the heart to tell her his love. But despised and dreaded as he was, it was safe to go back once more. So he slowly turned towards the enchanted Castle, and as he took the backward road, his feet were heavy and he hung his head. Dread went with him and he shrank from what awaited him. He was to go like one who passes from a warm lighted room out into the dark winter's night. To be henceforth alone with sin, given up to it; and his only counsellor, the Devil, to have power for ever over him, never more to be vanquished in prayer. The banished feel of it! And this was what being with Helen meant. But they might have his inheritance and toss his soul about among them. For his dear was waiting there. So gentle, so adorable; perhaps ready to love him—to love him. And Heaven declined down very close to him, when he imagined this last state. Nearing the house, he remembered how once that day he had believed he never again would see his beloved in the world; and now he was quite sure to see her shortly, if only for a little minute.

Safe in the quiet house once more, he laughed; saying, " My hat must rest on those pegs a while longer." Then he sauntered towards the drawing room. Mr. Tresham sat there with a heap of books by his side, on a sofa, which he had drawn to the window to catch the last of the twilight.

" Well, George, I've done my fourteen miles," said he, hardly looking round. " I hear you lost your shooting. I met Foster in the village. I had such a fight with our friend the Curate at Bexted, about a passage in George Herbert, I've been looking for an hour, and I can't find it now even. I know I'm right though," and he repeated the lines.

George, by a strong effort, swung his ideas back to the subject. " It is in his life, I think you'll find," he said, slowly, " not in any of his poems."

" Ah! perhaps you're right. I wonder could you pitch on the place for me, by this light?"

George took the book, and while he turned over the pages with stupid eyes, Helen glided into the room—dressed for the evening, and wearing one bright flower in her hair. Yet she was looking haggard and ill. She went quietly up to her

husband and gave him a kiss of greeting. The
two men were looking over the book together
—George's hot and throbbing head only a few
inches from her husband's. Yet it did not seem
to strike her as very treacherous to kiss him.
She had, perhaps, to do many little things like
that. George felt the kiss go right through him.
It was really a harsh and bitter sound to him.
It was now getting dark. As he had time to
think, he said, judging her impartially—' I miss
the servant with his ear struck off—alone.'
" Don't mind dressing, boy," said Mr. Tresham.
George and Helen stood silent, not daring to
look at each other: this was the beginning
of shame and silence for him.

By the candle-light at dinner Helen appeared
to have grown years older since the morning ;
and even her husband quietly remarked that she
was pale and out of spirits. However, he talked
away as a hungry cheerful man does, and George,
though he bound his thoughts down to whatever
the talk was about, made random answers. The
evening dragged on miserably ; till at last half-
past ten came in pity, and George went towards
his room.

In the passage he heard the rustling of a dress.
But he was hanging down his head, and could

not turn quickly round ; hence did not so much as raise his eyes until, thought he, "This is a silk dress, coming close to me, not a servant's cotton one." And when, at last, he turned and held up the light, Helen stood close to him.

" I want to speak to you," she said, trying with painful efforts to speak in a firm voice. "Will you come and talk to me—to-morrow morning—by the boats ? You will not come, I know. At seven I shall be there ?"

" Yes, yes, Helen," he said, being quite daunted by her eager and wretched manner. " I shall come at seven; and wait for you as long as you wish."

And then, quietly as she had come, the little creature went back. How wan and tired she looked! Until he had heard her voice, George had doubted if she were alive. For he might have easily seen her as a Ghost.

Then came another of his nights—backwards and forwards on the carpet of his pretty room, torturing himself. But in his inmost heart he had thrills of keenest pleasure during this new walk up and down. And now, though still accusing himself, he conceded that his remorse must be smothered for the present—till he had seen her this once more, at all events. So much

for him.   Here was the room in which, not long
since, he had sworn to put away the temptation
of loving Helen.   Now he loved her without one
trace of disguise.   The future was all blotted for
him ; but he might love her this once, and be thus
king of the world for a little while.   After this
walk he lay down to sleep.

At five o'clock he jumped up.   "If I sleep
again I shall sleep too long," said he, trembling.
And so he dressed quickly, and went out towards
the river.   He entered the boat-house, and there
he considered, saying " If I go to sleep in this
place, I'm not likely to sleep too long."   So he
lay down on a hard bench, and dosed till seven
o'clock came.   But the person expected was late.
At last the lawn of her house sprang into life,
and she came upon it, coming his way.   The sun
at this hour shared half the grass lawn with the
shadow from the shrubbery on the eastern side.
Dew diamonds twinkled still on the tips of the
blades of grass, and the fallen, crumpled leaves
were wet and shone like glass.   Most people are
dull and sleepy at that hour.   But these two
never thought of yawning. Such a quaint couple !
In the foggy morning by the river, by themselves.

It was going to be a hot day, and across the
water some women were already in the fields at

work ; a cart rumbled over the bridge, its heavy
wheels echoing in a way to catch the ear.

" Good morning," Helen said, wearily, and
then she turned her head away, not having yet
looked him in the face. " What had I to say to
you ?"

For his part he stood adoring her with his eyes,
' Let me look well,' thought he, ' that I may
remember her face when I am alone.'

She—" I have been so ill all day. And I cried
as much as I could all last night. Why did you
not come back when I called to you in my
drawing-room ? You wish that I should be ill,
and should always cry ?"—

He—" I have not made you unhappy. No, no,
no. Impossible. I *could* not."

She—" Did you hear me call and ask you to
come back, yesterday ?—after you cut my hand.
I had something to say to you ?"—

He—" No. How could I hear ? I was then,
too miserable."

She—" Do you know—I shall always hate you
in future ?"—This she said very sadly. " If I had
known what you were, I would never have liked
you in the least."

He—" I have been more miserable than you
have, Mrs. Tresham. I meant to go away and

never see you again, yesterday. But when I was some way off—Helen, I *could* not." 'Has she confessed to him,' he marvelled. ' She cannot keep my treachery from him!' And there they stood uncertain, at the early hour when many are turning over to have their last sleep.

"Yes, 1 cried all night after I saw you standing close to him," she said, mournfully. "You made me wretched by your cruel act. And you will tell Lucy Felton, that you kissed me on the hand," she murmured, looking up with apparently sad eyes. But by and bye a smile, which fatally finished her words, stole upon Helen's face. "Why did you kiss them?" she murmured.

George listened attentively, and for some time hung his head down, as though he sought for his reason. "They are so white," he said. When he heard his own voice and saw her still there, he knew that he was certainly to be lost for ever. "Shew them to me now. And forgive me," said he. And as she let her delicate hands hang listless, he took her fingers one by one again, whispering "Precious, precious hands!" They were now his entirely.

Thus they stood close together; but saying little. It was more than he had counted on—when his own voice faltered and his eyes would

stare open, like a child who sees a sudden streak
of moonlight on a wall—to find his dearest
trembling like himself; in all respects weak as
he was. His limbs were heavy with fear; but
he could not let her go away from him. His
shaking arm he put round her, and then with
wonder felt each sigh of hers press in and out
against his sleeve. Often and often he had noticed
the circle of her puny waist. Here this, then,
at last was the feel of it.

But Helen had twisted herself from him, and
stood a little way off, looking on the ground.
In a short time she came, not looking at him.
" Stay, and don't go away now," said she aloud,
and as if to herself. His heart fluttered more
than before, for she stood so close that she touched
him. Then, for the first time, he stooped a little
and kissed her forehead, which was her husband's.

They were not in this place long. Quite close,
Helen was ten times dearer and more adorable
than he ever could have imagined of himself.
Lest she should suffer from seeing, he had shut
her eyelids down with his finger. " You will go
away and marry Lucy, after this," was all she
said. He laughed. In a while she had to go
back. He watched her away across the lawn.
The gardener's bell rang for the workmen's break-

fast. She had some breakfasts to make for him
and *him*, too, and he remained dreaming. Well!
the world was full of bustling people, aiming at
this or that. And they got it and triumphed. Or
lost it, and were cast down. But he was well
above them all, for he owned everything worth
the having on Earth. He walked to and fro
before the drawing-room windows, thinking she
was far dearer this day than yesterday.

In the breakfast room there was the accuser to
be met and talked to again. 'Peace, now, to
my poor remorse,' thought George. There had
to be friendly talk got ready for Mr. Tresham;
and a smiling face ever forthcoming—to screen
what his darling and himself bore on their minds.
That was a very wretched work. But sickening
or not, it must be got through now. The best
plan was not to think at all. One can shut out
wretched things, if one tries hard.

After this he managed to stupify himself to
everything, save what concerned his dearest. The
days passed by, remembered just by what she said
from hour to hour. She, from having been the
weaker at the first, came by degrees to rule him
with her lightest word, now that he was grateful
to her, and considerate, and humble. Some days
she would vex him with little coolnesses; and it

did not take much to send him away miserable. Mr. Tresham kept him busy also, and planned expeditions from time to time; then he and George had readings of the classics together, which kept Helen and her votary apart. George, in those hours, used to marvel at his own patience, and at the skill wherewith he could bend himself to talk and attend to books while his thoughts were off on their own precious errands.

Helen's little body and soul were, together, a singular place for Deadly Sin to settle in. There were new things to be discovered about Helen every day, which made people increase in love for her. George could not help being contented and happy when she petted him; and watching her ways and words took up all his time. None therefore remained for remorse. Furthermore, he at this time gave up a former practise of balancing the week's results with his conscience, and making some attempt at a settlement, confession, and repentance. He suffered still when he was alone, and despised himself savagely at times; but he always came when she whistled, and she was there to console him with her laughs; and a kiss, ultimately.

George had by degrees acquired a kind of

cunning; finding out the exact way to change his
voice and manner, and make some careless
remark, when Mr. Tresham came up to them.
He took a miserable pride in doing that ably:
but about this time he also began to fear Mr.
Tresham.   Not physically; but the recollection
of his friend's face could at any time make him
tremble all over.   This, notwithstanding, that he
held his title most clear to be the possessor of
Helen's love. It was a bit of George's chivalry ever
to speak well of Mr. Tresham; what had he ever
done but kind deeds?   The fault was not his
that he was not worthy of this pure and perfect
darling.   George now confessed the power of
affinities on many occasions.

Although he had at length found a consolation
in the lofty passion which he said usurped all his
being, still self-respect, which had been among
his treasures, was languishing: he lost all ambition as well.   Once praying to remain fervent in
spirit, and to be before long ready for his Master's service, he now saw all that clouded over.
He was substituting for his long anticipated life
at Sawtry the *cultus* of his plaintive little Diety.
He was dear to her, no doubt, but still sighs, and
kisses, and such like were given to him sparingly,
and he had a right to be jealous now and then,

and tortured himself, saying 'she is not really mine.' But thoughts like that were sacrilege. So pure, so gentle a darling was still truly sacred in his eyes.

One morning he was musing to this effect: Mr. Tresham had gone away for some hours, and George and his hostess were taking the air in front of the house. After a while Helen, who was going about picking flowers from flower-beds, saw a yacht's dingy full of smart people coming up the river. "Oh, my! What shall I do?" she cried. "Heaps of visitors!"

George groaned wearily, and then vowed that he would go off and hide. It was the Baillie Baillies, landed from their yacht. And Mrs. Baillie Baillie had as usual a couple of young friends with her. One was a little soldier, supposed to be in captivity to her charms; the other, a Miss Dash, or Blank, or Anybody—who seemed to be very fast in her manners. Mrs. Baillie herself had been to Norton before, and George and Helen said that she was a noisy, harmless, ugly, little woman.

She had ever so much money; she had a double name, which besides being a great pleasure to her, impressed many, and arrested attention.

She liked to be thought fast; and loved the towns where people go for the purpose of yachting.

A woman's society in any shape was a change to Helen, who, we see, has had nobody to talk to but George Newmarch for ever so long; and while shaking hands, Helen took in at a glance, what a lovely suit of white serge, with black braid as broad as the road, Mrs. Baillie Baillie had on. Besides, a charming tarpaulin hat, with the yacht's name in gold letters, as big as theatrical posters, round it; then, three or four lockets, the size of oranges, lavender kid gloves, and a few bracelets, all for yachting in.

"My dear Mrs. Tresham," said she, "so well really, and the place looking perfectly divine, and Mr. Tresham out, I'm so sorry. We've had such a scorching pull up this jolly river of yours, a hundred miles I'm sure. We were becalmed in Leet creek, d'you know; and the poor men had to pull us all the way—and our crew are so stout, poor fellows; aren't they, Edward?"

"What a case of distress!" said shy Helen, laughing. "It's so good of you to come. I'm quite buried alive here, Mrs. Baillie. Won't you come in?" and so forth.

Up swaggered George; and while he was being

civil to them, he being a man, noticed that **Mr.
Baillie Baillie** wore a velvet suit; and a great
pink tie through a gorgeous ring, bearing an
enamel of a fox's head, as big as any Mr. Bur-
bidge ever bred. And glossy boots and shirts
of gorgeous kind.

'He seems a snob,' thought George, 'I'm
sure he has got lots of money, one can see that by
his contented eyes. The other looks like a gentleman.' Said George to him, " Why, aren't you
Parnell?"

" Yaeth," answered the little man, who had
not ceased to pull about his shirt cuffs.

" I remember you at Eton. You were at Woo-
ley's, weren't you?"

" Yaeth. I don't remember you."

" Newmarch."

" Oh! you were at Maryatt's."

" No; my brother. You and he were swished
three times in the same week, for bathing in the
master's weir—I remember."

The boy opened his great eyes. He was about
as big as a child of fourteen. He was perfectly
helpless, and went about like a little calf; but
was so pretty, notwithstanding; such lovely eyes,
such a little scarlet mouth, and such brown
curly hair.

George saw Helen looking with wonder at him.
They were all in good spirits, talking away.

"Why, haven't you archery, Mrs. Tresham?"
says Miss Anybody.

"And croquet?" says Mrs. Baillie Baillie.

"And lawn billiards, Mrs. Tresham," says
Miss Anybody. "and you could have such jolly
skating here in winter we skated at Walking-
thorpe all night by torchlight and some of the
193rd skated so beautifully do you know Captain
Dash? he's so good looking! and Mr. Dash
his father's a baronet but he's very plain but I
like the cavalry don't you? they all have drags
I sat on the 111th's drag at Ascot and Captain
Featherby would insist he had bet me twelve
dozen pairs of gloves to a kiss that Salathiel was
placed—and only three numbers were up all the
time! I didn't know it, of course does your
cousin always live here with you?"—

"But croquet; what a lawn, too, for it," says
Mrs. Baillie Baillie.

"Is it nice?" asked Helen. "We shall get
some Geor—Mr. Newmarch."

The other lady smiled innocently, and went on
chattering. "I must take some of that lovely
myrtle," she said, by and bye. "How it covers
the house! But we can't stop for an instant, you

know, Mrs. Tresham. We must be rushing back to the yacht."

" Oh! Mrs. Baillie. When I never see you from year's end to year's end. Indeed, it's too bad."

" But you know we only just rushed up here. Isn't the wind going to drop with the sun, Edward?" she appealed to her husband. "Mr. Parnell will be late for his leave, too. Won't you, Bobby?"

" Yeth, and get tried by court martial. And be reduced to the rank of a sergeant-major, and flogged," said he.

" Swished, you mean," suggested George. " The sun, Mrs. Baillie, has a trick of setting at any moment, here; there's no depending on it two days together."

" Dear! dear me," says the lady. And her husband declared the wind was beginning to die even then. " We want you so much to see our dear little yacht, Mrs. Tresham. Won't you come back and have luncheon with us? I know you have a boat, and your cousin will bring you back," she said, making everything proper.

After a little persuasion, this was agreed to, and they divided, George and one of the yacht's men taking the dingy. " You were in lower

boats, I know," says he, to Bobby Parnell:
" You can pull stroke in the other boat here."

And as Helen was in that boat, he had the
satisfaction of seeing her chatting to the little
soldier all the way to the yacht, which lay in
the mud-locked channel, right down at Leet.

They had a fine luncheon on board. Everyone
was made to drink champagne, which was so nice
after the great heat that it surely could not betray.

Helen did as they all did. Bobby Parnell said
nothing intelligible, but lisped and made a row.
Mrs. Baillie Baillie could not get him to look at
her, and wishing to show him off as her special
pet boy, found him perfectly hopeless and un-
tractable.   He would only make friends with
Helen ; she and he kept putting geraniums and
leaves in each other's champagne.   We may suppose he thought her more of his own age; anyhow,
these champagne cups and so forth immediately
got into his head, and he then became prettier
than ever. Helen began to get flushed, too. She
and Mrs. Baillie Baillie did all the talking.

George and the owner of the yacht had struck
up a great friendship, and were smoking on the
deck. 'I wish I were a snob,' mused George,
cynically ; 'and could afford such cigars as these.'

The sailing master declared it was time to be off.

How everyone laughed, putting Helen and George into the boats. When they said 'good-bye,' she was in the highest spirits. But George was in somewhat of a savage humour. Perhaps it was at having to scull, even an angel, three miles home in the sun. Brooding over the day to himself as they slid along between the reeds, ' She is not one bit good,' he repeated, ' and not what I thought her. Another idol broken ! and my conscience scourging me because I thought of her ! Only a fit friend after all for Bobby Parnell—the worst boy that ever we knew at school.'

Yet she had put him in a good humour again before they were half way back. Why should his jealous temper interfere with her harmless love of fun, and of a tiny bit of excitement? —" Why shouldn't I pet the little boy ?" Helen pleaded. " He kept asking me how old I was, and who you were. And if you were my husband. I'd like to have a little son of that age, George."—

And, over the thought of this, Helen grew almost pathetic. And it is true that her admirer was most easily soothed. But he remembered that hot day often, in after times, when asking himself whether she were really as good and as perfect as he had believed.

CHAPTER II.

ABOUT that time there was the usual September horse-racing at Doncaster; and on the morning of the great Yorkshire festival, it became known in the town that Mr. Arthur Felton's valet, on going to wake his master in the morning, had found him stretched on the carpet—quite dead. The lamented gentleman had been one of a large and brilliant party assembled at a neighbouring country house for the race week, and, being seized by a fit in the night, alone and before he could summon aid, had breathed his last.

This was very sudden, and it cast the amount of gloom which might have been anticipated. The owner of Rushworth was a man well-known to the elder generation, and he had his own kind of mourners. In the newspapers there was the customary notice taken. "Otis," in the sporting column of the "Morning Pillar," devoted a graphic little paragraph to the sad event. And the " Druid " jerked out an obituary of Mr. Felton in the next " Omnibus "—so full of italics, and void of stops, that one could not possibly make out from the tangle of sporting jargon, whether it was " ould Isaac Walker," who, by a double inversion, had bred the deceased gentleman from " Sea Pink ;" or some great coursing celebrity who had bought him—a short-horn yearling at Middleton-One-Row stud farm—and then " crept up from the distance," and won some tremendous finish on his back.

Thus Mr. Arthur Felton's place would be empty in future. He was one of the connecting links, it was said, between the men of fashion of the early part of this century, and the more modern school of sportsmen. He was a well-known fre- quenter of Poodle's, and of Grey's famous club in the same street; he was a member of the Jockey Club, too ; and—if he had not died and been buried—would have been a Steward by rotation the following year.

At Rushworth we can fancy there was grief of quite another kind. At all events, a day or two after the news came to Norton, George was sum- moned to attend the funeral. Bertram could not or would not go, Lady Adelaide wrote, and one

son, at least, must be there.   Then he must
leave Helen! Sometimes now he was so wretched
and desperate that no new blow could surprise
him much.

"We shall see you again, George, as soon as
there is nothing more to keep you at your
aunt's?" Mr. Tresham said to him, when he heard
that their guest must leave.

But George hesitated from fierce pride to accept this offer.

'I cannot force myself on people,' he thought,
even though he might lose Helen for ever by
going away. 'Well! so be it. If it comes to
that, I can always drown myself.'

Mr. Tresham, however, would have no denial.
"If we didn't want you, my boy, we would
tell you so; wouldn't we, Helen?" he said.
"Besides, you have to go on coaching me in my
Greek for ever so long still."

So it was settled that he was to return
the moment the funeral was over.   And yet,
leaving, even for a few days, was torment.   When
he stole a last interview with Helen, and lingered
over their parting caress, "Don't think me
foolish, darling," he said; "but it's just exactly
like cutting out my heart, and leaving it here till
I come back."

She was always sorry when he was sorry. "I will cry nearly all day while you are at Rushworth," she whispered.

Then he went off to the house of death, and was asked to be one of the chief mourners, no doubt. He looked sad enough in truth. His father was there; but he and George had little to say to each other. As for Lady Penelope and his cousins, they were visible only for a moment, and Lucy had cried till her eyes were, now at all events, dark enough. He never ceased thinking of his own sorrow, which was alive—while this for the dead man was to pass and be forgotten, and brooding thus made him silent and abstracted; that did for grief for his uncle's death, and so nobody noticed him.

At last he could leave Rushworth. And what a time the return journey seemed to take! The hours could be so long when they tried. He was too early at every railway station, and had to wander up and down platforms, fretting to be off. Coming near Norton again his spirits rose higher each mile of the drive. He chatted away to the coachman now about all sorts of things. He had not been happy for a long time; now he was perfectly happy for a while. It was strange to him that every one did not feel light of heart nearing that place; but George was in doubtful favour with the coachman, and indeed with all those below stairs at Norton. What was he doing there all this time? they wanted to know. So the coachman was not light of heart.

When the two poor lovers met again Helen was looking very anxious and careworn. How had she attained to this expression of countenance? We do not stay with her, and do not know; but George said to himself, seeing her thin cheeks, that he loved her only the more for that. "My precious!" he said, when they could steal half an hour to themselves, "I love the little lines in your face better than other people's smiles. Because those weary and sad looks come from thinking about me, I am sure."

"Darling!" she murmured.

—"When I was away," he said, "I was so dull and wretched; I used to go up to my room and try to sleep half the day: by that means I had fewer hours to live, and feel, and be wretched."

"I cried very often," she said. "Do you know —one thing terrified me. Shall I tell you?"

"Tell me what it was, my own."

"Well. . . . You won't laugh at me? . . . . . Why, you know, my maid came. And because I was crying—she talked: and at last she said 'she knew I was crying for you'; she said she would go away from me—if you came

back. I told her I would kill her if she said
that any more."

What could he say, even though this cut him
to the heart? " My precious, try not to be unhappy," he whispered, when he had been too
long silent. Yet to think, too, of his delicate
little Helen killing her great sturdy Yorkshire
maid!—" You know she is too fond of you to say
anything," he faltered.

It was not much of a stay to lean on, though.—
Helen whispered, " Mrs. Blacker said she knew
that I loved you, and I asked her why she thought
so. Oh! I don't know what she said; let us forget."

" Have courage," he whispered, very wearily,
however. " Tell me what people came to call on
you, and what you did while I was away."

Then, more cheerfully, she began to tell him
how the Rumbolds had come one day and she had
gone to Norport in their yacht. She had her portrait taken there for George. But it had not been
sent home yet. " Then the Hardicanutes called
twice and asked us all to a dinner; but Charles
had to be away, it happened, that time, so we
refused. Ought not we to have a dinner party,
too?" Helen said. " I do so want to do something civil for those wretched Hardicanutes."

" Send 'em a five pound note," suggested George. And Helen was amused at that, too. He was glad that people paid his Helen attention, and seemed to make much of her.

They soon forgot their fears of being noticed by servants and cruel persons. But the talk was only hushed down-stairs, not silenced. For the butler, meeting Helen's maid in the passage the morning after George returned, said, pointing to some of George's mourning which he carried, " More clothes to brush, Mrs. Blacker."

" You're right, Turner," she replied. " An' I do wish they were just aired elsewhere—I do that."

Turner took a cynical view of this and similar questions. " Makes me no hodds," he said, softly ; " I sees nothing. But if there wasn't two of the loveliest long fair 'airs that ever come out of a woman's 'ead, wisible on the collar of that coat Frederick was brushing this morning—my name ain't Matthew Turner."

It was hard for George to be happy. It is probable that Helen believed she loved him : she had told herself that she could not live without being loved by somebody, and his bigoted, impatient adoration had an immense charm for her. He desired now that she should be his love, and no one else's. A novel kind of hardihood had come to him, and it was, he acknowledged, a relief that Conscience plagued him no longer. He had throttled it, he said, and would never hear its whinings any more. Yet the life he led degraded him, he complained, almost beyond bearing. He could not read or think, and he had nothing in exchange, wherewith to satisfy his mind, besides, his tormenting passion. No wonder, therefore, that he was jealous of every bit of that love for which he had sold himself. When they saw each other daily—never quite alone, and having to blind the trusting guardian's eyes all the time—George often wished himself dead. Of course they were sometimes free. One day George made a pretext of reading as soon as breakfast was over, and by that means was left alone with Helen. He waited on the lawn till Mr. Tresham had time to be five miles away, and then walked slowly to the drawing-room.

He well knew who he would find there at this idle hour. Helen was sitting on a sofa with a little piece of work before her, looking distraught and weary, like a child who has been vexed. He came and stood before her. " Look! George," she said, trying to smile ; " hav'n't I finished that nicely?" It was some pretty sewing, and

she spread it out on her knees for his inspection.
But she could not long keep up the pretence of
thinking about work and sewing, or the like, and
turned her face to her lover, appealing to him by
her plaintive look. He drew her head to him,
and kissed her on the fair forehead.

"Tell me," said he, "do you sleep well now?
You look so tired, so tired—and you told me you
could never sleep. Do you?"

She shook her head: "Darling," she said,
looking as if towards some far off place, "whenever I fall off to sleep, I dream that you come and
kiss me. And so—I never sleep now."

He could scarcely bear that whisper. It did
wring his very heart. And he was sorry for her,
angry that he himself was the cause of this deep
grief. Still holding her hand, he sat, silent,
on the sofa by her side; and for such a long
time that she was forced to say something to
him.

"Oh! George," she warbled; "I don't know
where I am going, or where this will end.
Darling, don't be angry—but that Sunday you
were away, I went to church. And because I
never thought once of you—I felt so good and
then so happy."—

"Yes, precious," he said.

—" Are you angry ? I prayed that Sunday. But I can't hate you, if I try to, even."

" Why not, Helen ? I know I ought not to be here: *I* could go away, for I can bear being wretched ; but *you* can't, I think, my own."

" Don't say that. You know . . . . by and bye, I mean to be good. And to send you away. We will forget then, and never think about each other again all our lives. Say that we will."

" Yes ; I think it will be like that. I often think of the time when you will forget me. It will come, very surely. These things must be, Precious."—She went and kissed him. " Be happy now," she said.

He repeated that to himself.

" I can look at you for ever, Helen," says he. " Don't shake your head. Why have you such a little chin ? Do you think you have no faults ?"

She put on a suffering look. " My chin makes me miserable. And you sneer at my defects."

" Why, it's no bigger than a baby's," he laughed. " But it is mine, isn't it ? Come here close to me," he said, dropping his voice, as would happen, by degrees. " Tell me, do you like my kisses ?"

" I hate them, as you know. Once I pitied

you—when you were good. Then you were my boy, and I loved you. But now that you have become very, very wicked, I don't love you, George."

"Fancy!" he said, mocking her. "What a pity." And then they were unable to speak for a long time. George heard his own heart beating, and that frightened him. What was his duty now? He knew—and quickly forgot again. He was alone in the quiet room with his beloved. He also knew, 'It is ruin I am hurrying to. Welcome to it. Let it burn me up the quicker. I well know that she whom only I adore is mine. Can I lose her? Can I live without her? so near, and my Precious. And if I lose her—the doubtful future all we know of. We two must be parted, and grow old, and dull, and shrivelled—without any reward. Little pleasure we have here below, and when we can build another sweet delusion we are lucky. To fancy we both love truly! Is that to be wasted and lost?' Could she refuse him anything? No; by those peculiar dim eyes, opening feebly, he imagined not. It was too late to reason now. Between their kisses he murmured something.

"Ah! never," Helen cried, in her clearest tones. "Never, never." And then she could not look at him. George kept her powerless in his hold, looking at her pale eyelids. At that time he had strong shoulders—like a porter for strength.

"Oh! God protect me," Helen now prayed between her parted lips. "Oh! my husband, come to me," the trembling creature said. "Ah! my darling husband—why was I ever unfaithful to you, in thought or word" — thus maybe, quoting from some book she had read. Then her piteous head fell back. George pitied her. Twice that word *husband!* It blistered his ears. His hands dropped by his side. So it was on *him* she called. She loved her husband, then—when she was not acting. "Ah! yes," George said, feebly. "You are very right no doubt." Then he muttered bitterly, "Be happy now" (which was what she had said a few minutes ago). A moment more, and Helen perceived that she was left alone.

For a while she was too frightened to look about. She put her hand on her aching forehead, shuddering from time to time. While she gathered her ideas, he seemed to be still by her side. She almost felt the touch of his well remembered lips, and the outline of his arms— present in ghostly fashion. It was terrible. And then, too, she must be blushing still. Helen therefore rose to find a mirror, wherein to see her injured face. Perhaps there were the prints of his desperate kisses distinguishable still upon her check and forehead. The superstitious woman therefore dipping the corner of her pocket hand-kerchief in the water where some flowers flou-rished, rubbed away the traces of them. By rub-bing hard, you could abolish any kisses, she argued; and with truth. But nevertheless, they might rise up against her at the last. It was hard to tell; hard, for if it came to that, one's hands being kissed would be a sin. Who can draw such fine distinctions? But it is sinful intent, she had often heard, that will be punished. Why, then, every one who loved would be guilty. And such strictness as that was surely never meant. She could fearlessly say to her Con-science that she did intend to remain at the safe side. On the whole—and people who were the best judges thought so now-a-days—there was, said Helen, a fine ancient boundary line to be drawn at kissing. Or something to that effect. How all these hard laws confused and puzzled her timid consciousness. Despairing sometimes of ever being able to understand, Helen had said in her simple way that right and wrong is made down here on the earth—just arranged as society likes. And so what could poor women do?—tafe so hard against them. Was it her willing that George or she had not had a large fortune and been married long ago? The choice was out of her poor hands. Men were allowed to decide for themselves, hence, of course, Heaven would hold them bound to stand by their choice. But somehow women were ever slaves, and could only try to out-manœuvre fate, all their lives long. It tired her to death to think so much. And so she ended with a pleasant sense of thankfulness. But it was a strange, thrilling life this she led with her poor Geordie. Meantime she could smile a little, saying, "Darling boy! he talked nonsense. I dared not—dared not; and it is wild, wild folly."

Then, in the middle of these blushes and so forth, she recollected some letters to be got through. She must write to Rushworth, for one thing. "I sent that shocking old mad-woman a condoling letter," she mused, "and I must write to Lucy next, I suppose."

Sitting down to her desk, with a languid smile on her face, Helen commenced; and she wrote the most becoming letter that could be penned. 'For a beloved father's loss who could attempt to bring healing?' it said. 'Her dearest Lucy had all her smpathy indeed; but there were other consolations, better than she could offer,'—and

Helen mentioned them, across one page. 'Need she tell her dearest that to have her by her side now was her first impulse; but, alas! there are some things that we would like, and yet cannot do. Mr. Tresham was so occupied just at this unlucky moment; they saw absolutely no visitors.' And to add to their woes, their tiresome cook had just insisted on leaving them, and 'poor they' were actually living from hand to mouth—till another of those 'torments' could be procured. But by and bye she would take *no* denial. She must show Norton to her dear Lucy; and later 'it would be such a nice change to her, too.' So, with crossings, to the end of many sheets of condolence.

Probably the Felton girls were not left very well off. To be sure, times were changed since Lucy had been a fine lady, and little Helen a lonely dependant! She could not help just showing in a sisterly way, that she had lived to see changes.

Thus, it appears, two things were got through by Helen in one day, while poor George was not at all satisfied with his reckless morning's work. He could not but respect Helen and accuse himself; yet in the days that followed, she began to dread that he would perhaps come to love her no longer. He never reproached his darling, but he was often silent and cast down. And the recog-

nising that terrified her so that gradually she felt
she could risk anything on earth to win him
back.   Not that it was hard to whistle him to
her again.   What would he not believe that she
told him?   A few sighs and smiles charmed him
into quietness, and, moreover, now that she
feared he would grow cold, she became somehow,
doubly bewitching, without knowing it almost.
He had said to himself every hour of the day,
that living with her in the way he did was harder
than dying.   It was all horror on every side—
if he opened his eyes; but besides that, he was
sure that he would far rather go away than bear
this late torture.   Sometimes he told her this:
then she could not endure listening to him.   She
did not clearly know herself; but she would not
live without him.   That she knew; and yet later
on a day came—that he sat in the drawing-room
with her, and told her they must part shortly.
" And so," he began, " you love me very much?"

" Yes, my own."

He laughed quietly, from the arm-chair where
he sat : he frightened her.

" Tell me, George," she pleaded, when he
would not speak, " did you really believe that I
could *ever* be anything more to you than a true
friend ?"

He said nothing.

" You know—I often doubt—I often think you are one of those who would tire of a plaything and toss it away—in a month. Would you not? Look at me, and speak to me! Will you never speak to me again ?"—

" What can I say ?" he answered.

"You would tire of me—and marry those whom you would love better than me. And when you ceased to love me, what should I do ?" she asked, looking, as if to search round the world for an answer.

" Darling !" he said, " how can I tell what might happen—' when I cease to love you ?' My baby, you are right, perhaps—but can I go on living like this ? Hardly, I think. Don't fancy I blame you. Do you suppose I am happy now ?— do you suppose I don't know that I am a scoundrel, a scoundrel, a scoundrel to love you—a traitor every day of my life ?"

" But you would not wish to *kill* me," she said. " I would kill myself—if— Have you no mercy ?"

He was silent.

" Oh ! speak to me," she prayed, her face gradually growing white as Death.

" Helen," he answered, in a miserable voice, "can we argue about horrors like this ? I have nothing to say, not one word. Only I often think this—what I said—and wonder, if you loved me one bit—Well it does not matter? I wonder what *I* could refuse *you;* I often think of that."

She hid her face in her hands; at last, raising her weary head, she whispered—

" George."

He did not answer.

" George," he heard, after another terrible pause, " Forgive me. Will you forgive me? If you will not go away—"

The room was profoundly still. He heard her broken sobs begin, as soon as she ceased speaking. The utter, helpless abandonment of despair conveyed by her tone and manner frightened him. He wished to spare her: and there she sat with mournful eyes, filled to the brim, waiting for his answer. As he still stared before him, with eyes, struck open, they both caught the sound of the old and well-known footstep coming, and the door was pushed back by her husband. Well, they were sitting in two arm-chairs, and just looking as if they had heard bad news. Mr. Tresham had his daughter in his arms : it was so bright a day in the late autumn, that he had taken her from the nurse's charge, and then had carried her about in the open air for

a while. Now he was whistling, and rather proud
of his fine nursing. It was a precious little body
surely, that he held—a sort of bond between
them, growing up. Must not both care for it
most tenderly? In a way, it attracted Helen,
and, absent and tired, she had to fetch her
thoughts back to take all that in. Slowly she
turned her eyes to the father's frank, open face
—and then to the little lady in his arms. It had
the same kind of look, and exactly the same
brown eyes as Helen had; somewhat younger, to
be sure; and it was alone in having fat and
twitching fingers. George stared at the group,
as if he knew they were risen from the dead;
while the baby commenced to chuckle and laugh,
stretching its hands towards those on the chair.
"Come to me, my own," Helen said, mechanically; and George observed an entirely new
light of love now rise over her face. She took her
babe and kissed it, and kissed it as if it were to
be taken away from her.

Thus they remained, and he had time to watch.
One or two coaxing words from the father to his
child, and Helen silent over it. She had never
looked so old and careworn since she was born.
Meanwhile, he had her recent promise to think
about: by the rules of the fearful strategy which

they had adopted, they dared not speak to each other again—while he was present; they must keep a watch on their eyes. And so George got up and hung about the window. Mr. Tresham sang to the child, something it could not understand, and George smiled on them good humouredly, making his resolve for good and all, and saying to himself the while, " No, no ; I am not quite a devil yet! What would I deserve—after that sight there! Oh! Helen; I do love you, and therefore I would spare you." He must manage to tell her at once that he renounced the infernal favour promised to him : so he lingered, wearing out his heart. Just for one instant he had the chance to whisper to her, " Forgive me! Forget what you said. I have forgotten it !" then went to his room and communed how this was to be ended for ever and ever.

Sitting in a hard chair before the table, George rested his forehead on his crossed arms. Even in this agony taking pleasure in classifying the phases of his mind—he said, ' his thoughts were all choked by this bitter choice.' As sentiment had at that time most power over him, he turned in preference to the last picture—her helpless, dear face stricken by his cruelty: and on her lap—the little child, looking in turn from her to *him*, and he singing a song to it.

He thought—'how could I hurt this woman I loved, finding her at my feet? If she had had even one chance!' But that meek throwing herself on his mercy—she, the gentle and beautiful one. Oh! no! It should never be said that, for his infernal passion's sake, the sweetest person in England was dragged down to places of shame and infamy; but intruded—repeated two or three times —a whisper, 'What was it he asked?—If they were really appointed to love each other—only a very little. What would he not have done for her?' Hence the Evil Things had not done with him yet. Again he grinds his forehead upon his arms. And, while he sat and was weary of life, Mr. Tresham came there to him. 'Oh! perhaps she has confessed all to him,' thought George, (who was still a comparatively young man.) 'Perhaps the best she could do!' He laughed a bit, welcoming any sudden catastrophe as a change from recent torments; and, gathering his senses, held himself ready, having all the time the appearance of pondering the letter before him intently.

Mr. Tresham walked up and down for a few

moments; then he began: "George, I've a word to say." Getting thus far, he leant his hand on the back of the chair, through the wood of which came into George's bones an ideal shock, and a cold creeping. Well, what next? "Well, it's this way. You remember the sermon yesterday? You do, eh? Perhaps you found out I was thinking of you—about early helpfulness, that part?"—So this was it! George had lost sight of his catastrophe by this time; and now his thoughts wandered immediately away from this conversation, the bent of which he was so familiar with. "And," Mr. Tresham was saying, "it's a thing that I know you'd have thought out for yourself; but still, I want to see you started in something helpful. There's a vast deal you could help one in; you know I've been wanting a choral service here. That's one thing; and I want it done well, that's another thing. It's just a question of beginning, and here I'm sure is one recruit enlisted the moment the standard is raised."

"I shall be ready, sir," said George, hauling back his thoughts to the subject. Then, thinking of a choral service, he smiled, for the first time; for he rapidly called up a vision of himself, next to Betsy Candlish's long son, and Matt Snelgrove's boy, and the deaf boy from farmer

Lucas's, and the orphan with the swelled face—
who knew all Luke by heart—each in a white
surplice, ranged along the frozen chancel seats.
And Helen looking at him through her veil.
Mr. Tresham saw none of that. He went on to
sketch out a plan that had been a long time in
his head. They would begin with small ventures,
and if work could do anything, by and bye
would start a this thing and that in the parish.
" Helen thinks as I do, and I'm sure she'd like
you to help," he added; " you know you're a
favourite of hers. I can tell you the friendship
of such a woman is worth having, George."

' Oh ! will he never stop,' asked George, almost
stifled—while he went ringing on. " It will keep
you straight in many ways—when you have taken
the right road at starting," and so on. "The
great battle," George heard ; " stepping stones,"
this and that. He kept vacantly repeating sen-
tences to himself after Mr. Tresham. " I shall
do my best," he said, gently, at last. " Indeed,
sir, I have often thought thus ; but just now
I am bothered. This stupid letter has got into
my head ; indeed, I am obliged to you."

Mr. Tresham nodded, patted him once on the
back, and left him. He was nearly beaten by it
all. The mockery of this offer of a path of work,

when the counsellor ought instead to have killed
him in this room! 'How I love her,' he groaned
out; 'If I did, would I hesitate now. No, I do
love her, indeed; and can therefore vanquish
myself.' And now, it being nearly dark, a sweet
and peaceful smile had conquered its way to his
face, and with these signs of victory hoisted,
George wrote:—

"I shall never ask you to fulfil your terrible
promise. No, Helen, bad I am, but not quite
as bad as that yet. Could I ever look him in
the face, ever take his hand again, meaning to
do him that cowardly injury all the while? No,
my own heart's darling; we will love each other
as much as ever. At least, I can never change;
but God forgive us for ever thinking any sinful
thoughts when we stood in his light. And God
forgive *me* first. My precious! you will be my
very dearest friend on earth from this out,—my
sister, since I never had one. We will strengthen
and guide each other as long as we are alive—
will live near each other, perhaps, and be the
greatest friends ever in the world, and I hope
always good, my own; therefore always happy.

"Do not be angry with me! Do not think
less of me! (If you know, Helen, how I worship

you, and think of nothing else but your beloved
self when we are apart)—but I want to tell you
that I am ashamed of the cruel words I exacted
from you this morning.   I am never happy I think,
for a minute, except looking at you ; but do you
think I could really love you if I counselled you
to go out with me into the doubtful path of sin ?
You see, I keep thinking we are sure to die, darling ; and on the other side of the grave, what a
happy meeting ours will be, free from all shame,
together always, without any remorse to sting
us."—

He put down his pen, and smiling, let his
thoughts roam away into that happy future. And
yet—and yet, it was a long, weary time to wait,
and a faint solace registered—for all the years and
years till then.   The leaves would come out, and
the sun shine in spring, or the dead branches
fall, many autumns ; and how shabby the ultimate
day of reward began to look.   He might remember.   But she would grow stout, and then
would, may be, have more children—and would
neglect to recall how good he had been—and
laugh at him, perhaps.   Yet the picture of her
imploring, sorrow-laden face, and the child
smiling and raising its arms on her lap, re-

turned, and seemed to his wandering thoughts to beckon him. 'There is your work. Will you finish it?' he said, to himself. A little more, and people will tell this child when she grows up, that she has no mother. "*Dead?—no, not dead, but never ask about her.*" Yes, the first impulse was the right one; and therefore knitting his strength together once more, he finished off his task.—

" Darling," he wrote at the end, " I could talk to you like this for ever and for ever (prizing each word of mine because your eyes are sure to see it). A long space of time to be writing, yet not long enough to finish my Litany to you. You will not doubt me now, will you? and you will help me to be strong. Now, good-bye again, my own; God bless you also.

                              " G. N."

And now the triumphant smile settled permanently in his face. His thesis he folded and refolded, and breathing a sigh of relief, rose from his chair. The thick chains, he thought, had fallen with a clang at his feet. The struggle was over; he had made his choice—on the right side, with God's help, and again he could take a

turn at being a gentleman and a man of honour.
Now, he could think of himself without loathing.
Thus liberated, he quickly strolled out on to the
lawn and walked up and down till dressing time;
and the grass did feel more elastic and the air
clearer than for months past.

When the last dinner bell rang, he was musing
still; and so, having to hurry, to finish the tying
of his tie—for Mr. Tresham hated to be kept waiting—he forgot his letter in the desk, where it had
been locked. He said, when he remembered it
with a start, 'I will manage to give it to her in
the evening.' And all during dinner time he was
wretched, thinking of his duty still unfulfilled.
But she, for her part, was in strangely high spirits
again, malicious and talkative as she used to be long
ago. Was it that Mr. Tresham infused his cheery
and pleasant humour into everyone. He had lots to
say to George, about whom there was some story
of shooting a beater in the gaiters, at Farwell one
day. A version of it had got abroad, and Helen
would have it that Mr. Newmarch never shot
anything but young beaters. "You would like
French beaters best," she said; "they have red
legs. You are as bad as Stephen and Lord
Henry. Ah! by the way, if you shot a Lord
Chancellor in the stockings—do you think he'd

give you a chancery living? The present one lives in the next county, I suppose you know. Shall we ask him over here?"

So the evening passed. As soon as he got to his room he slowly took out his letter from the desk, and read it over. Was she worth all that? Ah! but it was his duty. Somehow it seemed late now, and the thing had grown very cold. *Litera scripta manet* came into his head, in still, small tones. He was angry at the voice. ' It was not that,' he said. ' No! no! no!' But he could tell her what he meant—in words, just as well as in a letter. So he locked it away again.

Sometime subsequently, therefore, he chose an opportunity to repeat to her in words the earnest promises he had put in his letter. His own clear eloquence surprised him. He had not known to what lofty heights one's nature can rise at times, until he found himself explaining to Helen how careful they must be from this out; how they must guard against sinful or ignoble thoughts; and how, henceforth, real happiness was within their reach, born of mutual respect and esteem. "There is a better world," he said; "and I pray that we may be judged worthy to carry our love unsullied with us thither."

As for Helen she was dumb; for he soared, she thought, too high for her. She was glad that he was going to be gentle and good again.   But somehow she never could understand the need for all this lofty bargain.

CHAPTER III.

WE will now quit the sequestered village where George was spending the important months before he was twenty-three, fly away to Stephen, and look down into the humble room, where he sits—on his wooden barrack chair before the fire, reading letters. He had some twelve minutes left to do this, because the 'dress' for afternoon parade had sounded; he was orderly officer, and wore his pouch belt, while his sword was already buckled on, and his cap was on his head. Of the letters which his servant had just brought in, the first had the Ricehope post-mark and a broad black border. It was from Lucy Felton, asking him to come there on the eighth of the month. The next, in a feeble, illegible hand, was from Berty.

"Dear Old Tiff (he wrote)—

"Get a week's leave and come down here and I can put you up in barracks Athelbury steeple ch's come off nex week and I'm going to enter the little chesnut mare the guv gave me in the military race and I want to put you up against them it's officers to ride twelve stun each and you have five pound allowance as you never rode a winer we've got a hop the day after all the county swells and lots of all the heirisses 'entered so you may pull off a good thing over both events so mind you come Pop your watch if you're hard up and we'll do a bill for thirty shillings for your fare back I've got lite spurs and no end of cullers don't forget your boots and breeches

"Your affect brother

"B Newmarch"

The last was from his mother, and was sealed up with much formality.

"Sawtry Marescal, Monday.

"My Dearest Boy,—

"You are unkind not to write to me. I hope you will soon, and tell me you are well; for the weather is damp, cold, and trying, even here, and I fear much more so with you. Not much news here; your father is an invalid again, quite struck down by his old enemy, the gout. You are causing me anxiety just now, my dear boy, for I fear that when you are ordered away from Athelford, you will find bills which you incur thoughtlessly must be paid, and then comes a crash! Just as with Bertram. Do tell me if you are now in debt. Poor George has been in great money troubles, as I could not help him with a farthing, and he was obliged to apply to your father, who is up to his neck in lawyers' bills; then such scenes! and I fear George will never be out of debt. Oh! money! money! but I hope all may yet be settled. I had quite forgot to tell you what has altogether upset me. It is the horrid revelations of poor Uncle Felton's will. It is, indeed, too awful. You, perhaps, never heard of Arthur Maxwell, who wanted to marry Sir John Bagborough's daughter last season, and has been a shocking *roué* in Paris and London. He was—it is really too terrible— Mr. Felton's son. I can hardly write on such a dreadful subject; but, the result is, he has been left every farthing that was not settled at Penelope's marriage, some nine thousand a year—almost the whole of poor Lucy's mother's fortune, in fact;

and William Felton has only about a thousand a
year to live on, and that enormous place to keep
up, which, thanks to your father, was settled
on the eldest son. Aunt Penelope has twelve
hundred a year out of the property, and each
of the girls only a hundred a year separately.
I think the law should be made to interfere,
but I hear, no use. We advise Willie to let
Rushworth at once, as soon as his mother can
leave; and I hear an American General, with
three mad daughters, is looking after the place.
But it has quite broken Penelope's spirits, and
mine, too. Your aunt wrote, wishing you and
Bertram very much to go there. I trust you
will, like my dear, good boy. You have never
been there, and it will seem unkind if you refuse.
Of persuading Bertram I fear there is no hope.
Lady Knaresborough tells me he is to be at Lord
Caterer's, in December, at one of those horrid
battues. He never writes. I send a five pound
note; it is all I have now. Give Simkins, at
Rushworth, half a sovereign; he lent it to me, for
the Feejeeans, the day the Bishop preached.

"Ever, my beloved son,

"Your fond, anxious mother,

"ADELAIDE NEWMARCH."

Stephen wrote an answer to each that night. The next day, he had got his leave, and arrived at the town where his brother was, by three o'clock or so in the afternoon. Berty met him at the station. I suppose those Hussars had been wandering; about, this therefore, was not the same platform where Phillips introduced that singular visitor, poor Mary Slowly, to his master, three years ago.

Berty was glad to see him, but Tiff missed the old frank smile, and thought that his eldest brother had grown irritable, and old-looking, and almost shaky. He began at once talking feverishly about the races, and his horse's prospects. " You're very fit, and well, I suppose," said he. " How much do you smoke now, a day?"

" Never smoke," says Tiff.

" By Jove! When do your fellows go to bed, generally ?"

Tiff told him, 'Not very late.'

" Oh! then—it's a certainty," says Berty; " you're sure to win for me. Lutterell wanted to lay me five ponies, mine. And then, a monkey to seventy-five—if I rode myself." So he went on. 'They must stop,' he said, 'to have one nip of cherry brandy,' at the principal hotel, on their way up. But even three glasses of this pleasant stimulant didn't raise Berty's spirits much.

As they approached the mess-room, a lot of officers were to be seen, gathered before the door. Some had come from hunting with the harriers. "Here's Chubby Newmarch and his jock," said they. "Newmarch!" somebody called out, "there's a very suspicious looking individual asking for you, with patterns of narrow blue paper for your approval."

"Don't you mind 'em, Chubby," said a short, dark young officer. "It's not a writ—only Bob Sloman's clerk."

"Thank you, Pat. I know; I telegraphed for him." And he was going off to meet his visitor, when at that moment a tiny stable boy walked a brown mare into the yard. Berty was all attention at once. "Is that yours, Major?" said he.

It was, and the major, a stout, good tempered looking man, went up to pat his horse. "Let her stand quiet, boy," said he. But she lashed out savagely the moment her owner approached.

"She's afraid you want to *scratch* her, Lutterell," said Mr. Pat Desmond, alluding playfully to his superior officer's well known habit of withdrawing his turf nominations at the last moment.

The other laughed, but said that he would bet about his horse winning, even now.

"I can lay you an even hundred, one two, major," put in that Mr. Eveley who, as we remember on a former occasion, knew no geography, and had such a strange establishment on first joining the service.

Tiff enquired if this were the favourite.

" Yes, the only thing I'm afraid of. Come along up to my room now."

" Who was that short chap—with his arm in a sling—you called Pat?" Tiff enquired. " *He* looks like riding."

" Aye, he does; broke his arm steering that same mare of Lutterell's, at Baden, last month— or he'd be up against us on Friday. It's Frank Desmond, our senior lieutenant. He's a capital fellow. Makes his money, I expect, for he hasn't got a half-penny on earth of his own. His father owns a lot of horses at the Curragh—sends him over a three-year-old occasionally from Ireland, to make what he can of. And he's got a wonderful five stone boy. Wish he'd give him to me. And that's the way he gets along. Every one likes him. Oh! you're waiting for me," added Berty, to a suspicious looking man, who stood bowing at his room door. " You've got *that* for me, I suppose?" And then some talk went on between them.

Tiff entered the room and shut the door. It was not easy to guess the calling of the man who occupied this room.   Apparently it was a tobacconist, carrying on a saddler's business—in a public-house; and keeping all his bills, memoranda, and love letters, on the floor.   A palisade of decanters round the walls caught Tiff's eye.   And Berty, coming in, said, " What'll you have to drink, now?   Here's most things about, I think. Shoot me! but everything seems going wrong. By the way, when I was in France I went in for absinthe.   It isn't bad at this hour.   You have some?"—

Tiff laughed.   " Not I," said he, looking about. He couldn't make out what had come over Berty, who, when there was a pause, kept walking restlessly to and fro, cursing to himself.   At last he seemed to remember where they were.   " Well, you're right not to drink, I daresay.   Let's see how your muscle is.   You will win for me on Friday, eh?   You know it's just about touch and go with me this time—if I don't pull off this thing—well.   Can you sit down and finish a race, I wonder?"

" Yes; I think so.   I had some lessons from Bill Ringall.   You know he trains near where we are; and I made friends with him last summer. Who'll be up against me on Friday? did you hear at all?"

" Ah ! that's just the worst of it. Lutterell's got Clancy coming. By Gad ! everthing seems going to the deuce. My room looks queer, don't it, Tiff? Just lost my man Philips. The fool deserted and took two hundred of mine out of my dressing-case. Sent word to him, I'd make it three—if he'd come back. Best hand at painting a black eye in England."

Thus they chatted away, and Tiff said he wanted a white tie to ride in, that was all. " You'll find a box full of white satin one's, never opened," Berty said. But Tiff did not require all that. His brother avoided the subject of Sawtry, and smoked away, rambling on about his bets and his ill luck ; and now and then drinking something. " I can't sit here," he said, restlessly. " Let's come down and see what they're doing in the ante-room, and have a game of billiards."

Meanwhile a couple of officers, who had been looking at the horse below, fell to talking about Berty.

" I suppose the two brothers back each other's bills freely," said one. " Queer people, the Chubby family, at home, I should say."

" 'Um," the other answered. He was good natured, and sorry for Berty. Indeed it was Bob

Sackville who spoke. "I don't think he can last much longer. Unfortunate boy."

"Well, I should say not, 'pon my word. Why, I was at that Bob Sloman's the other day, about some weeds; and as soon as I walked in you know, he says to me, 'Look here, Mr. Bagenall, what is a man to do! Just look at that, sir.' And by Jove! you know, Chubby had quietly sent an account of three thousand pounds—just what he dropped at Doncaster—copied out of his book on half a sheet of paper, and at the bottom he'd written, 'Please pay these'—to this man and that at Tattersall's. Bob Sloman did. But you can just fancy the rate of interest, can't you?'

"Well, well," says Sackville, "I'd do anything I could for poor little Chubby, because he's one's own subaltern, and all that. But *I* don't know what'll stop him. I wonder did he really give all those pearls to that red-haired girl at the Pindaric. Napthali, the jeweller's, man told me he *did* give them to her."

"Is it that woman who does the 'Genius of Lloyd's' in 'Dedœlus?' Not he. She wont look at him. I asked him whether her hair was real, and he didn't even know her name."

"I think he forgets his own name often. He

would not tell you, though. I believe, Charlie, that those really spoilt boys talk very little. It's only the men that get snubbed who boast."

Then they went in, and around the fire, the talk was of the everlasting races. Some one counted up the number of horses going. "Thought Newmarch had nothing but lame 'uns," suggested another.

"Is he not in mourning?" asked young Burnham Wood, whose father married Lord Dunsinane's daughter, and who, having been put into Parliament, talked, down here, a good deal. "His uncle is just dead. I knew the place well: not far from Athelbury—where your races are."

"Faith! if 'twas himself had died, Newmarch wouldn't be baulked of having something in the race," explained Mr. Desmond, who affected an Irish brogue when he chose, and delighted in shocking the last speaker.

Two or three people remembered the uncle.

"Didn't he leave his money to a poet—that offensive Arthur Maxwell—man with a lot of greasy black hair and a guitar?" some one asked. "A man that used 'go out hunting in a green velvet suit, last winter, at Rome."

"They say in town the wife got nothing but her jointure," said Burnham; "a man who knows the family lawyer told me so at the Reform yesterday. You know how it was. She was the greatest screw in England—saved thirty thousand pounds out of her pin-money; the husband knew it and left her noth—"

But at that moment in came the two New-marches.

"Here, Chubby, want your nomination," said Sackville. "Must send 'em off to old Hill to-night. How's it to be? Mr. Bertram New-broom's chestnut mare—what. Give the child a name."—

"What's she called, Tiff?" said Berty, "Becky Glitters—Lucy Sharpe—Lucy Locket—some-thing."

"I call her 'Sawtry maid,'" said Tiff.

"Sawtry Maid, Bob," chuckled Berty. "You know—fancy all our maids at Sawtry startin' for a big handicap! You know; we've got a lot of 'em. There's a little old woman, for one, if you ask her who she is—she says, 'Please, sir, I'm converted and carries coals to the top of the house;' she'd stay—"

"Here, stow your family affairs, little New-moon," says Pat Desmond. Then the racing technicalities were resumed once more.

Fortunately, Berty made no more bets. By the

time dinner was half through, he was wound up
to something like his old spirits, and his brother
saw his glass going up and down without ceasing.
Tiff had got next to Bob Sackville, who pitied
him; and they made great friends. On the other
side was Burnham Wood, who was enormously
rich, and, as was said, represented the Cutty
Sark Burghs in Parliament. Though not of long
standing in the regiment, he thought a good deal
of himself; he had hardly uttered a word to poor
Tiff, who sat next him.

Cecil Eveley hated him : " Chubby," he called
out from the end of the table, " ' Gummy' Burnham's been voting for the Radicals—and the Jews
gettin' into Parliament. Ask him."

Berty was chattering away at a tremendous
rate at that moment; but he gathered his political
ideas together.—" Now, Gummy," said he, judi-
cially, " what d'you mean by bein' an old Char-
tist ?"

The other regarded him with gentle pity.

" That's all deuced fine," continued Berty.
" Yes, now ! I suppose you'd let all one's Jews
into the House of Commons—or the House of
Lords, by Jove ?" It was but natural that the
claims of that remarkable people should be constantly present to Berty. " I've got a plan now,"

he went on—"tell me what it is, Pat?—Aye,
yes.—Suppose now, Government was to get every
fellah's bills and duns—I mean us sort of fellahs
—get 'em together, and register 'em. And then
let the Bank of England issue (what is it, Pat?)
—aye, issue certificates of indebtedness to each
fellah, which would be legal securities on which
we could raise money again. What effect that
have on a crisis?"

This remarkable proposition had drawn general
attention to Berty, taking the other somewhat
aback as well.

"M'Cullogh has a chapter on that very subject,
I know," he said, hurriedly. "But the best
thinkers are so divided on questions of finance."

"That's all deuced fine," said Berty. "I can
see how it is: I suppose you're in favour of
abolishing both church and state—that's the
fact."

But this was leading on to abstruse ground,
and a silence ensued, leaving Berty in possession
of the field.

About twelve o'clock, Tiff, pleading his nerve,
left Berty, settled down to a big loo in Cecil
Eveley's room—and went to bed.

When he awoke, about six next morning, there
was his brother in the same clothes he had worn

the night before, calmly working away at his turning lathe by the window. "Hulloh! old boy—slept well," said he. "D'you know, I've turned just fifty-eight pairs of candlesticks since I got this thing. And I don't know what the deuce to do with 'em, now. Fellows won't have any more as presents—I believe they've all got six pair of 'em in their rooms."

"Hav'n't you been to bed?" asked Tiff.

"Not I," said he. "I'll just lie down on that sofa there in a minute. Mind, we've got to find those harriers at eleven. I'll put you on Parricide, I gave seven hundred for him—after he ran second for the Liverpool, and then he *did* break down the next month, and no mistake! Pat Desmond says, vets come down from London to study his legs, and take sketches of 'em—they're so wonderful bad."

Then Stephen dressed.

"My servant 'll call me by and bye," added Berty, going off to sleep on the sofa. "Shame it is that fellows are made to learn to write—when they're young and know no better. I kept writing *such* a lot of I.O.U.'s last night, Tiff."

They found the harriers in due time—it was October then, and there were no foxhounds—and they had their three or four spurts with them. It was an enclosed country, with some big fences, and, notwithstanding Parracide's notable leg, Stephen thought he had 'never been so carried in his life.'

" Don't mind sending him along," says Berty. " May cure him, you know, and make the old beggar sound again."

So Stephen thought he might try how his own nerve felt, at one or two of the ugly places. ' I'll do,' he thought—as after galloping his old horse across a portion of plough, he caused him to leap a stiff post and rails into a lane.

Now it happened that Mr. Desmond, broken arm and all, sat on his pony in that lane. He also thought that Tiff would do. So when the next day came, and they were all rolling along on the regimental drag to the course at Athelbury, and of course talking of the race—he thought he might turn what he had seen to some profit, and settled down to business at once. ' If they wanted his opinion, there was just one in it— and that was Lutterell's.'

But Bob Sackville wouldn't allow this at all.

" All right, old boy," Desmond continued. " I don't care what other regiments have got, or what we've got—but I tell you a mare, that can win at Limerick, over that desperate country, and then shew the pace, on the flat, she did at Baden—is about good enough to eat your old military horses for breakfast—and not miss 'em. Why, I told you at the time, there was Count d'Yvetot, that same race at Baden—he was on the favourite, and he sung out, in chaff, to me, a mile from home—you know his queer English— 'Laisse moi, stand in un poney, Pat, mon brave; on te verra walk in.' And I would have, too, only for that cursed cropper. By Jove! I can see Oos station, and that Mercury on the top of the Staufenberg, upside down now—the first thing I twigged when I got on my legs."

Berty was listening anxiously. He said he should back Lady Alice a little : 'Clancy steered her, he supposed.'

'Yes, he was sure to ; and came from Belgium on purpose. Joe Levy had promised to see him through, if any one 'wanted' the poor fellow while over here.'

"Have you a book on the race?" asked Berty, proud of his business-manner. Desmond had; and thought he could just lay Berty 7 to 4 against Lady Alice, now; to hedge what he had taken at the club on Monday.

"All right—I'll take that. Ponies," said Berty, who never could get rid of a fallacy of his—that 7 to 4 meant two and a-half to one.

Eveley laughed : "There's another can't lose, Chubby, if you want to back them *all*," said he. "I mean 'Falstaff.' Why I rode against the horse in the Grand Military this year Pat, on a pretty fast one, too. And I went up to old 'Falstaff' three times, for a feeler, and never could live with him a hundred yards. I tell you."

Then they approached the race course : it was nearly the time. Away in the valley, the rickety wooden stand came in sight, already dotted with men like flies. The drag lurched through the slushy fields, and they passed close to some of the fences on the line,—winding, jagged, and sombre across the dead winter green of the fields. Out against the dull back ground—little bright flags marked the course. They heard the cry of the costermongers, and men selling cards, and the popping of corks and the clatter of sticks. Already the noisome clamour went up like a storm from the ring.

To Berty the scent of the damp earth, the smell of cigar lights in the air, and the very orange peel about, was delightful. How he enjoyed every second of a day like this! Standing on the box, he looked eagerly about, glass in hand. "Not a 'place' in the whole round," he said—for, he indeed, was not going to ride himself ; but Stephen, who was, only screwed up his eyes and took a survey of each bit of ground which the drag passed. This was the formidable line over which he had got to race in an hour or so. But then, that chilly feel, which the approach of an event of this kind gives to some—like stripping to bathe on a cold day to a young child, was utterly unknown to him. He only glanced down the card to see when his race came off: it was the third. " Hadn't we better walk the course at once, Berty?" said he. " We'll see 'em come over the brook, first race; and you'll be out of the way of dropping your money in the ring."

So they plodded round the fields to study the scene of operations; Tiff's quick eye chose out the softest place in each fence at once. That done, he would jump over himself. " The more you look, the less you'll like it—I'll know where to have it," he said, when Berty wanted to stare and exclaim at the ugly spots in the jumps.

Then they watched the first race—a family contest, as it were, between Sam Dale's two sons —on wretched horses ; and somehow, it appeared that the wrong one obtained the victory.

Then it was about time to get on his things, and Tiff jostled his way through the crowded weighing-room, and put on his brother's gorgeous colours with little delay. A well-built, muscular young fellow he looked when dressed. He was not, to be sure, a pretty dimpled boy like his brother—rather thin-faced and hard-featured instead, with short, curly, fair hair, and faint yellow whiskers round his face. But then he had broad shoulders; you saw power in his lithe and sinewy limbs under his jockey clothes, and his hand was perfectly steady.

Seven weighed in for the soldiers' race—after a vast deal of lingering. Seymour Puffyn couldn't find his boots for twenty minutes; then young Booke Muslyn of the Carbineers, had not been in a pair of scales since he left school, and was exactly thirty-seven pounds over weight. Next came Tiff, and took his place in the weighing chair. "Pound for the bridle," says he.

"Eh!" said Berty, who was trembling with excitement. "Give me a pound—somebody."

"Got nineteen shillings and tuppence in coppers at your service, Mr. Newmarch," said Jim So-and-So, and there was a gruff titter among the jockeys and servants. .But it was made right after a little.

"Captain Rolster declares a pound overweight for 'Falstaff,'" said the owner of that horse in a loud tone.

"You'll lose that, in 'natural trepidation' during the race, George," observed Mr. Eveley, who was 'going' for Sawtry Maid. "Fancy declaring a pound over in a steeplechase! You swell flat race men know too much for us poor steeplechasing beggars altogether."

And then the famous Captain Clancy appeared; he had just taken off a huge false beard and moustache inside the weighing room, and two or three staunch friends patted him on the back, as he got into the scales with his whip in his teeth. "You take it quiet, Captain," whispered Jack Magpie, the trainer. "Most of them others don't seem much 'used,' I think."

By degrees they were all mounted, and young Burdoon went by first, counting to get that ordeal over as soon as might be. Next came George Rolster, on 'Falstaff,' talking and laughing with Cornet Puffin, rider of 'Castaway.'

Captain Clancy was in no hurry to begin. He had ridden a tiring trial at Werghem, in Belgium, the morning before, and had travelled all day and all night. "Come and look at this rip I'm to steer," he said, to Harry Sloman—who has since become a very leading man. They walked down towards where the favourite was being led about, followed by a crowd. "Let me see—this is the one they made favourite at Baden, Harry. Breedy lookin' thing, ain't she?"

"She's about 'alf fit, Ted," said the betting man; for in their moments of privacy it was Ted and Harry between these two masters of their respective arts.

"Fit!" said the gentleman rider, witheringly; and he gave his opinion forcibly, and more in detail, but without record here, for better slang can easily he heard by listening about the saddling paddock at any race-course any day in the year. "By the way, who is this young Newmarch that I hear so much talk about? I'm so out of it all, over among those 'monseers,' Harry," Clancy said, despondingly.

"'Who is he?' Why, the same young chap bought old Parricide. *We* know how he spells his name, Ted. Why, Bob's got his paper for five-and-thirty thou. Five-and-thirty thou! My boy! what do you think of that?"

"Ah! then it's the same boy I mean. Look here, old man, put me a fiver on this mare of his," said Clancy, coaxingly. "You won't lose by me, Harry, so help me. And, you can slate this one of mine, too. I must go 'straight,' because Lutterell's in with all those Rue de Grammont chaps, and the field's so small; but this Lady Alice, or whatever she is, can't do Newmarch's one, not at three stone. Pat Desmond told me a trial he had with her, on the quiet, one morning"—and so forth.

The betting man squeezed his old friend's hand, and went. Then the boy brought up Lady Alice to be saddled. "Wet those saddle flaps, you," says Clancy, to the boy; "I'll settle the leathers. . . . . . Clear out of the way." He walked his horse out of the crowd, and cantered slowly past the stand. There was a rush to the rails at once, to get a sight of the favourite, with this famous horseman piloting her. Stephen came next, talking to his pet, and quietly noticing the quality of the ground to finish on. But of course, no one paid the slightest attention to him. When he and Captain Clancy pulled up, after their canter, they had to follow a lane, leading off the course, to the starting field. Here Lutterell caught them up, out of breath. "Don't back your horse for a penny more, old boy," said Clancy, good-naturedly; "she goes as weak as a cat." Then they approached the starter. "You'll just win this thing—if you can sit still," he growled to Stephen, after looking the pair over very carefully.

" Why, you are certain to beat me, ain't you?"
Stephen answered.

But this master did not condescend to say any
more to the youngster. And now Tiff noticed
that Burdoon was awfully pale—; that Castaway
rather wanted to graze; and then he got next to
Clancy, and saw how his knuckles shook against
the pommel of the saddle—as he handled the reins.

' What a store of pluck that fellow must have
thrown away,' Stephen thought.

" Now! gentlemen," he heard the starter say.
"Turn round, please, and walk up to me."

Falstaff lashed out at the favourite.

" I've dropped my whip," says Seymour Puffyn,
piteously.

" Stop and pick it up—when we're coming
round next time," Tom Burghley suggested, trying hard to get his ex-flat-racer to face the flag.

" Oh! Captain Clancy, please!—You'll be on
the top of me, Mr. Burghley," the starter pleaded.
" *Don't* break away, gentlemen.—GO!"

CHAPTER IV.

Now, when Berty had seen his brother's weight, and leathers, and surcingle right, and given him a leg up, and left him, with the worst possible orders, which Stephen calmly dismissed from his mind at once, he was almost sorry that poor old Tiff's neck was risked for it all. But, then, he was accustomed to people sacrificing themselves for h im ; and The Maid was going to carry all his desperate fortunes, he recollected. Pushing into the ring, therefore, through the crowd of bloated white-faced men, broken down publicans, stale pugilists, bankrupt shopmen, procurers, garotters, and other sporting persons who were enjoying themselves, and seeking profit in the place, Berty went to stake his money on his horse. He was only too well used to the fatal hubbub here, and gathered readily how the market was going—in favour of this or that horse, what-

ever it may have been.   There, anyhow, was Harry
Sloman, jostling his way about, crying continu-
ally, "The field—a ponny ! the field—a ponny !
the field—a ponny ! What'll you do, Mr. Newmarch ?" said he, stopping.

"'Take ten to one, mine," Berty answered.
But laughing, and shaking his head, Sloman
vanished into the whirl of jargon.   "I'll take
odds, 'Lady Alice,'" Berty now heard yelled.
" Wall ! I'll back the feel'— the feel' I'll back-k !
Any price soom o' these rooners.   Will ANY-
BODY back one? What 'you want to do, captain ?"
—This was from the great Mr. Jowler, a determined man, who was splitting his lungs here to
reap the young officers' sovereigns.   There were
only two or three large 'dealers' of Berty's stamp
present, and all the crush was their way, 'to lay
them a bet.'   He, for his part, stood serene, in a
short white coat, his glass slung across it, and a
wonderful hat upon his little head—the shrine to
which they prayed and waved their pencils : looking, in shirt collars up to his ears, like a prince
in a picture-book, standing to be admired.
" Now ! can't doo't, captain," the Jowler roared
in his ear. " Brey-ak 'ta Bank, layun' tens in
sooch a feyald."

Berty was very cool now, and his baby face

deadly pale. " I've done, then," said he. " You know *well* they back five of 'em, and you haven't written mine yet."

" Wall, here! have six fifties," or words to that effect, cried Mr. Jowler.

" Make it monkeys," said Berty, coldly. The other stared, and nearly swallowed his pencil, but wrote down the bet. Then there was a crush in some other direction. Cries went up from here and there, and the ferocious knot of men trampled about through the straw and slush; and Berty listened to the bell, which still swung, and swung overhead.

Then Lutterell came and touched his arm. " The favourite's price?" he asked also, of some betting man, and made a bet of some sort. After which he and Berty mounted the stewards' stand.

And, now, at this moment, a large man attracted Berty's attention; first, by bringing a strong blast of spirits thereabouts; and then, by a magnificent address.

"I think," he said, " I need hordly introduce meeself, Captain Newmarch—one of your dear fahther's oldest friends." This much was through a most peculiar atmosphere, and Berty stared at him astonished. He was tall and raw-boned, with ragged red hair—uncut for a long time—

about his head. He had blood-shot eyes, and the signs of drink. But one saw that he had been, at one time or another a gentleman, though his clothes were greasy and unbrushed; and he had a greyish shirt on—not grey by colour, but of an acquired grey.

Berty thought he remembered this face at Sawtry in old days. It was, indeed, none other than Dick Nugent, an Irish industrial, a man of birth, and at one time of some position, but who had long vanished from decent society, and now was known from time to time as claiming some dormant peerage, and troubling many men.

Anyhow, Berty nodded slightly.

"A chorming day," his acquaintance said. "I see, by reference to mee cyard, that you have an animal engaged in this interesting event. I was just going to ask you—these trains, you know, start at such absurd hours me young friend. I just hadn't time to change a cheque this morning, and if you could—"

"Was that mine 'Falstaff' kicked at?" exclaimed Berty, feverishly scanning the starting field with his glass.

"Aw, if you could lend me a mere five pounds —such a *canaille* here, can't even know them, much less accept a loan ; and, on the honour of an Irish gentleman, and I may say prospective nobleman, it shall be yours before the morrow."

Berty hardly heard him. He just thought, how the chap used to be at Sawtry once on a time. How forlorn and out at elbows he did look now! and so satisfied of his perfect title to a five-pound note that Berty gave himself up. "Eh! are they off," he was muttering. "Yes, of course, Mr. Nugent." And he pulled out a note, and gave it—almost blushing, indeed.

"Me dear boy, so like your noble father." And the comparison, no doubt, was too true here. "Let me give you an I.O.U. for the sum." And this he would have done faithfully—if somebody held his hand steady for him—only that, at the instant, down went the glasses. There was an ominous hush, and cries of "They're off," here and there. Then, loosed from the flag, they came at last, patching the hill with bright colours, all in a cluster, hard to make out.

But Nugent, seeing that Berty's eyes were on the race, seized a glass—with profound apologies —from the hands of a quiet elderly man beside him, and eagerly scanned each horse as, far away, they appeared to slowly pop over the tiny thread of a fence which, at close quarters, ran very thick and rigid. 'Castaway' was leading, and half hid by the fence for a second, took it the next, carrying away ten square yards of a patched up place on her knees, and blundering on into the field. Next 'Falstaff' swung over the gap, and rushed immediately to the front ; then came Tom Burghley with his one. Tiff had it wide on the right, and Clancy waiting, his horse yawing her head about and pulling his arms off, last of all. Rolster, on 'Falstaff,' made it hot for them, people said, while young Puffyn's horse was nearly away with him altogether. Once down the hill, they turned towards the stand, having the water for their third jump. Rolster gave a brilliant lead over; next came 'Detective,' and Tiff, fixing his eye on a place, went at it third. But here, in another second, 'Castaway,' quite out of her rider's control, rushed at the very same place, smashed into the Sawtry Maid's heels as she lit, and rolled the four over in a wisp on the landing bank.

Berty saw that. " *Curse him*," said he, " I'm ruined ;" yet he rushed down to help his brother. At this moment Captain Clancy took the favourite over clear of the heap.

'Castaway' was first out of the *melée*, and bolting over the ropes, knocked down that reduced gentleman and his wife with the roulette table—

finishing in a big salad, which Tom Buckler was just superintending on the step of the Life Guards' drag. Seymour Puffyn fell light; but as for poor Tiff, his first sensation was a terrific tug at his left leg, and The Maid kicking over his head, sending showers of mud into the air, as she galloped up the course. There was a low murmur of horror from the dingy crowd all over the race ground. It is a sobering thing to see a poor fellow horribly smashed before one's eyes; and the less brutalised people present feel guilty to be there at all. While, as for Tiff, knocked senseless at first, he might well give up, one cheek ground against the grass and his leg half-torn off; but he had hold of the reins still, though cold and sick at heart. 'It is coming at last,' he thought; 'but I'll have one good try—and I never *was* scared a great deal.' So, stiffening his arm, he attempted to go on pulling at his horse. 'I shall look such a fool from the stand,' was his thought. But then the crowd closed in on him. Not a bit had he given in; in truth, his remorse was for Berty's money, which had been staked on his riding, and was now lost. And now came his brother's voice, begging that he'd not think of going on.

Nugent watched all that breathlessly. " The

game lad," he cried, excitedly—alchololic tears
coming into his eyes. He was a nobleman again,
with that five pound note rustling against his
waistcoat.

"Badly hurt I fear, sir," the owner of the
glasses suggested, mildly. "Might I ask for my—"

"A moment, man!" exclaimed the presump-
tive heir to that Barony far away across the
Sea—his hot Irish blood kindling at what he
saw. "Here, Harry Sloman," he roared down
to the crowd below, brandishing the very five
pound note, "I'll take five hundred to five—the
boy that's down!"

There was a lull, and Bob Sloman was now biting his pencil to the quick. This cry from above
attracted attention, and Dick was recognised.
"I wish I 'ad yer somewhere—I'd put yer over
the railings," retorted a finely featured Hebrew,
looking up at him; "aye, and I'd make the
ruins too 'ot to old fawst men like you! Woy
don't ye pay yer corn chandler's bill? woy don't
ye pay me what yer howes me this heighten
months?"

"I declare to Gad I never saw ye before, me
good man," said poor Dick, hurriedly.

"Ah!" said the suitor, bitterly, "that's it—
where ever you go, you mace!"

" Here, I'll lay you, Irish," says Hulks and Co., the great ready-money people, seeing the real tangible currency. " Hundred to five, there !"

" No, no, Huggy," said Dick, remembering that 'twas to an ex-garrotter he spoke ; " I'll take your two, though," and he, getting a nod, booked it, and eagerly handed down his note—for at that moment, Tiff emerged from the crowd, quietly setting his horse going again. There was a somewhat derisive cheer as he passed, covered with mud, in pursuit of the others, now some quarter of a mile ahead.

" That fellah coopers me entirely," says one of the crowd, who had stopped the mare and held her while Tiff re-mounted ; " tells me ' I'll give ye alf a crown when I've weighed out,' just as cool as if he was buyin' a pennorth of greens."

Meantime they were up the next hill, Tiff taking each leap far in the rear. Away on the level ground opposite the stand, Booke Muslyn's charger went round at some white rails, and Tom Burghley's horse following that example, the pair, after turning their horses at the fence twenty times, to the amusement of the distant crowd, sat there in their bright jackets watching the vanishing race. When the starting field was passed for the second time, and Tiff, lying nearly flat back, flew the brook last, there were only three left with a chance, Falstaff, Lady Alice, and himself. Passing the stand the second time, he was last by about thirty yards, standing in his stirrups and taking it all quite calmly. There was a rush to see him and a faint shout of encouragement. Berty, back on the roof, saw it all with slowly returning pride and hope. 'He would take that bet again,' he cried; but Mr. Jowler shook his head. "Nobody places them!" the expounders now called out.

Where the straight course ended, there was a hedge and a bank, and once over that and off the grass, they had a stiff hill, just then under plough. As they crossed its furrows this second time, Clancy steadied the favourite, and Rolster seeing that, sent his horse Falstaff along, top speed, by her side; whereat Lady Alice, fretting all the way up to race with him, tired in the heavy land—and died away in her jockey's hands, as if she were shot.

"I'm beat like a sack, youngster," said Clancy, to Stephen, pulling his horse into a trot. "Creep up to him t'other side this hill; don't move on your horse till you're at the Stand, and you'll do him for pace, for he's on a slow one !"—

"Thanks," says Tiff; and when he had waited

up this slope, took the measure of Falstaff's pace on the flat ground, and nearly closed with him coming to the white rails where Tom Burghley still sat. They went over almost together, and then he could hear a tiny shout half a mile away in the meadow land. He was flurrying, for the first time, to get up to his solitary opponent. But presently he smiled to himself, and began to look at Falstaff's curb, as they sailed along side by side.

Rolster's condition and training was not like Tiff's, and when they came to the last turn for home, he was tired, and beaten, and let his horse run out ten lengths. Another yell from the ring acknowledged that. Making use of the ground he had gained, Tiff took a steadying pull at his horse, and, approaching the water an old dodge came into his head. "If I go like smoke at the place and take him with me, he may get a fall, and who ever stands up'll win." But he remembered Clancy's words, and the two horses kicked the sods into the water almost together. Then, at last, in the straight, only two hundred yards to go, Rolster on the right, in the middle of the course, slid back in his saddle, poised his whip, and began at his famous horse like a blacksmith. There was a dead hush as they came up between the wall of faces, threshing the turf with their feet, a cry or two from the ring, and Rolster's whip smashing like a flail. But he couldn't go faster. Tiff sat still in his place, and his eye was on Falstaff's head, which was just out beyond The Maid's. Yet he could hardly breathe; his heart had almost stopped, and he seemed alone, and the magnet of all those hungry eyes. He heard Rolster's short, sharp sobs, close to his ear, the creak of his boots on the saddle, and his whip going swish! swish! swish! He saw the level grass in front, the white winning post glaring against the board, and Falstaff's head, ever in the same place. Then, keeping his hold on with the left hand, firm, but reaching back, Tiff let his horse have two tremendous measured slashes with his whip. Her elastic answer brought his heel to Rolster's knee—who looked at him, and hung in a little. Their boots creaked together. Tiff felt himself jammed on to the cords—and in that stride, the judge's face was gone. Another, and Rolster, with one twist more, crushed Tiff in nearer still. The mare was on to the cords—and with her shoulder, snapped a white post short off —in amongst the crowd.

"Thank you," says Tiff, pulling his horse out of the tangle of rope. "That's a nice gentlemanly trick; but I've won, I believe."

Rolster said nothing at all, and they turned and walked back—both looking doggedly upwards at the telegraph frame, where, in a moment more, amid great suspense, Tiff's number was run up into the sky.

"The best race I ever rode," said Tiff, to his brother, as he jumped from the back of that little filly, which Helen Mallorie had once kissed on the nose.

There were tremendous cheers when he got to the ring, and more as, whipping off saddle and cloth, he walked in to weigh—quite a hero. "The gamest boy ever known. Where does he come from?" they asked.

Dick Nugent would have made addresses all over the ring about him—if he had been listened to, and claimed Tiff—although family differences had hitherto estranged them—as his favourite nephew.

Berty might well be pleased. On the top of the drag he declared he had won a million of money. Then Charlie Bedford got up to go a canter on Tom Seraphin's 'Rothley,' for the Grand South of England Handicap, and some other interest set the yelling and crushing alive again.

"You rode very patiently, Mr. Newmarch,"

said Lord Weston-Super-Mare, who had asked
to be introduced to Stephen.   He was here in
the quiet yellow suit, with the large red tie and
cigar.   His youthful heir too, was present,
learning to look about him a bit; and though
not more than twelve years of age, he had the
bigger cigar and the redder tie of the two.

"Yes, me lord," says Jim Doherty, who trains
in the Long Walk, hobbling up.   "I've been
sayin'—to be dragged fifty yards, and then get
up and win, ain't been heard of since me and
Bill Bean.   Come down and have a mount with
our drag hounds, Mr. Newmarch.   I've got a
horse you ought to buy, if we can only get you to
'face a stamp.'"

"I just waited till I saw we were in line with
'dover's tooth-pick on the steward's stand," said
Tiff, to Clancy, who was weighing in for the next
race.   "Then I went at him."

The gentleman jockey was delighted.   "Come
over to La Marche with me," he said.   "I'm
glad you chopped that booby, Rolster, anyhow.
They bought old Falstaff express for this race.
And now they tell me the party were backing him
last night—as if 'twas all over.   Poor old Lutterell
dropped two fifty, he tells me, and Detective
broke his back at that double, out of the seeds."

"Of course," insisted Berty, "you'll come back and go to the ball now."

But Tiff, who was dressing, refused. "I promised Aunt Penelope," he said. "My portmanteau is in the drag somewhere, if you don't mind coming home that far. Here's the white tie you lent me. Thanks." And he went on quietly scraping off the traces of Athelbury mud, with which he was plastered.

In his plain, dark suit, he looked as quiet and shy as ever. Taking his brother's arm, Stephen sauntered across the course towards the Hussars' drag, stopping to have a look at the horses which were already cantering for the next race, his honours not disturbing him much. Ridden out was his last race—over the last of these courses which he was ever to see railed and flagged ; nor was he ever to swing in scales, or buckle on a surcingle again. "By the way," Berty said, as they were taking leave of each other. "Who *is* Dick Nugent?" And he told Stephen of the five pound note, now, perchance, about to return.

"Why, don't you recollect ? He used to come to Sawtry, and manage to stay until our mother had to declare she was ill, to get rid of him. Claims to be Lord Clan-Gallowglass, in Ireland, and was always boring papa to help him in making the House of Lords do something or other."

So they said good bye. Stephen drove off to the station, and the rank and pernicious uproars in the meadows gradually died away in his ears.

CHAPTER V.

In the railway carriage Stephen could lie back and think it all over very placidly. The feat of pluck and resolution which he had performed, came to his even mind merely as an incident in the course of riding. He forgot it for the moment, in fact, only laughing to himself once when he remembered the queer sensation of looking up at the girths under his horse, and the *other* stirrup swinging about above. Now and then he felt with his finger how the scratch on his cheek was getting on, and whether it was swelling much.

Sometimes he used to wish a little that he had a few of Berty's fine things, for his luxuries were limited to a gratuitous mount with the hounds now and then from a friend; but on the whole he had got into a way of dismissing covetous wishes easily enough. ' I wonder what old Berty

did win for me,' he mused, just as his journey
was over: 'perhaps I shall be able to afford a
horse of my own, now. What robbers he's
among, to be sure! I suppose he and some
of his Ring friends will have the 'Maid' at
a trainer's, and backed heavily for the Liverpool, before a month. 'Tain't bad farming about
here. Those faggy woods, I daresay are Rushworth.' Then he counted over his money: with
what his mother had sent him, he had five pounds
nine and sevenpence left still.   'Let me see,' he
reckoned: 'Simkins, half-a-sovereign for my
mother—same from me; coachman, half-crown;
housemaid, ditto; fare back, twelve-and-six; fly
up to barracks, two bob. That'll leave me three,
ten and a penny to go on with. I'm quite rich!'
And in about two hours from the time he had
been dragged along the slushy meadows at Athelbury, he was driving up the avenue in the Rushworth dog-cart.

The dim October evening was just closing in
there; a smell of damp grass, and shrubs, and
fallen leaves loaded the air, and a soft haze was
over the meadows and woods.   How quiet they
are here, he thought, as he snapped off a rotten
branch above his head, and sniffed the air from
the fields: nothing seemed to be moving save the

sheep—great monsters, wandering about in the fog. Then the foggy avenue was passed, and the cheerful drawing-room windows flared down before him, throwing broad bars of light across the grass and gravel.

Lady Penelope came out to the hall to meet him. Tiff was a little shocked when he saw the change in her, and in the two girls beside her in deep black; while about them all remained a sense of something lost; and the bare and chill vibration of death had not departed from the house. " My mother wrote me everything, aunt," he said, quietly, when he was alone with them. " You know we have all felt for you, equally." So he was kissed, and Lady Penelope cried a little. Lucy looked very pale in her black dress; her eyes were darker than ever—too dark, Tiff thought—; and Cathy, as honest and frank as she always looked. ' When did he hear from his mother?' they asked.

" I think, on Tuesday," he said, colouring a little at the thought of intervening the week's work. " She told me some very sad things—for you know she tells me everything, aunt. Berty could not get long leave now, he wished me to say, but he sent you all his kindest love."

Then he talked about Willie, and any cheering

subject that he could think of. But though Lucy
was very nice, and sweet, and they were all fond
of him, the prospects were rather dull there.
' I almost wish I had stayed for the dance, after
all,' he said to himself. ' I wonder who won the
Handicap, too—' Rothley' never had pace, I am
sure.'

At dinner, again, there were sorrowful looks.
Lady Penelope asked Stephen, absently, now and
then about his Regiment, and whether he sat up
late, and if his Colonel were very strict and so
on; while he, all the time, was a little anxious to
hide the scarred side of his face from their sight.
Lucy was not slow to observe that; but kept it
in her own heart, dreading that something was
wrong. It made her unhappy—for she had longed
to believe Stephen different from all the others:
and now here was something he, too, had to
conceal. By God's permission—was he then, to
give his best days for the same bitter wages as
the others obtained? Her father's life and
death was hardly ever for a moment away from
Lucy's thoughts. Long ago she had learnt,
by some chance, the secret of his relationship
to Arthur Maxwell; it, and the like had made
her old and grave before her time. Trouble
and change enough had come upon her lately;

and once she used to ask herself why this were permitted in the world; but now she knew that it was the Devil's world, and that the Christian had no part at all in its plans and pleasures, nor should expect to find anything to be satisfied with here. It had been very wretched having to open one's eyes at all, and to learn more and more every day, that man, left to his own devices, imagines nothing but cruelty and weary folly. It was only by cutting herself off finally from the wearying mistakes and disappointments that come of friendship with the world, and looking alone to the sure hope promised, that she had even found rest. She had found it, however, and could have been bright and joyful all day long; but it was hard, even now, to think of entering into the Golden Gate alone, and having to see so many she dearly loved turned away. How she pitied Stephen as she looked at him—so simple-hearted, so plucky, and so honest. She did grudge him to the Devil very much. What was the cause of those scratches, she wondered? Had he got them in a prize-fight? Making many such guesses—which were comical: for she was unable to gauge correctly the depths men went to in their amusements; nor did she wish to be learned in these matters.

Lucy had much to keep her busy at home now. Thinking and acting for them all seemed to have fallen to her lot. Hence Stephen was left to himself the next morning, and he wandered about to places he remembered of old: it was rather melancholy work. Straw still littered the stable yard and coach-houses from the day when everything at Rushworth had been sold off; at the head-keeper's lodge the shutters were up, and no smoke came from the chimney, or from the boiling house close by. Empty kennels and stables were a sad enough sight for Tiff, and he turned away from it all up the hill, and through the plantations, putting up a few hares and pheasants as he went. On the crest of the great steep down, which overhangs the park, being tired, he perched himself atop of a loose stone wall that ran round a cover there, and took a look at the house below. He thought it had a dead and buried air; and this put it into his head that 'twas only for a short while that a fellow could enjoy a place, and then he must, somehow, die—no matter whether it was jolly there or not. All the years that his uncle had owned Rushworth were done with now, and the pleasure of living there couldn't come back; and the owner had had to go—no one knew where; but buried, there was no doubt of that. Those thoughts kept him whistling and thinking for a while. But the wide wind sweeping up the vale, and rocking the great firs over his head, blew too much oxygen into his young and ready blood, and cheered him too much, to let him dwell on sad things. Tracing the course of the broad trout stream in the park below, he thought how many good fish he and Willie had landed there; and how they used to quarrel about their flies, and make friends again, and get wet through! Some cads, he thought, would come now and try to fish the places; and wouldn't know the best ones, thank goodness. Then the landscape was done with, and he wondered if the County Paper had come yet, and what it would say about the races. So he made his way back to the house. In the long drawing-room, on a sofa by the fire, the paper was lying, uncut.—'Let's see the big race: by Jove!' (he reads aloud), 'Lord Ealing's Sable Cloud (Mr. Chaunter) first! I remember—little black mare. What do they say about me? Um! um!—'and, amid a scene of great excitement, Mr. Newmarch, who had waited with marvellous patience, came in the last three strides and won a terrific race, on the post, by a head.'

Rather gratified, Tiff leant back on the sofa, holding the paper before him ; and then a sigh in the room caught his ear.   He turned round, and there was Lucy seated at the window, nearly hid by the long curtains. She rose and came towards him with a smile on her face, though tears were collecting in her eyes, he imagined.

"I have read all about you, too," she said. "You were near being hurt—but you were not, after all, were you ?"

"No, not a bit," he said, confusedly.   She talked so quietly about his delinquency—'Why didn't so holy a girl scold him ?' he wondered. But this remained a puzzle, and there were many things inexplicable to Tiff, who did not boast so fine an intellect as his brother George.

" People run many dangers and arn't a bit afraid.   Death is an old wife's fable when we're young, I suppose," she mused, half aloud.   " We think it's a hundred years away, don't we ?"— (" So it is," said Tiff.)—" it is a fine thing to be brave."

" It was nothing," he said, shaking his head, and staring at her.

" Yes, I have been imagining that you didn't think a bit about fear, when you were— dragged."—

He saw her shudder at that word. Speaking gently, as if fearing to weary him, she said, "If I had been looking on, I'd have thought the devils clapped their hands then—because they hoped you were going to be theirs. *I* should have been afraid, though you were not. Don't you think Some one was very kind not to call you straight from that place, to account for all you've done? Was it not kind?"

"I don't know," he said, hanging down his head.

She came and sat by his side on the sofa. "Do I tease you?" she asked. "For I would go away if I did."

"No, no,—don't go," he said. And to be sure, 'twas rather hard on him to have to resist a beautiful creature like this. Scarcely fair, seeing that the Father of Lies now has mostly, and for long ages hath had, the monopoly of pretty, and wise, and warm-hearted people—scarcely fair that such a one as Lucy should be on the other side; such a one as she, made beautiful by a turn of the Maker's hand; by birth made delicate and most polite, and with it all cheery and talkative. As bold, as innocent. Not one bit afraid to say all she wishes or thinks, although knowing about as much of the slime of this world as young angels know.

In Lucy's case, ease and fearlessness were not
bred of cynical familiarity with horrors, but
came rather of having nothing to hide. She
sat meantime by the young jockey's side,
and was silent—praying probably, for words
to use to him. Since of herself she could not
contend with fierce, grown-up men such as he.
"You never thought of your soul during that
fall," she repeated, after a long time. "I know
the next world is the last thing in our minds at
times like that. It's about the littlest incidents,
close to us, we think."

"That's right, Lucy. But," as if trying to
remember 'something, " afterwards I did think
a little,"—he said.

"You know, Tiff," said Lucy, " God's patience
wasn't worn out with you ; for He called you back
that you might have time to repent and come to
Him."

He was touched by this, especially by the sweet
looks and manner and time specified above. He
knew he was not good at all, and would gladly
have read Lucy's books and pleased her—while
here. But it was very different to think of leaving all as she had done; for he had just won a
race. " Look! Lucy," he said. " I know I'm
very different from you and not fit to talk to you

at all. You were always good, Lucy. Much better than we can be. Oh! if I'd been like you, and
always with good people. I could bear trials
then."

"I am not good. My heart is as bad as yours,
Tiff," said she troubled by his error. But seeing
him shake his head, Lucy remembered that he
could not understand her meaning. "Oh! Tiff,'
said she, "don't wait for trials to be sent to you.
They never may be sent at all. You know what
I read once; perhaps your first trial will be hell
fire." When she told him this, she was no longer
in fun. Her words now seized and kept hold of
him. He was alone with her. The house was
perfectly still, and she sat close to him on the
sofa, as sad as though he were her own child,
and grievously ill. Her piercing sweet voice kept
telling him these ruinous and damning things.
Questions, forgotten from the days when he was
little, awoke and came out again to him. He
tried to clutch at the ideas and consolations
which used to uphold him; but they seemed to
have been broken short off, and he sank again.
He used to believe that he was among the fairly
good people, and while looking on at what
fellows did, it was his wont to pass many sins by
with a cautious laugh. When he grew up to be

a man, he was no longer afraid of God as women and children are. He feared nobody ; but had avoided grovelling and dishonourable sins, because he thought it was difficult or impossible to be a gentleman in the same boat with these vices. And now here, as he listened to Lucy, she made the long room a judgment hall, from the centre of which a voice announced how black and lost a wretch he was. His blackness of heart was written about the walls. He had never before seen the real hue of his transgressions. Would he be known for such an outcast beyond the room here ?

And Lucy besought several times that he would not harden his heart, that he would not wait for the blow which some day must be sent to awaken him from his lost state. And again, she seemed, although so slight and timid, his stern judge. It was already getting late, when she moved from her place. "Take this," said she, " and read it. I remember how I read it for the first time. Oh ! Tiff say you'll come now." She smiled, her smiles having such a charm as the sun, when it comes into a London garret by chance. She went, and left him sentenced in his own eyes, to death.

To death which he had merited. In that room

it was difficult to breathe. He walked out un-
steadily. "Perhaps your first trial will be hell
fire," he heard hummed in the air as he passed
the door. Then in the passage, the voice seemed
to confront him from the far end. These repeti-
tions must cease, or he must find Lucy again.
Perhaps he could leave these accusations behind,
inside the house. So he went out, and away
through the gardens, where those poor shabby
marbles and tablets were all damp and green now.
And taking the path along the trout stream,
Stephen quitted the park by the back gates.
Just beyond the lodge, he made out the direction
of a rough cart track, which leads from the
valley to an open down, where long ago they used
to shoot rabbits in the furze. He chose that
way hoping by tiring himself with rapid walking
to cure these fears. Hereabouts, a fine imagination like George's would have found enough to
distract him in the view opening up of the
water-meadows, and farms, and orchards—in
recalling the shooting parties there, who shot,
and what had become of them all. But Stephen
had no gift of fancy, and had in his mind hospitality for but one idea at a time. To his mind
there was merely the dark outline of the hill, and
then the sky, and Lucy so hard upon him, the

wind bringing her messages up after him. This fresh wind was here to give him life, and he could walk and climb ; while, but for God's long suffering mercy, he had never got up from Athelbury racecourse. Before now he would have had to give the account of his stewardship. The horse's hoofs striking a little farther one way, would have done it. He remembered some he had chanced to see killed. Harry Loft getting up to ride for a steeplechase in Ireland, and calling out, " Now, boys, it's either hell or the race." And he was killed at the second bank. Stephen had taken such things as that with a shrug of the shoulders and a grave face for a day. Now, where were these men, their first and their last warning given at the same time. And what a load of sin had he himself carried, through all his temptings of God.

He was trying to walk fast up this great hill to escape his thoughts. Were there any places far enough away, where sin could forget to follow, and weigh him down ? The wind, which blows here all the year round, turned into Lucy's mournful voice. He was wandering to and fro. Blindly, he stumbled down into hollows, and then toiled up steep places. The immense sky above, and the dark and foggy sides of the downs.

troubled him. During a lull in the wind, some heavy spots of rain dropped on his face, but the wet feel suggested nothing to him. By-and-bye his coat was wet, and that made him pause. Up above him—for he walked in a valley—there was a gravel pit in the hill side; over head vast rain clouds blotted their edges into each other, and he could not go back, but he might take shelter there. So, mounting the hill, he crept into the place, and there the rain would wet him no more. The night coming on, found Stephen crouching in this place, but he did not miss the light, seeing other things. When the wind folded back for a moment the huge black scarves of cloud, he knelt at the entrance, and, with trembling hands held towards the light the little book Lucy had given him, so that he might read what it said, as long as day remained. Pebbles fell from the roof upon the page which he tried to read, and rain drops wetted it through. He fed upon the words she had given him.

Meanwhile, after her mother had got her tea, and the servants were talked to, and the household cares all ended, Lucy had crept away, and locking the door of her cold room, she prayed hard for Stephen. He would be given to her prayers; she knew. Now, when she wished him taken from danger, now, when youth and health and energy were his ; surely she would not be required to wait till sin, having gnawed his flesh, should deign to cast the bones to God! This very moment, if it were possible, she asked.

This was the moment when he was reading her book in the pit.

CHAPTER VI.

IT was October then, and while the weather was cold and bleak at Rushworth, and where Bertram was, at Norton, which is far to the south, the days were still mild and cheerful.

George, we remember, had resolved to continue a thoughtful friend—and a guide, if need be—to Mrs. Tresham. He was never tired of rejoicing over the feat he had accomplished and gave thanks to his earnest and resolute gods for the victory. " *Liberavi animam meam*," he might have said at this time. 'And what a faithful expression that was of the relief, the deliverance effected by one strong effort of will in one moment of time. Broken off was the yoke of his sin, of his weakness, of his treachery, of his deadly covetousness; broken off by truth, broken off by one stout effort.' And now he had only to keep building the way, as it were, behind him, while he advanced; to keep rivetting those better resolutions by singleheartedness, by innocent free enjoyment, by watchful earnest work of one kind or another.

He was very happy then, and would gladly have seen Helen happy, and hopeful too. But she was, perhaps, a little wayward, and difficult to interest in the nobler path. ' It might be,' he began to fear, 'he could not altogether comprehend her sensitive intellect. She had not developed it as she might have done.' And he was forced to acknowledge by-and-bye (for he gave every order of thought fair play), that they had very little to say to each other, indeed, once they ceased to talk of love making. When it was all " darling," and " precious," and sighs and squeezes, conversation seemed to flow quite easily. But now, she was strangely silent and dull. I think, on the whole, she fancied that George was patronising her. Why, she asked, should he take airs, and insist on being so much better than she was? She did not care to be with him now, and he had no resources without her. He would try to take up a book at times, and before half a page was read, it had dropped in his hand, and he found himself going over the old, old track again. And yet, he could no more bear the thought of

leaving her now than he could have done a month
ago. At times he would mock at this sham
union of theirs—like a cheque unsigned after all.
Indeed, it threatened to be unbearable, now that
there was hardly anything in the way of novelty
to be said. All the brave and tender expressions
of honourable affection had been repeated over
and over—till their flavour went. He had looked
the same look of courageous hopelessness, fifty
times at least, and one could not be sighing both
in the morning time, and after luncheon, too.
Truth to tell, before a fortnight, a quarrel—or
what is worse, a yawn—had intruded itself more
than once. Our lady, on her part, at best but
appreciating dimly the great platonic idyll, which
George considered he was acting out, began to
fret in her unreasonable heart at this last fashion
of his. He was so dull, she querulously said,
wondering to herself if the lover might not, perhaps, be as stupid as the husband sometimes?
But this was unfair. She ignored the fact that
their affinity stopped so far short. Still, she used
to dread lest he was only a muff, whom she had
thought a hero, and used to ask herself " Is he
more afraid, then, than I am?" For generosity
and forbearance, some said, were quite incompre-
hensible to her, even from early youth.

It was that Helen, being a spoilt little thing, wanted some more fun after a while.   How could she puzzle her wee brain, comprehending his æsthetic notions of friendship, and what not? Her boy was twice as amusing when he was wont to tell her how miserable he felt.   She was vexed, too, at the loss of the piquant little despairs which had come after those first dangerous love scenes.   A touch of tragedy was excessively captivating now and then.   "And," she asked, " did conscience make so much disturbance, and upbraid one for nothing but this?"   Successive days of autumn weather, the same regular rows on the river, if it were fine, or rides through the forest; perhaps one set kiss at the end of their walk, and a long squeeze of the hand at night.

He was not slow to interpret that, and took to shaking hands in rather a sheepish way, each evening, Helen, as she took her silver candlestick from him, putting the least tinge of contempt into her " good night."   By and bye, he used to find himself laughing sardonically in his room at the whole thing.   But it is poor merriment laughing, ever so eclectically, at yourself.   It is close to cursing yourself, which by and bye he did; and next would acknowledge being ashamed of it all.   " 'Pon my honour, I am like the hero in some third rate French novel. He upbraids heaven and his mistress for things which are only the convolutions of his own infernal vanity ! No, come ; we will take an Englishman's way of fighting temptation and difficulties." And so, smiling, he would turn over to sleep.

He was on this heavy track of thinking, one evening especially ; and the day that followed he thought proper to remind Helen that he must keep up the part of a frank English man of honour, making this the more apparent, because the last day or two he fancied he had been borne away once or twice. It was his bargain they were carrying out, he remembered.

She did not like this mood, poor child, at all. Not even did he give her one of the brave and helpful kisses that day; and quickly noticing his reserve, she was very angry. If overtures to hard propriety were to be made, it was not from him, the boy, the college scapegrace, the Sawtry rough-rider—that they should come, but of privilege from herself. If anybody was to be prudish, she might have the option. Indeed, little Helen held sometimes imaginary dialogues, in which George's wicked advances were repelled by quiet, wifely dignity on her part; or rehearsed to herself, as a mental act of repara-

tion, domestic dramas, in which she was coldness
and decorum personified. Her memory had never
been trained, and was deficient. Meanwhile, all
that seemed now taken out of her hands, and so
they walked on the lawn; George went on talking such, such good sense, so quietly put. Of
honour he talked a little, and of hard work, and
its sure rewards. Of the beautiful lessons in the
trees, about them, too; and taught her the names
of those delicate ferns which grew by the boat
house.

She was furious. He should suffer for this,
and she would bring him back to her feet, or she
was much mistaken. The poor, obsequious, weary
tempter was summoned—from perhaps ever so
far off—to her aid. And of course he came, as
he ever does, to beautiful people who are bent on
mischief—no matter how they snub him. After
a while Helen's tone changed; she would hardly
even speak to her imitation lover, and grew more
and more reserved and distant as the daylight
went.

He was right, no doubt, in some of the things
he said, and she was afraid there would be talk—
the minute the sun set. Then, in the very middle of a generous rhapsody of George's, on some
of the social wrongs that our dear old country is

nigh dying of, and how all that is truest and best in us ought to unite to cure them—she went in doors to dress, without so much as shaking hands or gathering a flower for his coat even. It was quite too much. Was he always to be teaching her her walk in life? with his *réchauffée* of earnest slang, cribbed from the reigning Oxford latter day saint. " I," said little Helen, stamping her foot, " who have heard all this good talk since I could walk; why, I read prettier things than that in my Daisy Chains and pretty books before he had smoked his first cigar! He is tiring of me," she gasped, in terror, as a wind up to her irony.

Such bitter thoughts were Helen's, as the sun went down, and they parted. Him she saw still far off from her. What had he not been to her? And yet he was changed and hard. And George, at that very hour, scarce dared to look at her, vexed and silent, yet more lovely than words could express. He saw her turn away and stand some way off, her head bent in thought. Then he observed on her pale face a look so gently loving, so imploring, and so full of sorrow. But he withdrew his eyes, mistrusting himself, until his love was gone a little while. Then tracing the way she took, he thought her very walk was his—his own.

When the time came to dress, George pondered
long before the glass, repeating in a mocking
voice. "So much for the glorious sunset lessons
I told her of; and the next day to rise; and the
growth of all things as the ferns grow; and we,
the noblest work of all," he sneered. "I have
said, one single kiss of hers is worth all the
patchwork labour and sorrow of having a mind
and a soul at all. But she seems changed, too.
Oh! Helen! I wonder is there anything worth
living for, after all—even with her." And while
crumpling many white ties, George classified the
pleasantest things he had ever known; shooting
and hunting, and pleasant friends, and then what
he had once aspired to, sweet and noble things.
They were all delusions and failures. And then,
back here he came, and rambled on in the same
well-worn tracks. To this had come their pact of
ethereal friendship? "Lasted a week, and we
quarrel; and I hang on her slightest look—can
no more live without her than under the sea.
Wretched fool! And she is angry with me, because I am colder than once I was. And she's
wisest, I think. Transparent imposture! To
have one head, and soul, and mind in common;
and to stop short there. My darling! how cruel
and senseless I was to-day. And for what?"

So, as he harped on that morning and evening, he at last had to finish his dressing, yawning, and was very late for dinner; and found, for company, the Hardicanutes, from Farwell, and General Rumbold and his daughter, whom George rather liked. He sat by Mrs. Hardicanute, after he had, in an absent way, apologised for being late; and he stupidly listened, as she and Mr. Tresham discussed—with enthusiasm, almost with pathos—the charms of each dish which was tried in turn.

"Really, not a bad saddle of mutton that," said Mr. Tresham, gravely humouring his guest's special way of thinking.

"Not at all, is it?" answered the lady of Farwell, gracefully concealing the fact that her mouth was full.

"Frederick Hamby used to say that he could only help two people off a saddle of mutton' Two cuts, Mrs. Hardicanute—one at each side of the back-bone—and 'twas all over."

"Ah! yes. Poor Frederick Hamby. We have not many like him left. Now, I noticed your cook gives no flavour to these puddings; and so right. Some disguise them so absurdly, with one exaggerated flavour or another."

"Ah! no!" Mr. Tresham answered. "I tell

her particularly." And so on; while, with fixed and weary eyes the lady seemed to await the next dish.

By and bye George joined in a conference which they were having on the choice of schools for very little boys. She was a slow, solemn woman, and she fancied George smiled at the oddest times; for why should talk of Worthing or Littlehampton doctors make him laugh to himself? But it was something about Helen; some of her baby terrors of cows, when out walking, that came into his head. "I daresay my dear finds old General Rumbold very amusing. What are they talking about there, I wonder? I suppose he has hauled those guns over the Pyrenees by this—'and the Dook he said to me.'"

So George began thereon to drink his wine in a moody way, and he recklessly accused her of flirting with the General. 'She would flirt with them all,' thought he, observing her more flushed and charming than ever, as she turned in the direction of her neighbour's cumbrous speeches, not hearing one word, but laughing noisily all the time; so much, indeed, that Mrs. Hardicanute turned her head and her fan once or twice in that direction.

And Helen noticed it; and also seeing his

scowl, said to herself, "I cannot lose him," whereat she shuddered, though a laugh was on her face.

Yet, once in the drawing room again, she came to George with flashing eyes. "What a frightful temper you are getting," she managed to whisper, when they were together for an instant, in a far end of the room, by a table which held the tea things. She perceived his settled scowl, and laughed. "I never saw a temper so changed." Then she left him with a sweep, and fell in with the talk going on among the other ladies. "Yes, of course, Mrs. Hardicanute, you are perfectly right. Here is your tea—and she never would go there; and she said, an attack of her eyes; yes. But they declared, as long as Sir Patrick Balfour was asked, she never would put her foot inside Bullingworth gates again."

"If I have a temper it is you that have given it to me," murmured George, when she returned for more tea. "Why are you like this?"

"Like what, George?"

'His blood ran faster than by day,' she thought. And then he fixed his clouded eyes on her with a previous look in them. "You are not what you were, Helen." He left her the duty of defending herself. She, by way of defence, whis-

pered merely, " Darling," expressed in a be-
seeching voice—peculiar to herself—sufficient to
send a shiver through his veins, or nerves.   The
patient closed his eyes for a moment.   Then,
in   their   practised   secret   tones,   he   pleaded,
"Helen!   Helen!   don't talk like that.   You
know what it is to hear you call me that.   Don't
say it."

" Shan't I ?"

" Oh! am I not powerless ?   Look ! Do anything to me;   only continue to love me."   He
dared not look at her, but heard sweetly repeated,
in the same tones as his.   "You   know   that   I
do."

And after hearing that, he smiled, saying,
" My precious, what have I done to-day ?   But
I was wretched all the time, nor ever kissed my
baby even.   Go to them now;   curse this un-
steady saucer.   But come back to-night, when
they're all gone.   I have so much to—"

She looked, "I will;" and left him.   He
drank his tea, and then swung himself down on
a chair, with a flush on his face.   He knew how
to change his manner readily, and came to Miss
Rumbold, who was imparting to Enid Hardicanute some details of a new crochet stitch which
she had just learnt—interrupting them, perhaps

rudely, " Look, Miss Rumbold," he said, " I shall teach you to draw pigs with your eyes shut. Now, take this paper, and if there should be any difficulty in shutting your eyes by yourself, Miss Hardicanute'll hold them down for you. I beg your pardon, though ; it's one eye young ladies can't shut."

" Oh! then you don't require two needles," Miss Enid was saying.

" No, dear. What, Mr. Newmarch? Oh! my eyes are always shut—to anything that's going on," said Mary Rumbold, quietly.

" Mary sleeps with her eyes shut," said Enid. " No, I mean open. What do we mean, Mary?"

" Now, the great thing," George explained, " is to come back along the curl of the pig's tail the same way you went. And then you go along the curve of his back, and get his eye where it ought to be—"

Miss Mary laughed good humouredly. Her pigs were better executed than George's even. The other young lady thought him insufferable— always a younger son—with nothing, and no manners. Hers were mournful pigs, having eyes anywhere but in their heads. Mary Rumbold shewed George some puzzles, with numbers. He liked her well enough : but ' my eyes are always

shut—to anything that's going on.' What did
that convey? He hated double meanings. Yet
while Helen looked at him and this poor girl
together, she grew jealous; and, trusting him
not, proposed some music to be sung. Mr. Hardicanute had got close down to a picture-book in
order to yawn into it quietly. Then came his
daughter, and rustling up to the piano, with a
whisper to her mother, the two ladies began a
little duet: and a beautiful song sang Miss Enid,
looking as cross and fatigued as ever; her
mamma watching her, and making a sound of
voice of her own at places. A kind of hymn she
sang—standing decked with lockets, and heaving
pink-grounded laces, and wandering ribbons.
' Be-cause there is none other that fighteth for
us—but only thou, O Lord,' Enid warbled,
smoothing her pretty little elbows, and fluttering
a lace handkerchief, to the end of those well-
known words; and George, in a fine mood of
scorn, thought of the dire need expressed by the
flippant young lady's song. *None other!* And
for the people who sang it first—hungry and
wounded, naked and feet torn with flints—that
alone to rest on! to-morrow, with mother and
wife, to encounter, perhaps the lions—and no one
to help them in this evil world, but 'Thou, O

Lord.' Thus ran the song, savouring of the
rocks and deserts, and he thought of the pathos
in it all. So, forgetting Miss Rumbold quite, his
fancy strayed away—picturing Helen one of these
martyrs. And when Miss Enid rustled away, he
gave his applause, still looking at his beloved.

"Would the people never go away," he began to
ask. He was sure the clock had stopped—though
in truth, Helen, knowing one is bored on these
occasions, had put it on a quarter of an hour.

At last the Rumbolds' carriage came and took
them away homewards. " Sulky young puppy !"
said the General to his daughter, as they rolled
along. " To think that that's Brian Newmarch's
son !"

" How they do go on, papa !" says Miss Mary,
in awe.

" Nonsense, child. Bless my heart! You
women are always casting forward after some
scandal or other. You might give rational
people credit for a little sense. I suppose I must
ask the young prig to shoot to-morrow—write
him a note;" and the old soldier, who had heard
the Norton circle talked of quite enough, was
soon snoring soundly. As soon as their backs
were turned, Mr. Hardicanute had said, ' The
general fancied he was the only man in England

who understood farming. Had wasted a fortune at that wretched place of his.' Then the Farwell carriage came. And when their backs were turned, Mr. Tresham said 'his old friend, John Hardicanute, had never held up his head since he married Jean McTrossach. He told him how it would be.'

"Why doesn't Walter Hardicanute give them a living?" said Mrs. Helen. "I'm sure if we had a rich son—he should give us a living, Charles. Good-night, Mr. Newmarch." She looked hard at him, and went.

"I'm going to stay and read," says George, sitting down to a volume of Paley. Mr. Tresham wandered away to his study; and finished that article for the "Gentleman's Magazine," about three next morning: and George remained there alone—alone with the lamp, and a forgotten glove of Miss Enid's, and "the Book of Nonsense," and a workbox of Helen's, and "Hymns Ancient and Modern," and the "Churchman's Almanac," and the table cloth, which he buried his face in. 'She is never, never coming,' he said, biting his fingers. But at that moment, back she came; like a wandering little ghost; all her ornaments off, and a book held in her hand. She went straight up to him, with staring, anxious eyes; and, saying not a word, gave him a tiny kiss. "Why have you stayed?" she asked, meekly; then smiling, she inclined her face a little way towards him, which was sufficient.

"My own darling, have you come back to me?" he said, with those truisms lovers use. Then he pressed all her silks to his heart: "People will hear me rustling," she whispered, in a little fright.

"What a darling you are!" George murmured, looking at her. He needed to say very little. It was easy to talk now. "May I let down your hair?—you said I might some day."

"Look!" said she; "I wished to shew it to you. It is real—every bit!" and Helen shook it down to her waist, then drew herself away, that he might contemplate her, standing in the middle of her drawing-room with all her straight and drab-coloured hair undone. He and she believed that Norton at eleven o'clock was a fairy palace, built for one night by a waving of wands and a spell, where no one lived but their two selves alone. He also thought that this would soon be over; and she thought to herself, 'does he love me enough yet, not quite enough?'

"I didn't think you could look so sweet, if you

tried, my own," said he. "Come and sit by me here."

"No, George. I said I'd never sit there with you again."

And she drew herself away from him.

"You shall," said he, with a stamp of his foot; and winding his arm around her waist, he brought her near to him.

"If you make me, I must—but is it not so very, very wrong of you?" He, for answer, was trying to plait her hair like a ladies' maid would; and as he slid his fingers right through it, he said to himself, 'how it felt like tame and cold serpents tingling in his hands.' "Now talk to me," said he, brushing away some long threads which had ventured out on her forehead, in order that it might be clear; "talk to me. I know how unhappy I have made you. Shall I ever, ever be unkind to my darling again? What an idiot I was! You know everything best; whatever you wish I will always do."

Then they were both perfectly happy; she was nestling against his shoulder—never a word to say: quite contented with her first love, and her only friend. Resting by him was like the feel of floating down some brimful river in a dream. "I could stay here for ever safe by my own," she thought.

And "darling," she heard him say, " I am looking at you, so as always to remember your face,
just as it is now. How much shall I love you?
as much as I can love, I think."

" Yes, but more than that," she craved ; and
pursing up her little mouth, whispered, " I don't
like being looked at."

" Well, may I receive some kisses, then, if I
mayn't look at you ?"

" No ; it is forbidden."

" One ?" said he. And Helen slowly turned
her mouth upwards to him, smiling as though
'twould all be sure to last.

Then he said much the same as on that day
soon after his return from the funeral at Rushworth. They each looked upon the other's dimmed
and half shut eyes. But immediately they started
asunder, for there was a crash like all the glass in
Cinderella's kingdom being struck together. Both
their hearts stopped beating, as we say, while,
two cowards, they stood and stared. What was
it all? " Oh! Lawd! Lawd! 'Ere, Mrs. 'Olland,
where are you ?" they heard a gruff voice muttering in the next room. " My—my Lawd 'a mercy !
What have you done, Turner ?"

Helen vanished. The library, the drawing
room, and the dining room here, were side by

side, like stalls in a stable and opened into each
other. " So there is a Providence," said George,
reflecting impartially on the lamp's fall. Then
going to open the dining room door, yawning,
and with Paley in his hand, he saw Mrs. Holland,
housekeeper, on her knees by a kitchen candle,
gathering up bits of the lamp shade, while
Turner—who had been putting wine away, no
doubt—stood by, bemoaning the ruin he had
caused. " Good gracious! how you startled one,
Turner. I was half asleep," said he. ' Cautious
people, we,' thought George. " Half the servants
in the next room."

CHAPTER VII.

NEXT morning, Helen sailed into the breakfast
room, calm and abstracted. They had a few
minutes to themselves, and George marvelled she
could shake hands like that, himself half ashamed
to look at her. But with an air of tranquil
innocence, she poured out one cup of tea after
another in a row.

"See how Turner mended the lamp," said she,
pointing to the side-board. "He must have sat
up half the night, and got a new shade. He
brought it in with the most lofty air this morning."

"Turner had been drinking last night, Mrs.
Tresham," said George.

"I am glad he dropped that lamp," Helen
added, meekly. "What a narrow escape I had."
George scowled as usual. "Do you know, when

I went to see my baby this morning, it was very
ill. I was so frightened, George. But Charles
says he thinks it is nothing."

"I got a note from the general this morning," said the plaintiff. "They want me to go
over and shoot there to-day."

"I suppose you will marry Miss Rumbold now,
as you are tired of me. I saw that you loved her
best last night," said Helen.

George smiled. " After last night, of course,"
said he. " No, Helen, never," and he reflected.
" No, if she were as rich as one Croesus, and as
good as Lucy Felton is, and as handsome as
Cleopatra, and as well-bred as Bay Middleton,
and as clever as Talleyrand, I wouldn't marry
her, I think."

Then Mr. Tresham came in.

George's shooting at General Rumbold's was
very poor that day. The other gentlemen gave
up laughing at him before long. And, when the
men picking up the game scorned to look in his
direction after a shot, and he had blown a few
hen pheasants to pieces, something must
evidently be very wrong. Indeed the general
coming round a corner, lit upon George standing
stock still; his gun unloaded under his arm,
while just behind his heels, the hares were

scudding across in shot, and rolling over and over in the net.

"Cock awver. Mark! Cock gettin' 'oop. Ha! Ha! Whish! whish!' went the beaters all around him: but in fancy he was miles away. They asked him to stay to dinner. But, of course, it was found he had brought no clothes; and, as the general was a foot bigger than him in every direction, George begged to be excused; and ended by walking back, and being late for dinner at Norton too. There he found them very dull, the child much worse. He spent a miserable evening. There were no Magazine articles to take *him* away. George could not read, his select authors all repelled him—on such bad terms was he with himself—while every five minutes Helen was running off to see her child. Next morning was little better. George wandered away to the river. Down there he could look into the water and think. He had hardly spoken three words to Helen to-day. 'How long will all this last?' he asked. He did not want death to come interfering here. He found their own boat and tried to scull, but he had no dash left in him. Back he turned, and found Helen and her husband in the library, and the doctor trying with some faint jokes to cheer her a little. But she would not stay, and Mr. Tresham began walking to and fro.

"My wife has been terribly anxious all day, George, but no cause—no cause," he said. After a while, Helen came back and absently sat down to some work. Fear tied her weak tongue, it seemed. Her husband discreetly left her to herself, and George dreamt and dreamt in his own domain. Perhaps he was silent from good taste. Her child usurped the thoughts that were usually his, and he repeated to himself, 'Our love flourishes in prosperous times only. I suppose it's a fancy, born of idleness and ease, and has no place beside real trouble.'

'This is a judgment for my Geordie,' she dreaded, in her turn; wishing that she could avoid seeing his moody face before her. 'How angry Heaven is that I let my boy love me. And now it will take my babe away from me.' At last she said, in her little whimpering voice, "Charles, do you know my child had a blister on when I went up?"

"Well—well."

"Yes, and it stopped crying when it saw me. Emma said it had cried for an hour before. And I down here, laughing !"

"Now, Helen, don't give way." George walked

about the room. "Poor little thing," he said, simply, thinking how he could console the mother, for he was ever quick enough to pity. "I had a blister on once. Did it make your child all pink, Mrs. Tresham? It did me."

But Helen bent her head till salt tears fell on her work, and she sobbed, "Cruel, unkind. I know you're making fun, and laughing at my precious child." Drops gathered fast in her great eyes, till by-and-bye she gave way to a fit of crying. She cried for crying's sake. And 'twas only what his awkward quaintness always did. But Mr. Tresham, surprised in truth, begged her to reflect for a moment. "Surely George New-march meant nothing unkind. There was no real danger either; the doctor had told her so over and over again."

As for George, he was quite helpless. How could he be sorry enough? Laugh at her poor little baby! For what? he'd rather do anything. But she could only sob, and then hide her eyes. ' I'd like to be one of those tears,' thought George, ' to be crushed there and remain there.' And then he left the two together, and went out, musing on the last misfortune. And that poor little child in the nursery, he thought of its innocent interruption to their affinities with frowns.

'My worst rival it is, I always knew that,' he said, mockingly. But, indeed, he had not had much to complain of hitherto. Knowing her delicate and childish temper, he could understand how she had taken offence at his words. Yet he was very miserable and walked on to be alone. If she came to hate him now, what would he ever do on earth? 'I know I meant no unkindness, and she will remember that, won't she?' said he. But were these not wretched hours? 'Tears my love shed,' he muttered aloud, in one of his most crooked fits of remorse. 'Aye, but not the last she'll have to shed, perhaps.' Now he had got to his favourite river again. It was a soft warm evening, and a fog rose from the meadows opposite. Far away down the reaches, the herons and pigeons kept their toilsome flight over the reed beds, and a duck or two crossed the stream high in the air. 'What a happy place this ought to be,' occurred to him, during a moment's truce; 'no one to trouble us but ourselves.' Then he wondered what she was thinking of while he was away. 'Why need I ask, though? not of me, I know I'm never in her thoughts when we're apart.' Now that something had come between them, and she was angry with him, he had not to decide what he might, or might not, wish for.

And 'twas an inexpressible relief to have a truce from that strife and doubt for a while.

'These stones here should skim famously,' thought he; and, choosing a flat one, sent it sighing away over the smooth brown water. A few drops of rain fell; and he turned back once more. There was nothing to do. Helen was gone, and he could gladly have slept and forgotten sensation. Turning into the stables, he found the old coachman in his harness room, where it was warm. George saw little of the servants here, and now thought he would begin and make friends with this one, while he brightened up his bits. Perhaps he was sulky at first, but by and bye they had become the best of friends; and George learnt all about his sons, how one was apprenticed to a man who tried to keep back his wages, and how tall the other had grown—six inches in the year. This had a kind of interest for George, who, since he had left her angry with him, had moored his thoughts fast, just lazily taking in easy ideas that floated up to him. The short day passed in this manner.

In the nursery, poor Helen went through a dreadful season of watching. Her little child seemed gradually to get worse; each time she looked at it, more hot and restless. Her husband

had not come to the nursery for a long, long
time, and the doctor would not return till to-
morrow.   Perhaps, in the meantime, it would
die; he lived ever so far off, and doctors were so
unfeeling—just said a few words, and left hours
of agony, till they came again.   Sometimes she
would take her child from the cradle, and walk up
and down with it.   But it cried and struggled in
her arms, and Emma said it ought to be left in
its cot.

Poor Helen sat by the fire, fearing to speak to
the nurse, or to her maid, who came to and fro.
Those women did not comfort her, though they
rocked the cradle by turns.   Then it became
dark; and when next she felt the little round
wrist, the pulse there seemed to fly more fast
than yet it had, and the baby's brown, troubled
eyes, knew her no more, she fancied.   Most guilty
now, she could look at it no longer.   ' It will die
before my eyes, and I can't stay and bear it.'

Stupified with fear, Helen left the room—to go
anywhere—to escape seeing and hearing what
must come.   A little way down the cold passage,
she stopped and leant against the wall—twisting
her hands over her half open mouth.   But still,
at intervals, the querulous bitter cries of her child
followed, plainly heard through the lonely house.

To her own room they would not come, perhaps ; when the door was shut she might be alone here —if, indeed, those moans had not got into her head. The room was chilly, and little light remained, while the rain kept pattering gently against the window glass outside. Thrown on the toilet table, with her needle in it still, lay the pretty cape begun for her babe, and fitted once to the darling neck.

" It will never be finished now. Oh ! what shall I do ! Oh ! what shall I do !" cried Helen. And, falling upon her knees, she tried to make herself pray. But she sprang up again, and the pale young creature stood without power, and rocked herself to and fro. To whom now could she pour out her heart, and turn for help? Neither to the wise and good ones of this world, nor to God—whom people crawl to when out of work. For conscience kept sentinel across that door, and those promises, which the weary are allowed to plead, were withdrawn from her, she knew. " I did it—I did it !" the forlorn one moaned. " Oh ! I've killed my darling child. O great God ! spare its life a little longer. I didn't ever mean to be unfaithful to my husband —did I ? O God, have mercy—and do not take my babe; and I shall never think of George any more. I hate him now. Oh! do I not?"

But the rain continued to fall, the short day was turning to night, and under the lash—as it might be called—she threw herself upon the sofa, and, bending her head, this bargain she made: "If thou wilt give me back my babe this time, O Lord! I will never let George Newmarch love me any more—never!—never! I only loved him a little bit. It was letting him kiss me many times," she groaned, "that God is angry with. Yes, I am lost; for it was that—it was that."

Thus went up her gasping prayers, someway towards the throne, till her anger finished in passionate sobs, and her clasped hands were wet and cold with tears. When she had wept herself tired, Helen rose. Her baby might live yet, she thought; and worn out and frightened she stared about the room. What hour was it? No one came to talk to her, and that made her cry again a little. Sorrowfully, she wandered back along the passages to the nursery, and listened before the door. Not a sound within, but Emma's boots. The heavy nurse-maid turned round from looking at the cot, as Helen glided in. "It is dead," the mother said, half aloud; and then she noticed her husband there. " Hush! please !" he said, a little fretfully. " Do not make a noise, I beg."

And Helen now beheld that her babe slept, with its fat hands clenched, and a frown of pain upon its gem-like face; but still slept—safe and sound. Now it would get well, she was sure. There was no danger, and how needlessly alarmed she had been. She went to the window, and leaning her elbow on the sill, cried softly to her-self. Though she said nothing more, Helen thought her husband was brutal to look so cross when she had come in. He did not love his child—no, not half as much as she did. Every-body was unkind; but Constance would get well. She would finish the cape now—at once—and line it with violet quilted silk. Everything was smiling, it seemed though it was almost dark now. And then, with another joyful look towards the cradle, she stole away on tiptoe, and sat on the sofa in the drawing room—very happy, though it was chilly and raining.

After a time came her husband; and, sitting by her side, held her hand, not saying much. " I wonder where George Newmarch is?" she asked: " I want to tell him my beloved child is quite well."

Her husband was not thinking of their guest, perhaps. "You had little faith," he said, with a smile.

"Oh! I was not frightened. Now, you are going to be cross and brutal to me again, Charles. Mayn't I love my precious babe, if I like?"

Her husband patted her hand good-humouredly. "My dear, all that is beside the issue. How little you are used to trouble, Helen."

Then lights came, and by and bye George Newmarch joined them; so that it was a far brighter evening than the last had been. Indeed, everybody's spirits returned during dinner; and George had to relate all he had done at Farwell the day before, and what he had shot and didn't shoot.

"Foster's son told me, in great confidence, that Jack Rumbold goes out and shoots all the best fields, about eight o'clock in the morning, before we begin," said he.

"What a horrid boy that is," Helen remarked, in a chastened tone. "He used to be so nice before he went to Eton. I think Eton ruins boys. I know one it did, I'm sure."

"Thank you," said George. "I'm very fond of Jack Rumbold; can't help it—he's so like Mary."

"Ah! I forgot," Helen said, resignedly.

"Well, I suppose we ought not to say much," Mr. Tresham observed, "for the general told me last night that two of my dogs get loose—and go over and hunt his covers, regularly, on their own account. And he's given orders to have them shot. Do you hear that, Helen?"

"Aye, there was a brute of a Newfoundland yelping about Satchel wood just before we went through it," said George, "I had a shot at him, but he was too far off."

"How cruel you are," said Helen, plaintively. "I daresay that very dog was my pet, Ralph."

"I daresay it was," said George, reflecting; "for he did look an oppressed sort of poor wretch."

CHAPTER VIII.

AND now that her little girl was over the late small danger, and that the sun came out at Norton, and Helen could ride and walk about, she was quite happy to have her boy by her side once more.   As to her bargain, the fragile little creature simply forgot all about it ; nor ever, it is to be believed, even recollected how she had promised to give up her offending, till long, long after ; then, no doubt, with smiles.   Indeed, what else could she do ?   She would be ungrateful to be afraid now.   He was always thinking about her, she could reckon upon that : and it was so nice here now that nobody troubled them at all.   She liked him when he amused her with his queer fancies, and was docile and not fierce.   She used to delight in saying she was certain he did not care for her a bit, just on purpose to hear him persuade her that he did.   I suppose he gladly bore such tyranny. It was so sweet to him to find the approach of sickness and sorrow had not changed her, and that they could be fond of each other again.

That was the first thing he thought of, and the only thing he had time to care about. For in face of the danger of losing his Helen, when the child was ill, he had not once as much as considered whether their last reconciliation was to be repented of or not. It is to be believed that he read hard after this, and, on the whole, had not been so bright and cheery for many a day. He would never be really happy till he was certain she loved him. But it was hard to be exacting, when she was so joyous. So he just passively took each day as it came.

Thus weeks went by, and as long as she would say sweet things to him he had an equivalent for those chance fits—jealousy, and self-contempt, and despair—to which he was now, indeed, getting a little used.

Mr. Jack Rumbold, who had left Eton and was, we saw, selfishly making use of his liberty among his father's partridges, became rather a friend of George's. In the raw November days, when Helen's little white nose would have run risk of getting red in the open air,

and she preferred to stay in doors, the two
young men would pass the time rabbit shooting, or occasionally in expeditions along the
coast after wild duck.   Once, even, they went out
trawling with some of the Leet fishermen, and,
to Helen's terror, were away two days and two
nights.   Jack Rumbold was going to Oxford in
the spring, and looked up to George with a
certain respect, as to one who knew all about
those places.   But when they went out on
rough work George could not help envying his
companion's sturdy ways, and his utter want of
imagination.

"I wish I were as stupid as he," thought
George.   "Oh! how happy blunt witted people
are.   If I could dismiss everything with a 'I
say, coom out o' that now,' as Jack does!"

Sometimes Helen would be cross if George
went too often shooting rabbits.

"I know you long to be with Mary Rumbold,"
she would say.   "You really spend the days with
her instead of shooting.   And you love her, because she reads poets to you, whom you understand.   You despise me, because I am ignorant."

"My darling," he used to say, "did poets ever
dream of such a sweet, sweet as you?   They
never had the chance, poor fellows."

She liked the custom of being pressed to his heart, while he had a gun in the other hand. He looked so strong in muddy gaiters and thick boots, dear boy! Indeed, he grew to be at all times so tender and gentle to her, that in addition to making George her tame domestic lover, Helen got insensibly to like him as well. She missed him when he was away, and she found nothing to supply his place, although she was allowed to do just what she pleased, having only to look cross one minute for her husband to yield good-humouredly to every fancy. At that time, about the beginning of December, it was bright wintry weather. The mornings were so fine that George thought no more of shooting, but often took Helen for walks or rides. Once away from the house, and well in the forest, it was a joy to breathe the very air. On each side near them, the heath land stretched out clear and wide, in ribs of brown, and grey, and gold. Birch trees with emerald heads, speared on dove coloured stems, rose out of the heath like tall creatures feeding, while bounding the view tender blue tufts of copse and wood stretched all around, away back to Norton Manor. Thought Helen once: 'The sky is so blue and clear to-day, and

the sun shines so—surely it is perfect to be loved,
now of all times.   I would not care for this dear
place, if my boy did not love me so much.'
" You'll never tire of me, Geordie?" she said,
suddenly, when they had ridden a mile or two.
" You'll love me whatever happens to us?"

He thought he could decipher this mocking
humility; and well he knew he was long past
the choice.   But still, he looked down reproachfully. " My darling," said he, " I told you
long ago "—he pulled his horse into a walk, and
turned away his head from looking at her eyes—
" I told you once that we would have to part, my
darling.   Look; how can I stay here with you,
and doubt that you love me?"

" Do I not 'love you?'" said she, turning
to him her cherished face, whereon the blush
raised by their last gallop still flickered.

" Yes," he said, half aloud, " you do, perhaps."   And then he asked himself—how
much?

" And if you really loved me, George," she
went on, " what more would you ask than that I
should give you all my heart?   Is it because you
care for me so much that you have no pity on
me?"

' But when did genuine love argue readily

like this?' he asked himself, as once before. Well, be it so! Very sure he was that she would never be his own true love. And that being his fate, what did anything else matter? "Yes, darling," he said, "you are wise, I think. But it's all a puzzle to me, most times. For you simply require—isn't that it?—that I should love you, and not love you, at the same time."

"Oh! this is cruel, Geordie. You know that I would peril my hopes of Heaven for you. Am I ever happy, do you think, save when you are near me, and good and fond of me?"

"Is that true, baby?" he said, gratefully. "I wish to submit to you. But, still, I wonder often why you like me to kiss you? It also is wrong, I know. Besides, I wonder why in the world you have such a darling little face, which must be kissed often."

"Oh! but," said the lady in her troubled voice, "I shall be able to repent of being kissed, Geordie—by and bye. But, you know—if one became thoroughly wicked in heart, it would be no use repenting."

"And can one repent of certain things, only?" he asked, languidly.

But Helen was ignorant of ethic, we may think, and, as there was a silence afterwards, he drew his left rein till the horses touched, and took her right hand in his to hold. Thus they rode for a while, both dwelling on their own anxious thoughts. 'I am quite sure she loves me,' said he to himself. 'She tells me so, so often.' And she had for her consolation all those magic gifts which being loved confers upon a woman. If that ride could but have lasted for ever! the horses, knowing the story, would surely never grow tired or lame. But sunny mornings will never come back; the chord is broken, the touch is lost, and may not be felt again. It lasted but a little, at best.

They went for a good long ride that day, staying out till it became dark and cold. Yet, when they could hardly see each other, they had ever so many things to talk of. They were sure they had always been destined for each other since first they met—been born for nothing else, in fact. " And yet we haven't lived so very long in the world, after all, Helen," he said.

" Do you know, Geordie, I often think how you and I were little babes together—just at the same time—though I was born miles and miles away."

" Yes, you are just as old as me—I remember."

"Geordie, tell me more about your travels, and how you used to go to Saint Andrea delle Fratte, when Aunt Blanch was asleep."

"Oh! there was music; I hear it now," he said wearily. "What do we care for my travels, though? They're over and gone. Come here, close to me again, and give me your hand to hold."

What did he want more than this? He had no ambition now. Why, there were great men and clever men in plenty, and still, which of them on earth would he change places with, if he were only convinced that she loved him?

Once back in the house something he saw may have pleased him, too. When he got to the drawing-room it was empty, but presently Mr. Tresham came.

"One does not think how soon the daylight goes now," said George, while apologizing for not coming home sooner. There was really no need, but some lie of this sort was the daily toll to be paid, for the delight of being with his darling. As for Helen, reclining on the sofa, she left the falsehoods to George, for she felt a little fatigued, no doubt.

"You have not got a chill, I hope?" her husband said, touching her cheek with the back of his hand.

"Chilled! no. Why should I be chilled?"
she answered. "And I do so hate being pawed,
Charles."

He was not a little astonished, doubtless.
And what George had to remark was how
differently she used to run to welcome her husband in former times.

It had long been settled that they were all to
be at Sawtry for Christmas; now it seemed as if
that plan would fall through. Letters came
saying that the squire was far from well.
Dreadful things had happened to Berty, and there
had been one communication in particular from
his Colonel to Mr. Newmarch, which had nearly
been the latter's death; in fact it had brought
on so severe an attack of the gout, that it was
feared he could not bear the strain of having any
visitors at Sawtry this winter. Helen was glad
that they were to stay at Norton—she said she
was happy; and yet George, whenever he for-
sook his unreal paradise for the contemplation of
sober prospects, began to have a foreboding that
the coming spring would very surely sweep away
all those pretty silver cobwebs which, in the last
few months, had spun here and there. A settled
sadness fell upon him by degrees. There seemed
to be heaped up the ashes of many burnt precious
days; while but a scanty store of future ones

remained in his satchel, to be drawn out and enjoyed. These gone, he must go out into the naked world, once more, to resume living the life of ordinary people, who have not much money of their own. Once Helen had said to him, " Why need he ever go away from her? could he not come and be Charles' curate here?" " I never, never could," he had said, with a shudder. He had tried once to make up his mind to some such plan; but he could not face the blasphemy of that. He had resolved instead never to be ordained at all. And yet he must earn a living somehow. So much for that pretty church, waiting for him at Sawtry; and all his long planned work—mapped out a while ago! He had traded away his hopes of that for his Helen's peculiar sweet lips, and cheeks, and so forth. Hence, he practised not to think of what he'd do at all, but aspired now merely to enjoy the more what days remained. She noticed how silent he grew, and one day questioned him.

" I will have to go soon—and we will see each other no more, Helen !" he answered, humbly.

But she could not bear the thought of that.

" Oh! George, do you wish me to die? Don't say you'll leave me. Listen to me, Geordie." But his thoughts were wont to stray far off.

"Geordie, on my birthday shall you be here?
Geordie, *won't* you stay with me till then?" And
the simple little angel hung down her head.
These hopes she would give him; yet with an
honest reservation all the time to postpone her
boy's wicked wishes to the haziest future date
imaginable.

"When is that day?" he asked.

"Oh! in spring; when it is clear and bright,"
she said.

And he marvelled how meekly and yet pre-
cisely his darling talked. What a *naïve* way she
had, poor child. 'I wonder has she a soul at
all?' he used to ask, sometimes imagining that
a little toy soul, which could be kept in a box
and wound up, had been given to his beloved.
His scepticism was all thrown away, though.
But if 'she hath no soul,' he used to say, after an
argument of this kind, or ' if indeed, the devils
are the same kind as she—I hope they'll let me
come among them when I die.' But that he now
judged altogether blindly, from vanity and
impatience, and selfishness, we may well think;
because Helen must have had a very warm heart,
and appurtenances indeed, to shed the tears she
did, when he talked of leaving her. 'Why,' she
would ask, looking up—a great height—into

his face, 'need he go and work and toil, far away
from where she was ? Why could they not be
happy by themselves ?' These were to her such
peaceful days ; she never cared to hear another
voice or to see another face. But he—though
long afterwards regretting that precious vanished
time, and finding it divine when irrevocable,—did
not share her peace, and could not learn her
patience.

There used to be news of Sawtry and the outer
world sometimes. Stephen, it appeared, had
taken some extraordinary fit of conversion or
something into his head ; and no one could say
what lengths he was likely to go. He had cut
himself off from his old friends, it appeared, who,
though making every allowance for the poor boy,
could not help being repelled by these wild
extremes of bigotry and dissent, into which he
had rushed. Lucy Felton was entirely to blame,
people said ; but of course, that poor girl was to
be pitied, rather than blamed—deprived as she
had been of a father's influence, and leading the
solitary life she did. The Feltons had left Rushworth altogether, and Lady Penelope was already
half way into a law suit with the new tenant,
about the shooting. She and her daughters
intended to pass the winter at Shelveport, where

they had taken a cottage; and Helen said, all
the consumptive people who resorted there would
form quite a congenial society for poor dear
Lucy.

"I wish my lungs were hopelessly affected,
George," she said, after first preparing her little
speech. "I would be so good. They look so pretty
—propped up by pillows, and repeating sweet
sayings, and short hymns. Then I would send
for you, to say good bye to me, when I had a red
spot on each cheek. And you would come, just
as the sun was setting; and I'd tell you to be
good always."

"The Feltons will be quite neighbours—over
at Shelveport," said George, grimly.

"I'm sure I hope not. After all, they say one
gets to Paris almost as soon as to Shelveport,
from here; there is less changing they say. But
you know, George, I don't want to go anywhere,
or to see anybody but you."

But to Mr. Tresham their coming so near was
very pleasant news. "We must see a great deal
of them, Helen," he said one morning, as he was
reading his letters.

"Yes, Charles," said she; "I hear," he continued, "Stephen is going to pay them a visit,
too. I think I shall make him stop with us for

two or three days on his way ; and I say, George,
you must give him a scolding about his ana-
baptist ways ; d'you hear?"

But George was reading his own letters ; and
with frowns, no doubt, since they were from
Sawtry. "Oh my! poor Mrs. Pringle is dead,"
he said. "She dropped down dead at her
sewing."

"Will you have some more tea?" interrupted
Helen, who had at first concluded from his eager
manner that somebody must have left him a
legacy.

"What do they say," added he; "hem! hem!
disease of the heart. Poor thing!" and George
let the letter drop for a little, going off into
dreams.

"She used to make me wear tight boots, and
brush my ears with hard hair brushes," said
Helen, shrugging her little shoulders.

Whereupon George looked at her with curiosity,
remembering how the nurse, who was just dead,
had very often sat up for nights and nights with
little Helen long ago ; and how she used to spoil
her little girl, and screen her from scoldings, and
worship her, indeed—as they all did. It was
strange. Perhaps, though, the balance was more
even than some might think, for as Helen had

certainly once loved the good woman for a while, she could not complain, should she hover about and hear the last remarks.

It was while he was thus in doubt about his darling's temperament—sometimes picturing her as wicked as himself—that Stephen came to Norton. It wanted but a few days of Christmas then, and Mr. Tresham had arranged that the two brothers should spend Christmas day together; after which Stephen could go across to Lady Penelope at Shelveport; and George, as we saw, was to endeavour at this time to get some of the Calvinistic notions out of his brother's head. Mr. Tresham had said, "I hear poor dear Stephen has actually taken to preaching publicly to his brother officers and to his men. Nothing is more delightful than to see a young man early taking a decided stand on the right side: but for a layman to put himself forward like that, courting notoriety, why it is—to say the least of it—bad taste. And yet I believe a finer fellow than Stephen never walked—he'll get sense though, George; he'll get sense."

It was all very well for Lucy Felton to have her little say about separation from the world, and all that; people tacitly overlooked a woman's religious whims—no matter how wild they were.

But for a man of sense—whose opinions always claimed a certain amount of respect—to rush headlong into those excesses, why, it was altogether too much. As for George, he dreaded his brother's coming intensely. Of old he remembered to have met some of the people whom Stephen now copied; how pertinacious they were, and what terrific names they gave to things at times; while Stephen specially—whatever he took up he put his whole quiet resolute strength into. And—as if he did not suffer remorse and jealousy and torture enough already—there came a cruelly irritating letter from Tiff. He wrote, that he wanted to warn George of the change he must expect to find in him; not for the sake of forcing his own views on anybody, but because he couldn't meet his brother in false colours—now that they had not seen each other for such a long time. He did not now care for the same things as he once delighted in. He had enlisted in another service, under a different master, and looked for quite other rewards. So, God grant that there might be accord between them, and at the end, he hoped that they were mainly agreed in the essential things, after all.

And George was afraid and angry at first. For a long time he had shut his eyes to those subjects.

Indeed, he had hardly had leisure: they had dropped away from him, or rather had been over-grown by the things which concerned Helen. And yet he could still be moved by words such as Tiff's. He was afraid that Stephen would shake and disturb him, so he tried to harden his heart, as is said, wrapping himself up in high contempt. 'After all, what does the boy know of the iron passion which I feel? Has he ever been vouch-safed a soul-absorbing love such as mine?' How easy it was for his brother, who had escaped fall-ing into the net of Destiny, and had not met one Destroyer like Helen—to court fancy faiths and dogmas. He had room for them in his soul. George had not. And as he sat in the library thus musing, Helen came in to see him. " Would you like to hear what my Puritan brother has got to say?" asked George. " It'll suit you. All women take to these things naturally, don't they? Look how cheerful he is!"—and he read a portion.—

'Some say it's very easy to be a christian, but, George, I don't believe them a bit. I find it awfully hard sometimes; and I seem to be losing hold on everything now and then. But after all, one's enemy is the biggest coward ever known, and he'd safe to give way if one stands up

to him : you know the text I've got that idea from.
But whenever I'm bothered or inclined to give in,
I just take a look in my Bible, and I'm sure to
light on the very thing I want to help me.'—
Well, don't that please you, my beautiful
baby?—it does me," George sneered, and Helen
stood utterly without speech; indeed, at first listening to the extract, she had fallen into a frame
of mind as if she were at Church.

"Does Stephen say all that?" she asked at
length, very coldly.

"Does he?—aye, ever so much more, too.
Why, I believe you are my enemy. You, with
your sweet ways; you, little charmer, with the
brown eyes. It is you I must pray to be delivered
from! Listen to the rest."

But she wanted to hear no more. Again, he
made her out worse than himself. And now this
Stephen—it would be horrible. "He comes the
day after to-morrow, does he not?" she said,
with fear and loathing in her voice.

"Yes, temptress," George repeated, with sorry
laughter. And Helen, angry and wounded,
turned from him.

"Oh! I know what the other will do; I know
what he will do," she moaned, when she was by
herself again.

CHAPTER IX.

WHEN they had Tiff in the house at last, notwithstanding the disagreeable things that had
been said of him, he gave very little trouble to
anyone.   He was gentler, and also more cheerful
than he used to be—that was all.   He had a pro-
voking look in his face, as if he always possessed
something wonderfully pleasant of his own to
think about.   Mr. Tresham was surprised by his
ways, and, somehow, could find no opportunity
to take him to task.   It was Helen who steadily
disliked and dreaded Tiff from the moment she
set eyes upon him; because George, noticing
from the first that he seemed inclined to say
very little of any kind, quickly got back his
courage, and began to look down on Tiff as a
mere boy—indeed, ceased to think about him at
all, after the first few hours.   Once or twice, it
did strike him as queer, how utterly indifferent

he was to old Stephen now. To be sure this conversion humour had given him a gentlemanly shock, and he might well feel aggrieved; but he used to love Tiff, and now wished him drowned. To be sure, this preaching and giving tracts was as if his brother had gone into trade almost; and, brought up as George was with a public school-boy's horror of Jews, Radicals, and Dissenters, it could not but grate against his feelings somewhat harshly.

As for poor Tiff, the quiet of this place was pleasing to him, no doubt. 'I can understand people growing fond of Norton,' he thought. 'By and bye, I'll have a chance of talking to George, I am sure.' And though he could not be quite at rest while that was undone, he talked modestly to Mr. Tresham in the meantime, about the village, and his church, and schools, and neighbours. At breakfast, two days after he came, they had an argument; and Mr. Tresham asked him straightway to go for a long walk with him.

"The fact is," he said, "I'm going to Farwell —a village near here—and it's a secret, because I'm going to look at a house where I think your brother George might live. I want him to stay here, and be my curate—that's the fact. Some-

how, I believe we'd miss him if he went altogether; and I'm getting terribly old to look after
a whole parish myself, you see."

This was as they passed up and down the lawn
after breakfast. Tiff looked at him, taking great
firm strides—longer than his own—and laughed
a little at this complaint of getting old. He
could understand Lucy Felton being interested
in this man. They continued to stroll backwards
and forwards by the river till it was time to start.
Tiff went back to put a lighter coat on for his
walk, for Mr. Tresham advised it.

"And wait for me here, when you've changed,"
he called out. "You'll find the shortest way to
your room through the tower, there."

So Tiff went round that way, and in at a side
door. 'What a pretty place this is,' he said to
himself, 'and what a happy couple they are apparently.' Yet all these easy and pleasant things
of this world choked a spiritual life, Stephen
believed. He was not one who read Helen's, or
anyone else's real disposition, at a glance. 'I
believe I've forgotten my room,' thought he; 'it
must be at the far end somewhere.' And turning
out of the sun, down a dimly-lighted passage,
looking at each room door, he heard whispers
such as these, coming out of the wall.—

"Oh! Geordie, don't stay now. I tell you
you cannot. He will be gone in ten minutes,
and then you can talk to me all day."

"Kiss me, then, baby—once."

These whispers were somewhere in the
darkness, close to Stephen's ear, and they were
from living people. The voices he knew well—
only whose were they? His senses said whose
they were; yet was it real? He stood and
sighed; and to make it real, in a moment her
dress, and no other, was noisily swept back, and
a door was softly shut, as he turned the angle in
the wall. There now was George's back, just
before him, and Stephen heard him whistling.

And he whistled faintly and more faintly, till
the air turned into mutterings such as these.
"Curse him—and curse me for a coward. He
never saw us. I know he did, though. Curse
him—he came here for this. Oh! and I've put
her in another person's power. He tell, though?
No, not Tiff. Why he could not do such treachery.
Did he see us—did he see us, though?"

And now George was in the entrance hall,
through which, in a moment more, came
Stephen, wearing the other coat which he had
gone to find.

"Are you—going to Farwell, Tiff?" asked George, turning round upon him.

"Yes—I am—going," Tiff answered, looking on the ground, in one of his absent pauses; and then he went through the library, and out to the back of the house.

George followed him into the library, and watched him across the lawn. He took some book up, and commenced to read it, mechanically. It was a gardener's hand-book; and how miserable the man must have been who wrote it. There seemed shame and despair in the first paragraph he read over, though he did not remember it as he read. Oh! how horrible it was to read; and how dreadful to think. And then his sweetheart came there to him. She stopped and looked about her, breathing in a manner that was frightful to look at. It was all known now.

"My husband is in his room still. Where is he?"

"Look!" said George, pointing to Stephen pacing up and down outside.

"He saw you kiss me," she said, with eyes full of horror.

George gave a savage laugh, and did not look at her.

" Oh ! you are laughing at me, of course," she whispered, wildly. " You would like to see me ruined and despised by my husband. It would be all a joke to you."

" Look, baby," George growled out, quietly ; " if you like, I'll get my dear brother there to come out shooting with me, and I'll blow his brains out, 'fore he can tell anyone. D'you believe me ? Oh ! if you're afraid—I would, very surely."

" Madman ! you would not," she said, with a slight shudder, giving him a look of curiosity and fear at the same time.

There was a long silence ; at last George spoke.

" He will say nothing. The Newmarchs don't betray trust, Mrs. Tresham. They're all men of honour "—he laughed slowly—" all of the name, except one. I haven't got a great deal of honour now — your husband's best friend still, my dearest."

" If I could be sure he would not tell," she mused, not noticing George's last words. " No, he will not, I think. Stephen—yes—he used to be always far the kindest of them all, except this boy here. Darling," she added piteously, " I am frightened. I have only you to trust to—they all terrify me so. You won't be cross to me, Geordie, if I tease you with my fears? I used to pray, you remember, darling, when I was frightened. Now I can never say my prayers any more, Geordie."

She seemed to be so weak at times, it was hard to keep from pitying her. Her eyes would fill with tears, and, straightway, one would think her injured, instead of much to blame.

Now she took George's hand—meekly—so that those who looked towards the room would not think it strange—and held it between hers, taking strength therefrom. They had to settle the matter between themselves. As she bent over his hand, her hot tears began to fall, patter, patter on his flesh—scalding it, he thought. It was not all ease, this partnership of theirs.

"This misery was brought about by him alone," he said. She was suffering – not wilful and coquettish now. She wept salt tears—only because he had once traitorously won her heart; and because there was a gulf between them which she was killing herself trying to pass. He wished once more that he were dead; he wished that she had never seen his face. After a fashion, there was coming punishment which he had denied would ever come, and he shrank back from the first approach of it.

While these two remained at Norton, not comforting each other, but trembling—Stephen was walking. And it was an endless, tedious day. He had to keep on talking, because he dared not say why he wished to be left to himself; but when he had the chance of being silent his thoughts would slink back to what he had seen; until he felt himself a sharer in that treachery and shame which he had discovered. He had never been so unhappy—never once since Lucy's prayers were answered that time at Rushworth. And now it was only because he still clung to something earthly; because his heart was still moved by such things as love for George that he suffered. A sort of shame pricked him at having heard what he should not have listened to. And yet their voices had come to him suddenly and unsought for, from round the angle of the passage as he groped his way along, thinking of nothing. Hence conscience acquitted him of the meaner charge, and he was left free to think, when not chatting with his friend. It was some time before he could master the sense of it. His brother had been here since July, he remembered. Why so long? No one could tell. Was not there a dim recollection of Helen and him long ago? Aye, this was planned in those days. Oh!

it was frightful. And then he would look fur-
tively at Mr. Tresham. There he trudged along
in utter darkness—and how much ought he to
know? George, Helen's lover! He could not
forget from old days the symptoms, although he
had decided to detest all those things. It was
impossible, he tried to believe. But they had
seemed to be accustomed to hiding a plot—to
understand each other so well. Was innocence like
this? Helen he could not judge at all. If there
were sin, George alone was to blame. A great
reverence for women was a habit of Stephen's.
He wished to know no better; and he had got
into this way from knowing nobody but Lucy
Felton well. And yet if he were angry with George
'twas not for long. What right had he to judge
him, or to boast that he was better than his helpless brother? But, for God's grace there stood
Stephen Newmarch, hiding in some passage with
some miserable, poor wretch. He neither wondered nor was angry that—warring in his own
strength alone—George had yielded. Nevertheless, he prayed that it might not yet be too late.

It was past four when they were back, and
Helen was there to meet them in the hall. To
see her tripping cheerfully across the oil-cloth to
take her husband's hat and gloves, who would

think, by the light of the lamp, that she was so
subtle of heart.   By this light, she gave Stephen
one steady look, which he could not return for
shamefacedness.   Can this woman be guilty?
Oh! no, he thought; and she in her turn read
at once by his face that he had seen all in the
morning without a shadow of doubt.   She carried
her husband off to learn quietly about the house
he had been to; and Stephen found his brother
in the library.   It was usually dark in there, and
George all but dropped his book as the door was
shut.   "It is I, Bo," said Stephen, and he
wearily sat himself in an arm chair.

"Had you a pleasant sort of walk?" George
asked; and he wished that he had not so wretched
a tone of voice.   Stephen made no answer, nor
did his brother much desire to hear him speak.
Why could George not keep quiet, instead of
finding accusations in the darkness and the presence of the others?   There they sat though, and
not a word was heard between them for a long
time.   At last George rose impatiently; he knew
not why, came to his brother, and stood between
him and the light; whereon Tiff turned half round,
and reaching out his hand, held George's sleeve.
It was now too dark to see the sweet smile on
the younger brother's face.   It was an expression

which came there whenever he prayed. This happened years ago, and at that time the finer recipes for self-regeneration, invented since, were unknown. Hence Stephen could think of no re-scource but the common one of praying away. "Dear old fellow," he whispered, and when George seemed to listen he went on. "I have been praying for you all day. You know I think more of these things now than I used to do once."

"Yes, I know, old boy."

And then Tiff's heart nearly failed him, "You ain't angry, are you, Bo?" he gently asked, turn-ing his face upwards once more. "I ought not to care, but I do pity you so; I don't like pain-ing you."

"I am not angry. Not now, at least. I've hardly seen you since you've been here, and I havn't been—happy, thinking, and one thing and another."

Then there was a long pause, and Stephen sighed several times. It was terrible ground he wished to tread upon. This was a matter of one, he well knew, who was, as it were, sacred by name and birth; and he was the while her hus-band's guest. He could not talk of things like that with indifference or a sneer. He wanted to speak plain to George. He longed to warn him —and yet it was all a sore trouble and strait.

And George was not in the proudest place. How ready he had been to give his passion a loose rein—lead where it might; and now that he had grown a little afraid and tired, he was about to make the hastiest repentant sinner ever known; glad to borrow any other person's strength to guide his feebleness, or to obey if any one would think and act for him. Tiff may have read this too, but to him that helplessness, that broken and guilty voice, only revealed one willing to confess his fault and ask for forgiveness.

While Tiff was still in this doubt, George came and sat on the arm of his brother's chair, resting one hand upon his shoulder. " I must talk," he said impatiently. " Who have I to talk to but you, and I'm so wretched. What are we to do; tell me, Tiff; tell me something." When he said " we," he heard Tiff draw his breath, " Well, there you've heard me now. What's the good of lying to everybody for ever."

He sprang up, and went walking to and fro, trembling from the concussion of his own thoughts. " Oh ! Tiff, look here. It's just Hell this, whatever I do."

" Dear Bo ! You must not, must not. I guess

why you are unhappy, and I blame myself for not speaking before. I was as unhappy once, and don't you think I know how to feel for you? Oh! poor fellow! poor fellow!"

How could he go on; what was he going to hear next? He therefore prayed again for guidance in his speech. Meantime, George gripped his hand, and feverishly began once more. "You pity me, don't you? You don't believe I ever meant to do wrong. Look, I went on from one thing to another. Look, it began, half with fun, just to amuse her, when it was so dull, till I came to be with her always, and I found I loved her. I never meant to tell her. And then one day I did tell her, oh! that day, and she loves me so, I found—"

"Yes, Bo."

The clock was ticking away, and Stephen kept praying as we have seen. So it was all true!

"Do you believe me? Look, I did love her so. Do you understand?—it's not like ordinary love, with us; we're more to each other, and it's quite different loving her to anything I ever knew before. Oh! the morning she told me!" Then he bowed his head and thought for a while of that sweet hour, "but I know, Tiff. I know that it's ruin and folly. I wouldn't harm a person I loved for all the world. Don't you believe me? I never would, you believe that?"

"Yes—yes, Bo."

"Oh! I'd give anything if she'd forget me. Why, she cries sometimes. And I could kill myself. Now, what d'you think of me?"—Was it not wretched to hear that, to hear his brother frightened at the sound of his own voice, whispering his confession. It is no light thing when one is quite unused to it, to listen while the secrets of a man's heart are shown, and worst, when he treats of such matters as these.

"Think of you, George," said the other. "Oh! I think you must ask for help to be delivered from the body of this death. Do you suppose I wonder at it all. Only chance, or always meeting people more selfish than yourself, could have kept you from such as this, while you were what you were. Trusting in your own strength, you prosper—till you meet some sweeter sin than you ever thought of meeting; and then, you have not one bit of chance, Bo. Oh! no chance at all, believe me."

And in this fashion he went on, heard eagerly by George who now thought that in a moment he had freed himself. Then Tiff made his plans.

"You'll do what I ask you, George," he said. "You'll leave this place and come with me, at once. Look, for her sake, you'll make it short, won't you? Leave this to-morrow, finish it off, and in six months you'll forget it all, and she'll forget." George humbly shook his head. 'I gave a long, long margin,' Stephen thought. "If I put it on lower grounds, Bo, what could you do, even here, for her? Ruin and poverty and death is all you could offer the person you tell me you really love. But I'm ashamed to think of that; that's not it."—

"Tiff, I will go to-morrow," George said. "Only you mustn't leave me much to myself. How early can we go?"

"Have you got strength, Bo?"

"Oh! yes. I can do it now, I know, I know." And then the wretched conversation ended very soon. They left each other with as few words as might be, and 'twas a miserable day for both, think of it as they would. And George was glad at first. He tried to think that a great danger and great sin was put away for ever. But when he followed up the little channels of his mind and found nothing but memories of her sweetness everywhere, he was dismayed, a sullen despair came upon him, and he no longer cared to live.

It was done now. He could not resist Stephen—
the stronger will and cause was there attending
him, and he could not go back. A kind of numb-
ness fell upon him, he wished to be alone, but
the small round of the day's events would not be
put aside. Dinner came and the lights, and
they all must meet and talk again.

Helen guessed the truth almost the instant she
saw the two brothers together. And then she
felt a horrible certainty that he would go for
ever. It took her wits away at first, and she
quailed before the dread sight of Stephen. How
terrible he was, when all looked up to him. She
scarcely dared to hate him now. Despite of all
that had passed—he had power to take her boy
from her. Quite cowed, she did not look at
George. He avoided thinking of her. And it
must be done. So when the chance came, un-
moved, he heard Tiff say, "I think I shall go
to-morrow, Mr. Tresham;" having said that, he
looked at George.

"I'm thinking of running over with him, to-
morrow, too," the elder brother said, firmly, and
his own calmness astonished him.

"Oh! nonsense. You were to be here for
Christmas, and I won't hear of it," Mr. Tresham
objected, carving away busily.

George's courage rose, though he could see his darling listening to catch if there were any reprieve for her. "Well," he said, "I'd like to go with Tiff, very much. It's years since I've seen Aunt Penelope, and we'll all be together at Shelveport. I know she'd like it." And he saw how there shone in Helen's eyes, a look of withering contempt. "Will you be very much offended if we spend Christmas there, instead of here?"

"Offended! no not I. I can't make all this out, though. What has happened now? My dear George, you know, I like to see you do just whatever you like best. And with your brother just the same. I daresay this is a very dull house for young fellows. But do just as you like, I can't say any more. Come back here the minute you're tired over there. And then tell us, whenever we bore you. Isn't that it, Helen?" She had a great self control at times. "Yes, undoubtedly," she said, laughing excitedly.

"Well, you're awfully kind," George continued. "I'll—that is, I shall come back, of course, when Tiff has to leave, in a few days. It's very, very kind of you to ask me, I am sure."

"Very good, George. How dull we'll be, Helen. We'll have to eat all the plum pudding ourselves. Have you made it yet, I wonder. I think George had better take his share away with him in his pocket?"

No one was listening to him. Stephen was thinking sadly of his brother's poor pretence for escaping, and George was wondering how long forty or fifty years of life from this out would be. As for Helen, she was now quite subdued. A little dragon vanquished.

CHAPTER X.

THEN rose another day, and it was Christmas Eve.
At Norton even in the mild southern country,
there was a frost that morning.   All down about
the river the air was foggy and still with the cold,
leaves and grass crackled under one's footsteps,
and men watched their own breath rising like
mist.   Nothing save the house itself seemed at
all cheerful, its long dwelling room windows always had a safe warm look, with their show of
bright glass and trimly painted sashes.   Inside,
the rich red curtains hung lazily down to the
carpet, making one envious as one looked in from
the raw world outside.   Birds, were outside chirp-
ing about on the broad red gravel paths, prospec-
ting for seeds or 'crumbs along the borders, and
they were very cold.   Now and then a face came
to the window pane and stared through. One face
was very sad and thoughtful, and from it I dare-

say these birds had hopes. Another flattened itself against the glass and with tired eyes observed the hazy scene outside; that was George, and he was not likely to give much to hungry birds.

Inside, the urn is brought up at last, and then the three men turn to the table. It is quite early but the two brothers had resolved to walk over to Trele, where they would meet the Norport steamer, and their luggage was to follow in the dog cart. It was a fine day for a three hours' walk and now the time was drawing near to start. Men are poor hands at making tea and when Mr. Tresham had spilled the hot water, and knocked a cup or two over, he looked at his watch to see if his wife might be coming. He had left her asleep; to be sure, eight was an awful hour to get up at this time of year; poor child! how she sighed and talked in her dreams last night.

They were all rather silent. To do an act of high moral courage very early upon a raw winter's morning is hard. A kind of apathy, though, had fallen on George, and he sat there staring out of the window, and complaining how raw it felt.

Mr. Tresham told Stephen not to be surprised if he came over and paid them a visit at Shelveport himself some morning, provided he could persuade Mary Rumbold to keep Mrs. Tresham company.

Tiff hoped he would; and then the two talked about Willie Felton. "He had behaved so nobly," Tiff said, "settling such and such a sum upon his sisters, after his father's will was made known."

How weary George was of the Feltons. Could not Tiff manage to spare him, even for a little while, till this was over?

"Willie had just returned from the East, and was going to travel again for two years in the spring," Tiff added; "though Lord So-and-so, Secretary of State, had wanted him so much to be his private secretary."

But Helen came in while they were yet on this. She was cold also, and the one who loved her most saw her shiver. She kissed her husband, saying, "Good morning," to the others, with a kind of smiling face.

"I didn't like to disturb you," said Mr. Tresham. "We thought we'd manage tea ourselves; and look at your fine table cloth now."

Helen again smiled; indeed, everything made her laugh that morning. "I suppose I slept so soundly," she said. "No, I won't have any breakfast now."

Then it was nearly time for the departing guests to say good bye, and Mr. Tresham had just a word to say to Tiff in private. "Now, you'll remember to give all those messages to Lady Penelope, from us," said he; "and you'll tell Lucy I am very angry with her for her heresies and schisms." There was, in addition, a book or two which he must find to put into Tiff's hands before they parted.

In this way George was left alone at the table with his thoughts. When he looked towards the window, Mrs. Tresham stood there, turned away from him, and looking out, playing idly with the ribbon round her throat; while the saddest landscape almost ever seen at Norton, was beyond. Over all hung a dull fog, and the trees were quite bare and dead. George could summon up a kind of daring now and then; therefore, he rose and went to the window where she was; but Helen's eyes followed those little birds which still twittered about, seeking for crumbs outside. "They are cold," he said; "shall I get them some bread?" But she gave a start, and shrank away when he spoke to her; nor did he dare to meet her eyes, but muttered, looking straight before him down the river all the while, "You know why I leave you; because I love you, and was killing you. I shall be wretched while I live. Will you try to forget me? Will you try to be happy, and love your baby and your husband?"

"Wretch!" she said, softly, biting at the thin sinews of her wrist.

And this was all spoken in the gentlest whispers, neither looking at the other once.

"How they are talking secrets," said Mr. Tresham, who at last had found the books and given them to Tiff. "I believe they're the greatest allies imaginable—Helen and your brother. Now, you men ought to be starting, though, 'pon my word. "You'll never believe that I love you," George was rapidly muttering to her. "Oh! will you let me go like this? Won't you believe I only go because I love you?"

"Liar!" she said, with the same unreal smiles playing about her face.

And then Stephen said, "George, ought we not to go? You say it's twelve miles; and the boat starts at one punctually."

"Good-bye," George began; but she did not move, and then Tiff came. "I am going, Mrs. Tresham," he said, whereon Helen turned round and lisped, "I'm so sorry you must really leave us, Stephen. Give Lucy and them all my kindest love. And, laughing causelessly, she shook hands with him. However, she did not touch George's hand, nor did she look at him again. Therefore, he went, hardly knowing what he did or said; and thus was free; and it had happened that they never said good-bye at all, except at the window—in the poor way we have just seen. From the moment George resolved to flee from his temptation, he had not had one chance of turning back.

It is a long stretch from Norton to Trele, and George plodded steadily along the half frozen road, saying scarcely a word. When those two did talk, it was about the commonest little things —whatever came first to their minds. Tiff did not cease to vex himself with the remembrance that his brother had made a sort of promise to go back to Norton. He wished that had not been given, for he prayed that it might never be kept. As for George his wounds were bleeding, one might say, internally; but the return smart of misery kept off as yet. He let his mind drift where it pleased, in the meantime. On board the steamer it was bitter cold. Had he been happy, George could have stood in the bow and gladly faced the Channel breeze; he crouched, however, this time on a bench, among the lug-

gage, without raising his head. "Come and sit
by me, Tiff," said he; for he had observed a
woman and her child, looking as though they
would be his neighbours on the seat; and the
sight of a woman made him shudder. He hated
the very looks of one. 'There they were,' he
said, with loathing ; 'all the same—timid
treacherous, and accursed.' "Tell me about the
Feltons, Tiff," said he. "Will they be glad to
see me, I wonder?"

"Why, of course. You hardly know Lucy—
you will like her so much."

"Is she like—" He stopped suddenly, and
would have got red, perhaps, but for the December
cold. "What is she like? Tell me, Tiff; shall
I go to Sawtry after this? Is Berty there? I'd
like to see him."

"Oh! no! Berty's not at Sawtry. There's bad
news about him, Bo. Don't you know he has
to leave his regiment?" And thereon Tiff related all he knew of the story of Berty's recent
follies and misdeeds.

It set George thinking ; there were other folk,
then, as wretched as he was. What could become
of poor Berty, he wondered. Everybody seemed
going wrong, except his strange brother here.
Musing thus, he allowed Tiff to talk on without
heeding him or answering him much.

A trawling smack or two was beating up the Channel, and, in the zenith of his misery, that set going a queer little wheel in George's brain. ' If I had to go off trawling now,' thought he ; 'and my dinner depended on how I worked, would I have time to go sighing and regretting, I wonder? Or, if I had to drive a cab all day, could I afford to be dreaming about my darling? Ah! but I would, though—and of nothing else. I'd be wool gathering, while the people called me to come and drive them.' That made him smile, for the first time since they had left Norton. ' How little I would earn on that system,' he thought. ' How hungry I'd go to bed after the first day's wool gathering, too. But I would not care, I think.'

By four o'clock they were at Shelveport, having had a long drive in the coach, from the place where the steamer stopped ; and George was tired and worn out. It was such a great mercy, in Stephen's eyes, his brother's yielding to him in this matter—that he had been very loth to press things on him, or to tax him with further efforts. He hoped that the peaceful life and ex-ample of those he was with would soothe and interest poor George. By and bye, there would be a yet greater change, and a real awakening,

he trusted.   He greatly desired to be able to
tell Lucy all his anxieties for his brother; but
George had hit the mark, when he said the Newmarch's knew how to keep silence; and Tiff remained, what is called a gentleman, in spite of
the mighty change in him.   He never, therefore, told Lucy one word of that—never in all
his life, indeed; and she was left in extreme
wonder at many of her cousin George's ways.

At Shelveport, all the talking devolved upon
Stephen, and he had to answer questions about
Norton, and about Helen.   George had coldly
announced, that 'he had just come over for a
day or two;' he said 'he hoped they were all
quite well,' as if he were with strangers.
He was trying hard to bear their presence, as
one does that of wearying fellow travellers, on a
long journey.   It required a strong effort to
speak at all.   Lucy and Cathy longed to see
Helen again, they said.   They wanted to hear all
about her little child; and thus they tortured
George unconsciously.   He found it hard enough
to accustom himself to new people.   Indeed, he
had been so long at Norton, where there was no
change of society whatever, that he had come to
feel awkward and ill at ease with strangers.   His
day's journey and the changing once over, too,

old thoughts by degrees marshalled themselves together afresh, cruelly recalling that which was lost. The recollections of his injured darling, left there across the water, rushed back upon him overpoweringly, and he became each hour more lonely and sullen. When the time came for prayers, he sat moodily listening to what Lady Penelope read, and staring at them all one after the other. What a queer woman his aunt was. He could see her now—the first day he remembered her at Sawtry; she used to talk out loud in church in those days. There was Cathy, she looked a healthy girl, with red cheeks. 'What were they to him? why was he here, so far away?' he asked, grinding his teeth; this was not the place he delighted in, there was nothing binding these people to him, though he knew them all well. The words which were being read, but made him rebel the more stubbornly; and by degrees as he listened he marvelled what sort of man he could be to have come here at all. He cursed himself slowly; and then observed Stephen with wonder. His brother was a poor wretch, he began to see now; and this Lucy—he supposed those two carried on a lean, tepid sort of flirtation of their own. Had that fellow ever any blood going about his

strangled veins? he asked. Not much in all'
likelihood. His temperament and his sluggish
brain and his nervous system—working half
times—made him cold and cautious and respectable. He might take his own paltry profit from
it, and yet George had allowed himself to be
brought here, and had just broken his darling's
heart at Stephen's beck and call. He glared
about the room as he thought thus: it was his
prison, and he could scarcely bear to breathe
there. He said 'good night' to them, having
spoken hardly a dozen further words; and got to
bed, as quickly as he could, knowing the while
what time was in store for him when he would
be alone.

The little cottage where they lived, stood in
pretty grounds, having the cliff behind it, and
land planted well with trees, curving down
towards the sea. He opened his window, cold as
it was, and looked out. There was no pleasure
in the sight; the shrubs and tree stems brought
dearly loved Norton to mind—only everything
here was foreign and altered. Again, he asked
despairingly, why on earth he was here? Why
he had done himself this dreadful injury? and
for a long time, he stood leaning his throbbing
forehead on his hand, planning nothing and

hoping nothing; till drowsiness came upon him by and bye, and he fell asleep.

In an hour or two, George awoke, and the air of the room was strange to him, and the very sheets felt strange to him. For a moment, he forgot why he was here; then opened his eyes wide and remembered. Would he ever see her again? Oh! never, never! she was lost, and they would talk together no more. How dear she used to be, how lonely being without her was; he considered how could he recall her best, and recollected that her portrait was somewhere in his desk. Getting up, he lit a candle and found it presently. Putting the light and the little picture on a chair by his bed head, George lay and looked at it. This was the portrait she had got to give to him, the time he was away at Rushworth at his uncle's funeral. When she was always near him, it lay in his desk, perchance on the top of that repentant letter, which he had decided not to send. Now she was far off, and only the shadow, say, of his darling's face was here. Dulled was the picture with his kisses. ' She was thinking of me at the moment it was taken, she often said. Yes, she was, I think. Well, I know that look in her eyes—that look! that look!'

He put his hand across the mouth and chin, and saw only her eyes and forehead; then he hid these in turn, and gazing upon her little lips, could not say which portion he loved the best.

Each way the candle light fell on it, there was a new expression; sometimes, he thought grave looks came; and sometimes smiles. Was he never to hold his darling in his arms again, and feel her heart fluttering within his grasp, as when he carried pet birds in his closed hand? The smooth silk of her dress seemed to be slipping away under his touch, even now. There was not a waist in the world exactly like hers. Thus he moaned and muttered, until he fell asleep a second time.

CHAPTER XI.

NEXT day, there was the sweet tinkling of the Christmas bells close to this pretty place. The Feltons had chosen a different church to the kind George delighted in; but he had known he might expect something of the sort. After morning service, the four cousins took [a walk, and only common place Christmas subjects were talked about. Poor Tiff did not yet see his way to having a long talk with George; and how could Lucy help him, or guess why he was so anxious about it? The occasion would come by and bye, he prayed and believed.

In the afternoon, George found another church more to his taste; it had irritated him having to go where the Feltons took him, and he would not be thwarted now. In fact he longed to be alone, because he almost hated the sight of his brother and cousins. As the hours went by, he continued to grow more and more scornful and desperate. He could not listen to what they talked of—only planning how he could leave that horrible place.

Thus passed Christmas Day; and after another night of suffering, he said that he could not stay longer and live. But when the morning came he was not yet strong enough to tell Tiff what he had determined.

That day there were some visitors, who of course had to be entertained. George did not know them, or look at them much, though they seemed congenial friends to Lucy and Stephen. It was another trial to Stephen, being occupied with strangers all day; for he had noticed how weary and impatient poor George looked. Yet what could he do? perhaps they would be left more to themselves, from this out.

The third morning he had at last a talk—which was what he looked forward to. It was a mild and bright day in that fair climate, and the sitting-room windows could be left open, on to the lawn. When breakfast was over, Tiff thought it would be a good day for a walk through Shelveport, and along the coast, where fine views might be got. He sought his brother to propose this, and in the drawing-room found him.

George stood at a table busily poring over Bradshaw, and Lucy sat reading, on the sofa, by the fire. It flashed across Tiff in an instant, 'why does he look at that book,' and going up to him, he asked, " What's the cause of your deep studies, Bo ?"

The other gave a slight start. " Me ! Oh ! I'm thinking of translating Bradshaw into blank verse !" Lucy looked up and smiled good-humouredly. " No," George added, quietly, " I'm looking out the steamers from Norport— for I shall have to go to-day, I think."

Into Tiff's face came an expression of sudden and intense pain. He turned away, and walking to the fire place, stood staring at the bars for a certain time ; while he heard George still turning over the leaves of that book. At last, Tiff went back to his brother, and laying a hand on his arm, said, " Will you come and walk on the lawn with me?"

George looked at him coldly. " Yes," he said, " in another minute, when I have seen all about this."

Meanwhile Lucy rose and went, so that the two were alone together.

" Oh ! what is this ?" said Tiff, despairingly.

George got up from his chair, took a step or

two, and then faced his brother. "You want to know," he began, biting at his hands to keep himself cool. "It's this; I'm going away—I mean to go. Yes, you ask me, and I've only got to say, I do what I please—quite, without consulting anybody in the world."

"Yes, George," said Tiff, who now hardly knew what to say to such a man as this. "You can go—that's true. But d'you forget like this what a—what—you have only just fled from?"

"Ah! yes, no doubt: I can take care of myself, though; and I'm very sure there is no call for you to interfere with me. No—none," he said, very wrathfully, for all he wished was to lash himself into a rage; since, if he were drunk with anger, he would not fear so much the step he meant to take.

As for Tiff, he felt how powerless he was now. All his fierceness was gone in these days, and scenes like this distressed and wounded him. George's savage manner could not rouse or enrage him, and he knew not what appeal to make. "Oh! George, is it come to this?" he said humbly, after a bit. "Do you remember all we said to each other? You won't harden your heart again, and tempt God. You cannot be safe at Norton. Oh! no. Look, Bo, man's

honour may be touched, he may be moved for a
moment; but I think God can never trust him.
Can you trust yourself?"

"I can," he answered, and then there was a
dead silence between them. "Yes," he went on
at last, in a loud bold tone, "I can trust myself
to be a gentleman, and no infernal blackguard,
that ever I heard of."

The rooms there opened into one another, and
Tiff thought how these words might go through
the house; they rang in his own ears very cruelly.
"Oh! Bo, take care—take care; my heart and
yours are both deceitful above all things, and
desperately wicked."

That was all he could think of, and it lost
something by his frightened voice.

"Aye, I know what you mean—thank you," the
other said, turning deadly pale; "thank you for
your nice opinion. I'll remember it—I'll remember you, believe me; and this charming
place you brought me to."

Then he had completely won the day. Tiff sat
down at the table, and remained gazing before
him, without a further word; but George's
hardihood lasted to the end. "I suppose I can
find them to say good-bye?" he said, half de-

fiantly and half to himself, and then he strode away to pack up his things.

By a piece of good fortune, his aunt as well as Lucy and her sister, were all in the drawing-room, and he constructed a fair excuse for leaving Shelveport so soon.

Lucy looked at George curiously, as he was making his apologies; she wished much that she could have known him better, but he had avoided her. She fancied there was some trouble between the brothers, something which Stephen could not talk about, and that alarmed her. How much she did discern, it would be hard to say; but it were a rare fault in her woman's nature, if she missed guessing what was at the root of this new sorrow. Little things presented themselves to Lucy, even from the days when Helen had come to Rushworth the second time in childish disgrace. She believed that her cousin had been fond of George, once; but to Lucy it was a monstrous and loathsome thought that a woman could care for other people when she had once sworn to love her husband. 'Thou art of purer eyes than to behold evil, and canst not look upon iniquity,' fitted Lucy exactly. Still, if Helen had come there then, I do not think Lucy could have kissed her, or have talked to her. She was alarmed for George, and yet she pitied him. What if he had been enthralled by a perjured woman's snares? She, too, had looked forward to the working of better influences. But on a sudden he had chosen to hurry away from them, no one could tell why.

As for him, in an hour from this time he would not so much as know what coloured hair his cousins had. Those three days with them had been a hideous kind of trance, in which he noticed nothing and decided nothing. At the threshold of the door Stephen dared to speak to him for the last time. He whispered something most beseechingly, but what it was George hardly heard. He stared in his brother's face, and then drove away on his long, long journey.

Away at last from that prison, whereunto he had been beguiled, a great sense of triumph and freedom returned. He had delivered himself from them now, and they could never vex him any more. As yet all plans but whirled round his head. He was going, though, to Norton, without turning back now. Where else could he rest, or bear to live and breathe? By and bye he would decide on the future, and the whole day remained to him for that. Perhaps she would

turn from him, and refuse to speak to him.
That made him frown and tremble, but it did
not turn him back. It was only at Norton that
she could be found, in her own familiar rooms.
By her little table she would be sitting before
the fire, at the side she always chose; perchance,
was walking now in her garden, along the yellow
paths. He knew the places where she would
walk by herself; he could see her, in her dark
winter dress, taking little hurried steps, and
swinging the muff she carried, her eyes all the
time on the ground. What friends they had
once been. And now, perhaps, she would despise
and avoid him, remembering that he had deserted
her. It might be; and yet if he could only see
her once, he trusted to find words wherewith to
show her his repentance. 'How will she talk
and look, when we are enemies?—we never have
been yet,' he wondered; 'what will she say?'
but he would risk everything. He was a coward
we have divined by this time, but truly a most
reckless one, who ran headlong into the way of
the greatest hurts and dangers.

As his journey was ending, and the steamer's
course set for the opposite shore, he grew light
of heart; he could almost catch sight of Leet
Creek, away there down the coast. Iuland, be-

hind that faint fringe of woods, was the place of places, where his darling stayed. Well, he had tried hard to leave her, had striven his very best, he knew. But he could not resist any more. He was entirely in the hands of fate, he said, looking most generously on himself; and something that no man can fight against drew him on. For this reason all doubts, and contentions, and charms to divert his thoughts were but vain and powerless.

At Trele it was nearly dark. His luggage and his ticket and the petty cares of travelling took up his thoughts here, and made him cross enough. His story could progress only after the slow and matter-of-fact pattern of other tragedies; porters there must be to carry his things, and a musty fly to draw him along.

In that accordingly he went back. And now 'good-bye' to him. Once he was meant to be a hero, and a friend. For we saw, at one time, how he had chosen earnest and worthy companions, living, indeed, a better and purer life than any of those with him; having his difficulties, of course, but well able to fight them out. At times a little sarcastic and singular, but tinged, in reality, with nothing more than a boy's cynicism—come of reading more critical writers than he could digest. To start with, in the main most loyal and true, and brave withal; relying on it that he had the free choice, 'either to let into his heart and give the reins to all sorts of devil's passions, or the spirit of God;' satisfied, as he grew older, that, spite of daily troubles and vexations, he was getting on, was growing in moral stature and advancing away from the meaner vices. Lo! and behold! he came here and met Helen (who was but a handful at best) in her garden, and afterwards he bowed down to her and worshipped her.

For this cause he is never a hero, nor shall he have any of the cribs and helps which heroes get; nor their large fortunes.

That day, though, one thing did happen which was all in his favour. To understand it we must return to Shelveport, where, just about twilight, poor Tiff was taking a walk up and down the road before the gate of Lady Penelope's cottage. He felt very, very sad, dissatisfied too, and vexed with himself. He could not settle down to anything, thinking miserably about George. There was a long bit of the road visible from where he was, and down this he saw coming a man in a black coat, a figure which Tiff knew quite well.

It was none other than Mr. Tresham, and he

was walking briskly, on account of the cold. It was fortunate that he should light on Stephen at once like this, and as he got up to him, he called out cheerily, "Well, Stephen, how are you? Very fresh, I hope. How's every one here? I told you you might expect me one of these fine days, and I've got Mary Rumbold to take care of Helen. So I suppose Lady Penelope won't turn me away. But what have you done with George?"

"Have you not met him, then?" said Tiff, growing sick at heart. "He went to Norton about eleven o'clock."

"What a pity! We must just have crossed on the road."

"You must just have crossed on the road," Stephen repeated, staring at him, as a dull child stares.

CHAPTER XII.

CAN YOU FORGIVE HER?

A LITTLE way back, when Stephen and George were crossing together to Shelveport, there was mention of serious troubles which had come upon Berty. We must not lose sight altogether of the eldest brother and his affairs. He last appeared on the day of the steeple chases at Athelbury, prosperous, and occupying the coveted, although really barren position of the winner of a race. He, undoubtedly, had his meed of success on that occasion, notwithstanding that he had lost a few ponies on the other races, after Stephen had left. He could afford this, however, and was, as anyone could see, with half an eye, in a fair way to make a handsome competence. So eagerly, in fact, did he go in for the thing after this, that he quite forgot Stephen's existence, and never, subsequently, alluded to what he had won for his brother in bets on that race. Indeed, speaking of those matters, he always maintained that, if anything, Tiff left off in his debt : because Berty, shortly after Athelbury races, made some match, counting that his brother would be sure to ride for him, and, getting a firm refusal at the last moment from Stephen, who was, by that time, of quite a different way of thinking, he had to ride himself. Just then, poor Berty's was, by no means, that hard condition requisite to carry a man through a four mile race. At the last fence he rolled off, from sheer exhaustion, as he was leading too, and lost altogether a large sum of money. This he always blamed Stephen for; and such it may be remarked here, is often the fruits of adopting extreme opinions, without giving warning to friends and relations.

Berty in these times lived away six days of his life in the twenty-four hours. Indeed his career was like a cracker or squib, after it is lighted.

Upon receiving his winnings from Mr. Jowler, he did make an attempt to take up some of his bills, and discharge a debt or two; but he kept a vague account of those promissory notes of his, and somehow, there were so many other things to be done with ready money, that the amount he had gained at Athelbury soon melted away. 'I can't say I'm actually losing while this lasts,' he used to reflect; 'if it does all go—why, then I'll only be starting even again—at all events, as regards racing.'

It is said that he had seventeen steeplechase horses in training about November, when the season had fairly began—and this in itself is a tax upon a moderate income such as Berty's. He and another man took a cottage near Leicester between them, when the hunting began, and Berty at once decided that he must build new stabling to it. Then there had always been other drains upon his purse, such as constantly buying jewellery, and giving it away on the smallest provocation. He acquired a fixed habit of doing this, and came, by and bye to look on the price of things as a mere abstraction. Living in London must have been expensive to him also, for he was always at the dearest hotels, and giving dinners there to many persons.

On the turf he was not uniformly successful. There are said to be endless uncertainties and disappointments in those matters, and Berty was often almost disgusted with it all. "Why, Frank," he used to say to his friend Kerseytor, who though not generally prudent himself, would comment

very forcibly and even grossly, on the career
Berty was running—" why, look at my luck.
If I do have a good thing, by any chance, I'm
certain to be on duty that day, and can't get
away to back it. And when one does go into the
ring to put a thousand or two on one's horse, ten
to one but some of these ruffian betting men
has got all the money beforehand, and you're
requested to lay 13 to 8 on your own nag."

" Yes, what else can you expect, you blank
young booby?" the other gentleman would
respond. " You had one good horse—that thing
you won at Athelbury with. You gave her away,
I suppose, for a hack to carry some of your deed
old ballet girls."

" Ah! that was a nice business about Sawtry
Maid," the other answered, pensively. " I backed
her at Shrewsbury autumn, old boy, just like
smoke. Well, and the day before the race, that
simpleton, Jack Strangles, who was doing the
commission for me, comes and persuades me to
put her into a selling race, to have her beat, and
get a better price. She was beat nicely, of
course, and, by George! sir, Sam Dale claims
my one the very moment the saddle was off her
back, almost, after their all swearing to me, sir,
that there wouldn't be a claim. Of course, old

Sam just took a couple of hundreds from the book makers next day, put Johnny up, and she never tried a yard—I needn't tell you."

"Ah! yes; I always did think you a gory little ass, Chubby," murmured Frank; and then he would caution Berty still further. But, somehow, he kept on, in spite of it all; and, wherever white rails, and green sward, and a bell, and a judge's box were planted, there Berty's dimples and dark eyes and curly hair were sure to be seen.

But, though Berty attributed the trifling difficulties he was in to luck alone, it cannot be denied that he had one sheer extravagance—he was always playing *roulette.* The people who carried on that game used to follow him, and write to him, and find out where he was going. He was always ready for it, and he was never quite sober when he played *roulette.*

So he was utterly ruined very soon. Then came a time when he had no money in any of his pockets; when his account was hopelessly overdrawn at Wynn Ellis's, and at his agent's, and no amount of Grandison or Newmarch blood could move the former to cash another of his cheques. Then he had to begin to classify all transactions into those that demanded ready money, and those wherein " tick" was a legal tender. He has advanced this theory that, only for the circumstance of railway fares, ready money would be a commercial superfluity, and a drug even. This was plainer to him as time went on, because at that town where he had entertained Tiff, Berty was so well known, and the old station master was such a friend of his, that he actually gave him a special once or twice on credit. But the Regiment moved; the station master at the place they got to next, was a hard-headed man, who knew not Berty, and was cross and over-worked, and haunted by a block of coal trucks, and so in dealing with him cash had to be forthcoming. Now, in London, Berty went in debt often for his Hansom cab fares.

That autumn, his name was flying about London on reams of protested bills. He would get hints that bailiffs were looking for him, and would have to dash off to Bob Sloman, and persuade him to talk to the people who had judgments against him, and by cajoling the money lender, and being civil and penitent before him, Berty used to gain a little time. From Bob Sloman, however, all supplies had ceased by this. He had advanced some four or five thousand pounds and had got bills, and *post obits,*

and agreements just sufficient to soak up the
whole of Berty's interest in the Sawtry estate.

And now Berty had very nearly run out all the
line on his reel; in a little time something was
sure to bring him up with a jerk. If he had but
chosen to go home at times and give some sign of
being sorry, he would have had his mother, for
one, on his side; but no one at Sawtry ever saw
him, from the time hunting the woodlands was
over, about " the first Sunday after Craven week "
—one of Berty's red-letter days—till the Sawtry
covers had to be shot in November, at which
time he generally used to come down for a week,
appearing at home as cheery and light-hearted as
ever, and utterly oblivious of debts, difficulties,
and scoldings. With him there came, now and
then, a company of sinners, little better than
those who had driven Lady Penelope Felton to
her room in former days—only Berty's friends
had no money whatever of their own, and were
small of stature, and gloomy and drunken.
Whenever young Lord Teddington had no room
at Shandwyck, he would transfer some of his
irregular body guard to Berty to be entertained,
and their language and their ethics were more
than the Squire and Lady Adelaide could quite
put up with. But this winter that we are in, it

had come to pass at last that the squire would neither see Berty nor give him any more money, and he returned all bills unopened to the tradesmen who sent them to Sawtry. A few of the later bills had been enough for the squire; for instance £930 to Messrs. Baffin and Dent, of Oxford Street, for cigars. The squire kept that in his desk, and used to take it out and look at it every day.

I think it was in connection with this bill that Berty went into business, about that time, becoming very particular as to the quality of cigars he ordered, and getting large quantities on credit. These he would sell to his friends for ready money, or the nearest approach to it known among them, and in this way he came to understand how people in business made such large profits. About that time, also, he took to pawning a few of his watches, and would drive up in his brougham and make a capital bargain with the different pawnbrokers.

There was a young lady to whom he had given some jewellery; and at one time, when he was desperately hard up, seeing a ring which he had presented to her, on her finger, he asked her for it. She looked at him, "All right," said she, sadly, "here it is." So he took that, and pawned it, too, whereby he was able to get down by train in time for " morning stables" next day.

This was the same young lady—with rough red hair—whom Bob Sackville and Mr. Bagenal talked about the day Stephen arrived to ride for his brother. It was Miss Vane, an artist at the Pindaric Theatre, and it was she who acted the genius of Lloyd's, in the great nautical burlesque of " Dædalus. "

Miss Vane was very 'graceful, and unaffected, and ladylike.' In those days people were almost persecuted for having red hair, and she used to hide hers as much as she could, and make it darker with a comb. She had dark grey eyes.

People who cry out against the immorality of the stage would have felt how much wickeder they were themselves, and acknowledged it, had they known Miss Vane; for though she used to dance in that nautical piece clothed merely with something to represent marine assurance, and the sense of what she owed to her position as artiste and girl alone in the cold world—yet she had probably as great and high aspirations as others. And why our hard working sisters of the sock and buskin should be exposed to the taunts of those who cannot sympathise with their mission and their work, is a thing not easy to understand.

Can it be that the fault is with those who teach them no better? Here was this young lady (whose mother had been a dancer, and now charred, and whose father was in the wide, wide world, not to be signalised), without a protector, and therefore looked coldly on. In early youth she used to run of messages about the theatre. Then her mamma took to beating her; so she ran away, became a tramp, and did some hop-picking. Then she came back to London, and used to sell flowers, which business she left to go and live as maid-of-all-work to an elderly Scotch tobacconist and his wife, who kept a shop near Leicester Square. She told her mother when they met again that she was married to a gentleman, but not being able to bring any proof of this, her mother, who was still strong enough, gave her another beating, and they parted. I have often wondered why the high-born lady does not take the ballet girl and educate her, instead of looking down upon her. However, Miss Vane lived with this elderly couple, till, after a while, she took lessons, and came to dance very well indeed, and as she had a good memory, we will see that she was promoted by and bye.

At one period those Scotch people used to beat her and cuff her, upon Sundays and holydays.

But all things considered, she was well fed. She
made friends among the other ladies at the theatre,
and was very contented. Indeed, after a time
her good temper and patience and a certain
amount of shrewdness, got her on rapidly, until
her salary was considerably increased, and she
got thirty shillings a week and upwards.

She then became a lady, and was saluted as
such. It was at this time that Berty knew her.

When Nelly was about nineteen, and was sav-
ing a little money, she again found out her
mother, who was doing washing, though not to
any great extent; and these two hearts, which
had been estranged, beat together again; whereupon Miss Vane took a little house of her own in
Brompton, and had a lodger in her parlour; while
her mother did the cooking, and sometimes opened
the door.

By degrees Miss Vane made a great many
friends, and one or two celebrities took notice of
her. She picked up the best manners, besides,
and learnt to dress really well; so that she could
hold her own at any of the entertainments or full
dress balls she went to. Undoubtedly she had a
quaint, straightforward, untamed air that was
very attractive, and some people said she looked
quite handsome at times. Bob Sloman—who

knew everybody—remarked her specially. "There's a touch of nature about that Nelly Vane," he used to declare, sententiously; " she has a fine 'eart, I do believe."

After a while, Colonel Wellington Footlyte made Nelly's acquaintance, and would have fallen in love with her had he not been in such awe of the young lady of the corps who at that particular time had him under her domination. Anyhow, he asked her to his Richmond parties, and thus Miss Nelly was quite launched into good society.

It was at one of these dinners that she first saw Berty. And when she began to feel at home and notice the people, Nelly thought she had never heard such a nice, pleasant voice as his. He was in the best spirits possible, describing how he and some of his brother Husssars had entertained Mr. Calcraft at breakfast, after he had turned off some fellow up at the jail of the town where they were quartered; and on a hunting morning, too. " I offered to mount him with the hounds," said Berty. " Told him 'twas easy fencing, and no drops." And Berty chuckled uproarously at this, as he did at all his own jokes. " But he couldn't see it. Good old chap, but rather slow."

What a dear old boy this was, Miss Vane thought. She kept looking at him and forgot

the rest of the company, trying to catch every
word he said; not that they mattered much, for
it was really only the sort of talk that all young
swells talked; but he had such a darling way of
bringing out his words and laughing at his own
fun.

She could not take her eyes off him, and during
dinner was strangely silent and reserved; but
towards the end, she managed to make him talk to
her, and later in the evening, to her delight, he
took her to row on the river.

The last time she had been to Richmond, she
had come with her tobacconist couple—one stifling
Whit-Monday long ago, when she was poor and
ill-treated; then she had worn a shabby dress
and bonnet, and they had had tea and some
shrimps, which were not fresh, in the town. But
now this little swell was sitting close beside her,
showing his pretty teeth and making a row and
amusing her, while the moon shone so nicely on
them. She had never dreamt that Richmond
could be so heavenly a place. The little soldier
promised to take her back to her mother's house
in his brougham; but no doubt he had made the
same engagement with more than one other
lady of the party; and when they got up the
hill he somehow went off with the first who asked

him ; so Nelly, waiting about the corridor of the hotel very disconsolate, was found by Miss Fitz-Vernon, who offered to give her a lift up to town in her trap. " Little Truefitte, of the Foreign Office, was with her," she said. " But he was nobody ;" and he went to sleep at once, besides, so that the two ladies could talk as much as they pleased on the way.

It was a sign that Nelly was getting up in the world, when so great a lady as this was civil to her. Miss FitzVernon, after dinner, was a little talkative and incoherent, and couldn't help patronising the lesser celebrity somewhat too much. But Nelly was thinking of other things, and listened quite defferentially to the other's criticisms on everybody. " What did you make of your little soldier, dear ?" said the superior of the two, at last, in a whisper.

Poor Nelly didn't know what she ought to say. She looked at their sleeping friend ; but he, poor youth, was fondly dreaming that the Tories had come in again, and that he had passed in French for a paid attachéship after all ; and he heard them not.

" Newmarch ? isn't that his name," Nelly said, softly.

The other laughed. " Why, dear, you ain't

going to get spooney, are you?" she said, with
superiority.

"I call him such a noble kind of face."

"Pooh! he's nothing.   Freddy here told me
the women all call him 'Little Giggle,—among
the real ladies, my dear."

"He's in the Guards, ain't he?" suggested
Nelly, desiring to exalt her new acquaintance.

Miss FitzVernon shook her head.   "I know
all the men in London, and he's not a Guardsman,
dear—more of a plunger, I should say.   Why, I
know those men so well, Nelly.   Show me a man
in the street, forty yards off, walking towards
me, and I'll tell you at a glance if he's in the
Guards or not.   I think it's a way they get of
carrying their heads, dear," she mused, "wearing those big furry bear-skins down over their
eyes."

Thus poor Miss Vane showed her ignorance of
the world.   She was undoubtedly in love, though,
and did not struggle much against it.   Berty
had asked where she lived, and she wondered if
he would remember it, and would come to see
her.   Now, what had Berty ever remembered
yet?   In either case she loved him, and began to
feel troubled from that day out.   She feared for
herself; she knew not why—because she had

never been in love before, and hitherto had only known it as a very common misfortune—calling for compassion, if anything.   Girls whom she had seen taking on about a fellow, were generally made very stupid by it, and were sure to get treated badly in the end.   If she had read the novels other girls did, she would have got the condition off by heart, and known exactly what she ought to feel like; but Miss Vane could hardly read or write at all.   Now she felt for the girls that she used to laugh at once; she knew what they must have gone through.

It was her first taste of that which keeps one awake; and then, which has to be thought of the first thing to start with in the morning.   True, there was Mr. Sloman; he was a would-be lover of hers; of course he was a very handsome man, and, of late, had gone on tremendously die-away about her.   But she couldn't bear him now. There had been, too, that nice little German, who used to wait at the Mesopotamian Divan off the Haymarket; he had been a good little fellow, and had offered her his savings and his hand. But he got taken by the police, and she had known it was all spite—that pale fellow in the A division, with the black whiskers, hated him, she remembered—and then the poor young fellow

went and let on that he had taken the gentleman's watch, and got three years. Those police
and magistrates, she believed, were all in league
—every one of them. Yet, after all, had he not
been a mean-looking sort of young man, at best?
and, indeed, since she had met Berty, most of
her former admirers contrasted very poorly with
that noble, sleek, and unembarrassed young
dandy.

Thus Nelly threatened to become a great
aristocrat, and to acquire a habit of detesting
people of her own class.

"Lord, Tilly," she used to say to her friend,
who helped her to learn her parts, when they went
to have their supper after the theatre; " wouldn't
you rather wait on a gentleman, and black his
boots, than live grand, and be made much of
among those 'coster bred 'uns,' as Mr. Sloman's
clerk calls them?" And then she would feel
herself quite carried away by an enthusiasm for
the upper classes.

"Has he been round at your place lately,
Nell?" her friend asked, inquisitively.

"What—Bob Sloman? Don't bother me
about that 'orrid fellah. I can't bear the sight
of him. And I said I wasn't to be at home, if
he called. He's a horrid man, I do think."

And yet, what would not Miss Tilly have given to have had the great man driving down, day after day, to call at her lodgings. But the unpardonable transgression of not having so pretty a face as another, is ever sternly before the eyes of a woman like this. She never thought of disputing that Nelly should have her choice of any number of admirers. Certainly, Nelly Vane was growing into a very handsome girl.

Berty Newmarch owned a box at the Pindaric, and also had the key of a door by which he could pass from the house to behind the scenes. He was well known there, and, with his companions, was much about the place. In this way, Nelly often had a chance of talking to him for a moment. He did not remember her face in the least, when she used to try and remind him of their day at Richmond, and generally mistook her for somebody else. At last, however, he fixed her name in his head by some accident or other, and suddenly was very much taken with her. That was one time when she had to come on as a parr in some grand ballet of fishes. Her scales won his heart; and, indeed, fitting quite tight, made a very glittering and becoming dress. It was then that he gave her the rings, and when he went back to his box to look at Nelly and the other little fishes, she turned her face towards him, and dexterously kissed the rings once or twice, keeping perfect time all the while.

However, about then, he had to go up to Scotland for the 12th, and she did not see him for many weeks. She used to send him letters, however, which her friend Miss Tilly wrote out for her. Meanwhile, she had only the company of those beautiful rings—his present—to remind her of him; and she used to keep them near her pillow, in a small box—quite apart from her other ornaments, side by side with a shabby little prayer-book, given to her long ago, as a death-bed present, by a poor young lady in the hoop-skirt making line, who had died of consumption.

If he were only sure to come back, she would be so thankful, and would never complain again. Each night she would look from the wings all round the boxes, seeking his face. It was never there; but he would come by and bye. Her life didn't amuse her now as it used to do. When she thought about him—lying awake half the night—she felt strangely softened and changed; and there came to her an intense longing to be thought good, and pure, and worthy of him. If it were only possible that he should respect her and think of her, the same as he did of ladies—

then, perhaps, he would love her, too. Why wasn't she a lady? then she'd never have been wicked. She would try and become good; and to this end poor Nelly wandered off one Sunday and went into a quiet church, a long, long way from where she lived. She had never been before, and the silence kept by the people, and the coughing from one spot and another, and the great bell buzzing in the tower, frightened her. She looked with envy at the ladies, gliding in so quiet, and at home here. To her it was all confusing; and she crept away, as humbly as she might, to sit among a lot of small children in the free seats.

And then all the people stood up suddenly, and it began. She had to glance about nervously to see if she were doing as the others did. Her Prayer-book was in her hand, though, to be sure, she could not understand the arrangements of it; very shy, she strove to turn over the leaves the same way as the others did. She never got beyond the calendars at the beginning; but when all knelt, she thought she would pray of herself. About Berty she would like to pray, but there was a thick crust over her mind or soul when she tried to begin.

While she was endeavouring to spell out these

things to her profit, Berty was shooting in the north somewhere, and not praying, it is quite certain. All women are good, some author has said, and, believing that Religion is the winning side, they wish to be of that division. But men are far otherwise. Hence Berty used to read those letters that Nelly Vane caused to be written, lying on the heather, about luncheon time, and not caring whether she became good or not. They disappointed him, and their respectful tone and monotony of style became wearisome. He wanted very much to see his good tempered little red haired actress again some time or other. She was more amusing, certainly, when one could see her close.

Being in London one day not long afterwards, and walking along Ryder Street, Berty had to stop at the corner to let a grand carriage, which was coming slowly down Bury Street, pass before him. He thought he knew the horses, and then, looking from the coachman's legs up to his face, he was sure he remembered him, too. Meantime, a lady in the carriage was nodding in his direction, and at last she stopped and began to speak to him.

"Oh! Bertram, how are you? Why do you never, never come to see us? Your uncle was

asking what you did with yourself—only yesterday."

" Now I knew that I had seen that face before,"
said Berty to himself. " I've been in Scotland,
aunt."

She shook her head sadly. " Can you dine
with us while you're in town ? I must give you
a long scolding some day, Bertram. You will
never be steady, I'm afaid. Mrs. Harvey Broase
told me you promised to dine in Hill Street twice,
and didn't appear at all, or send an excuse. I'm
sure Eustacia Broase is such a nice girl, and will
have quite a fortune. Shall I drive you anywhere ?"

' Now,' thought he, ' I hardly know this woman ;
and she seems to be talking in a very odd sort of
way, as if she was one's tutor. I shall go and
see Nelly Vane, for my part. There's nothing to
do for an hour. I wonder where the little girl
lives, though.'

" Will you take me as far as Brompton, aunt ?"
he said, in his frank, candid fashion. His manner reassured Lady Blanch, and she told
the coachman to drive westwards. Then
Berty lay back in the carriage and searched his
betting book for Miss Vane's address. Luckily,
Lady Blanch was very blind. She doubtless would

have liked also to hear who his friends in that
far-off quarter were; but her nephew, with all his
lisp, had a certain dignity and reserve about him
at times that put inquisitiveness out of the question.

" Armageddon Villas, please," Berty called out
to the servant; and the heavy Ellis chariot, with
its great hammer-cloth and spreading coats-of-
arms, plunged through the gravel up to Nelly's
little house.   Just as they turned the corner, Bob
Sloman's mail phaeton whisked by them, and
Berty thought, ' How black he does look.'   The
capitalist's head was bent down, though, and it
is to be supposed that it never was worth his
while to look at big lumbering respectable car-
riages such as Berty was in then.   So those two
did not greet each other.

" Mrs. Vane at home—I mean Miss Vane,"
said our hussar, when the footman had delivered
his fusillade of knocks at Nelly's door.

There stood a tall, shabby woman, staring over
his shoulder at the great carriage which had just
turned and was driving away.   She might perhaps have resented his free and easy manner, but
plainly, a person who came in such a turn-out as
that was to be received with deference.   " No,
sir; she's not at home," the woman said, putting

on her best tone. "Ch! then, I'll wait. Won't
be long, I suppose? Up here am I to go?"
Berty said, making for the stairs.

The woman followed him up to the sitting
room, and began moving the chairs about and
pulling up the blinds uneasily, while he swaggered
through the room and settled his hat on, opposite
the mirrors. "Miss Vane know your name, sir?
Who shall I say when she returns?" This was
meant to be a severe hint, but Berty was too
busy settling his tie in the glass again to take it.
"Miss Vane is very particular about her visitors,"
added the servant.

"Ah! I daresay. Wasn't Bob Sloman calling
here just now? What does he want?"

There was no answer. "I say, are you Miss
Vane's mother?" asked Berty, turning round on
a sudden inspiration.

"No, sir," she answered, speaking with that
serious tone and manner which the lower classes
assume when telling a lie.

'You are, though,' Berty thought to himself.
'Got the same eyes, too.' As for the woman, her
face had a cross and care-worn expression, and,
from looking after the kitchen fires so much, was
somewhat shaded and grimy. Still, she had a
grand, erect way of walking, and had a straight

figure, for all her black-lead tinges. Berty pitied her, and he thought, since she seemed to keep hovering about the room, that he might as well make friends with her. " You've a very nice place here," said he, giving her one of his sunniest smiles. " How prettily you have got your rooms furnished. I'm sure Miss Vane's very well taken care of." To be sure, he was so good looking and highly finished, and had such a sweet lisp, that, for the sake of old times, the other could not but admire him. "Miss Vane ever speak of me?" he asked, when he had got the talk into quite a confidential flow.

Probably she never did; her fondness for Berty was too precious a treasure to be displayed to anybody, it may be suppposed. " There's a many gentlemen admires Miss Vane," the servant said, proudly. "Ah! there's Mr. Slo—." Berty looked at her with a laugh in his eyes. " Well, 'tis Mr. Sloman. Why, he's a dying for her, and hoffering jewels and presents, and writing and messages, hall hours, some days; but, Lord bless you," she continued, excitedly. " My young lady won't look at none of them. You know how young ladies is sometimes. She's very 'aughty, is Miss Vane. Dear, dear me! there was that foreign gentleman—a Grecian gentleman, I think they said he was—went on at the door in despair one night, positively awful; and Mrs. Gussett sent one of her young ladies in the shop round one night to say as how she'd heerd he was waiting with a knife to stab Miss Vane and do for hisself too. What they'd do in jealousy's awful, them foreigners, particularly the Greeks and Italian ones, I've heard."

But at that moment Miss Vane was heard opening the hall door with her key, and Berty was left to himself above.

In a minute or two Nelly came, a glow still on her cheek after her walk, and her eyes wide open with pleasure and surprise at finding him there. It was a wonderful thing that she, with her audacious manner, gained during her hard life, trembled at the sight of him, and was unable, in fact, to say two words, as she held out her hand. She began to bewail her sad fate because, well knowing who she was and what she was, her love could mean nothing but weayring sin, which she had heard so much of, and longed to be able to get away from. She continued looking at his face with gentle affection, noting the extraordinary grace of his head and throat as he stood rapping the table with his knuckles and laughing at her. Quickly, however, Nelly recollected that this was not the way a lady would receive him, therefore she walked about for a little, taking off her gloves. "Excuse me, won't you," said she. "I knew you would soon return to town. Won't you be seated, and take a chair?" Thus ladies speak, she thought.

"They're too small," said he, knocking over one with his foot. "What a beauty you've grown! I was in Scotland, and went to Baden, and got back in time for Doncaster, and thought I'd come to see you."

"Who told you where I live," she asked looking at him, and smiling, perfectly happy, her eyes still delighting themselves with the sight of him.

"Oh! I saw it in the Court Guide," said he. That was not very witty, but she laughed. The plainest things, when he said them, were amusing enough for her.

"I began to think we'd never see you again," she went on. "There was two of your fellows down at our place last night; I forget their names. But we didn't talk. One was a little fellow with funny blue eyes, and fair moustache like; don't remember his name. Charlie Bedford told me he saw you at Doncaster, and you lost all your money there. Is that true?"

"I'm sure I don't remember," says Berty. "Give me a kiss, Miss Vane." She drew herself away, poor thing, and blushed. Rusty were all Nelly's blushing powers, and her confusion grew worse and worse when she felt herself getting red for the first time for many a day. Berty looked at her with mild surprise, and observed how serious she had turned all in a moment, growing paler and paler.

"Don't ask me," she had said. Accordingly Berty drew her towards him, and kissed her twice; each time he did, she gave a shudder. 'How very nice a person she was,' he thought, and whispered, "Come and sit here."

"Don't ask me," she said, in a faint voice. Yet she came to sit by him, as he remained expecting her. He had previously admired the furniture there, and praised her good taste.

"This is not how I meant to act," she thought. "Will my darling ever respect me, if I give up to all he tells me to do?" She was more unhappy than words could tell, and she shook with fear. If there is any pity to be given, bestow it upon her sad state at this moment. If he could only have gone away and let her cry, or stayed and fallen asleep, so that she could cry unseen, and watching him. We know what his end will be; but he was at this period undaunted, and she looked lovely to him. He said deliberately, "What a lovely face you've got."

She said, "Oh! do not. Oh! leave me."

He said, "Yes, darling, I'm going."

She said, "You will leave me; won't you?"

He said the same as before.

She said, "Go, Mr. Newmarch; leave me."

He said, "Those aren't the same ones that you wear, as the bounding Bayadère of Bessarabia, are they?"

"Oh! Captain Newmarch, you forget yourself," Nelly cried out, struggling to go. But he only laughed. Then Nelly spoke in wrath. "Don't touch me, sir!" she said. "You forget that I'm a respectable girl. You forget yourself, I think, indeed." Shaking off his arm, she rose, and striding across the room, seated herself on a chair and looked haughtily towards the place where he remained.

Berty raised his eyebrows a little, and then, approaching the mirror, gave a twist to his glorious curly hair, set his tie to perfection, and stretching across the table, took up his hat. When he glanced at Nelly, that—to his eyes—

supernatural and grotesque look, still disfigured her face. "I have to dine with some fellows," he lisped, taking out his watch. Had she revealed to him that she was in reality a white elephant, and not a girl at all, he would have lisped still, and not said much. Therefore he was about to leave, having almost forgotten who she was by this time, when she spoke.

"Listen to me, Mr. Newmarch."

He bowed coldly. "You've made a mistake I think," he said. "You took me for what I'm not. However, I think I shall drive down to Richmond with Charles Gournay, and have grouse and a magnum of this champagne they give one, and get back in time for some hazard at one's rooms."

"Berty!" she said, looking with imploring, filmy eyes. "Berty!" Yet she did not rise and come to him, and so he went. She now really loved him.

See what Berty thought. He was all but excessively angry and annoyed. To ask him to come to this house, and then to drag him into long explanations! Why did she live there? He had been let in for a drive with his Aunt Blanch, in order to arrive at this neighbourhood, the look of whose shabby genteel, suburban streets, forbade the suspicion that a resident there would have behaved in this double-faced manner; was all that nothing? Hansom cabmen coasting along, saw him, solitary, and waved their whips. He shook his head angrily. Could anyone have foretold such fraud as Nelly had practised? This weighed on his spirits, and he spoke his mind candidly about it at dinner. He and his friend were rather silent on the whole. It happened that they had backed each other's bills—a lot of them here and there—and had just recently been served with writs on account thereof. It had been settled that they were to go into their affairs together on this occasion; accordingly Charles Gournay, after a long silence, said, " Is it true that Nelly Vane has gone into a convent? A man swore 'twas true, at Strong's yesterday. Then, on the other hand, George Wygmore declares she's been married to Bob Sloman for months."

" Well, I can't say, old fellow. I'm never told of these good things. But, I was just going to say, I think the girl rather too bad, and a most forward, presuming little woman, 1 mean to say. I hardly know the girl myself, and I find she goes on as if she had known one all one's life, and could take any liberty she chose." Then he mentioned how unfairly she had behaved that afternoon, and it was settled that she was anything but a safe person to have as an acquaintance.

Thus Nelly had triumphed. Nevertheless she was most wretched afterwards, and repented of what she had said and done. He had gone away, and she would never see him again. But she had done her duty. She said that she was a martyr, and now began to understand what were the consolations which good and self-denying people had. When at first she felt resigned, she had ranked herself with those honest women whose upright life in face of temptation she had happened to witness from time to time. And then Mr. Sloman began to call on her again. He managed to see her a few days after Berty had been there, and he told her wildly that he couldn't live without her. That day, he had got through a fabulous amount of business. The 'second October' had been an atrocious week for the " gentlemen," and down he drove, almost confused, after the endless negociations crowded into the morning. Now, he came to pour out his vehement adoration at Nelly's feet. Why did he bother his head about the woman? He couldn't tell, and yet this girl's little finger was worth all the others put together.　As for Nelly, when he talked, she took it very placidly.　Her heart's darling she had driven from her, and after that, to hear this man talking !　It made her laugh. Anyhow, she could practice on him, how to be stern, and to reject people for by and bye.

"No, Mr. Sloman," she would say, quite calmly; "don't you talk nonsense.　I'm not going to hear it, and I won't have it."

He used to look and look at her, and then frown and stamp his feet.　"Listen," he'd say, " I would do anything reasonable for you, Nelly ; I would now.　Look, you may see my banker's book if you like, and you can see what I'm able to settle on you ; and I would, too."

But she could not bear more than a certain quantity of this ; and said at last, " Look, I 'ate the very sight of you, Bob !" grinding her teeth, and flinging his hand from her.

Still he would persist whenever he had the chance; and it was very hard for her to speak indignantly to him, for many reasons.　The man she did love, knew not a word of her old life.　If she had declared to Berty that she went straight from the position of Sunday school teacher to dance at the Pindaric Theatre, he could not have contradicted her.　No doubt Berty had heard men sneer her character away; but what was it they did not sneer at? A word from her was sufficient to abash him, in reality. But 'twas different with this Sloman, whom she well remembered long ago, coming in and out of the dingy parlour behind that shop where she had lived once; it was little use, indeed, saying to him what she said to Berty.

And he, for his part, put all this obstinacy down to one of those well-known but unaccountable whims women take. Somebody had said that she was spooney on that young Newmarch, who was going at the time. It must be something of the sort, and so he must only have a bit of patience; thus he put it. It was sure to be right, by and bye, if her lover were really a young booby of this sort, who hadn't very long to last now. Out of Nelly's presence, he could discuss the *pros* and *cons.* calmly enough. But when he actually saw her close, she was a wonderful girl!

Bob Sloman is like a minor villain, described just to whet one's vengeance. Later, a puissant young hero might appear to smite him utterly; and even, by a little perversion of the law and a few simple snares, to wring all his ill-gotten wealth from him. But Bob, in reality, knew the law well, and always kept on the safe side of it.

At this time, it is plain that Nelly was forlorn. She shut herself up in Armageddon Villas, and stole discreetly home from the theatre each night, quite alone. As for that Greek gentleman, he strove desperately to meet her several times; and, indeed, succeeded, for she could always be seen, smiling and chatting to everybody, when not actually before the footlights. But she steadily forgot who he was whenever they met. Look at it from his point of view, this was his story—his tragedy! So, one day he said good-bye to his friends, went straight to the " Baltic," and, taking the advice of a gang of his own people congregated there, sold a ' clean bear' of two hundred thousand Brighton railway stock. This was years and years ago; things rose and rose during all the next five accounts, and that Grecian gentleman was never heard of any more.

Once, Nelly Vane met Berty at a breakfast party—the only place she had gone out to for weeks. She meant to refuse, but a young lady persuaded her to go to this one; and, since it was some City man who gave it, she had no fear of meeting Berty there. But his appetite for

breakfast and so forth was now eclectic (he
knew several of these people; indeed, things
have tended that way of late); and Berty had
dined with this man for three days running,
and had slept at his rooms the night before. Not
having been home for some days, he had only a
collection of dressing gowns to clothe himself
from.

Nelly trembled like a leaf when she saw him.
He certainly avoided her, and she resolved to
keep firm to the end. Somehow though, she
found herself by his side, after all, when no one
was looking. Said she, " Why are you so cruel ?"
He stared at her. " Berty," she whispered,
again. But he gave an incredulous sort of laugh.
" 'Pon my honour, Miss Seymour," said he, forgetting her name, indeed, " 'tisn't quite good
enough. I take the trouble to drive down to
your house, or wherever you live, and in return,
you take liberties—sending one away and that—
that, 'pon my honour, one can't look over."

She sighed and gazed at him most fondly.
But he had other things to think of, and would
not even notice her further. After she got home,
she repeated, " Was it not a lie ?" or words to
that effect.

She went and put on a black silk dress with a

quantity of flounces, and casting herself down—
" Was it not a lie ?" she said.

Later on, when Nelly wearied of staying in
doors and doing nothing, she used to get letters
written to him, explaining why she had been
harsh; but Berty had forgotten all about her, it
is to be believed, and he had plenty to occupy
him in those days. So her letters were never
answered, and she grew very wretched and
lonely. Going to church had pleased her well
for a little; and when she heard the organ
played, she used to wish herself in Heaven,
where everything was weird and sweet like that,
she fancied. As time went on, though, there
used to be no change in what they did at church
service; always the same things, learnt by rote—
breaking off in the middle, and the clergyman
taking it for granted that one knew all about
them beforehand. She longed to ask questions;
but instead, she had to go out with the others,
who looked so satisfied. Doubtless, there came
nobody to the place as ignorant as she was. The
novelty of the church worn off, therefore, Nelly
got tired of trying to be good, and dreaded that
she had lost her love, and got nothing in return.

CHAPTER XIII.

CERTE CAPTUS EST : HABET !

WE have been going back a long way while talking about Miss Vane; because it was in the early part of one summer that Berty first met her, and now, we see how well he knew her at one time, and also that about Christmas, when he came to have no money, she gave her rings to him. She would have given him the pupils of her eyes if he had wished; but there was nothing to be got "on" these eyes, and what Berty wanted was sterling money. He had, in the last few months, ruined himself utterly. He began to look about and see that he could not raise a shilling in the world, and all the fun of being hard up vanished; now and then he got hold of a few pounds. He put on a bold face and ordered a lot of wine at Strong's; this he

M 5

sold to a young cornet just joining the regiment,
and with the proceeds paid something at
Buffer's, on account.   He then reversed this
financial operation, getting the wine next time
at Buffer's, keeping himself thus pretty well in
funds.   Money he knew he must have.   That
was all miserable work, though.   The poor opera-
tor got haggard, and careworn, and nervous ; he
became irritable, too, and quarrelled with everybody in the regiment, till no one cared much
what became of him.   And now his soldiering
was drawing rapidly to a close.   About that time
he formed a very bad opinion of his colonel, who,
he said, had grown an unbearable old brute—
always down on one now, if one got into a scrape
of any sort.   To be sure, Berty's way of treating
a difficulty was with a lot of cursing and a great
deal of drinking.   There had once been a day
when his colonel was wont to sit, sipping hock
and seltzer, of Sunday mornings in Berty's
room; and yet before this year was out, it came
to pass that he told Berty he'd try him by court
martial if he didn't sell in twenty-four hours.

It began, the last time, about some nasty scrape
Berty was involved in—something about a cheque,
and a servant, and a bill stamp, and a tradesman
in the town. It all came to be reported, anyhow;

and one afternoon, Bob Sackville, crossing the barrack square, saw the colonel sitting at his window in his shirt sleeves, smoking his pipe, and sketching, as was his wont. " Oh ! Sackville, just tell Eveley I want him," called out the great man. In one of the passages, Bob encountered the colonel's private servant. " Do you know what's wrong now, Palmer ?" Bob Sackville asked quietly. " It's Mr. Newmarch again, I'm afraid, sir," the man answered in a whisper ; " the colonel's had the major, and that tobacconist hout of the town up for an hour ; and *I* heard something. It's a bad business, captain, I'm afraid."

" I can guess what he wants the adjutant for," said Sackville. The faithful Palmer nodded his head ominously.

In a few minutes Mr. Cecil Eveley, who had gone in by chance for learning his work, and was now adjutant, came along that passage, all dressed in velvet, with a tame monkey sitting on his shoulders. " 'Vise you to get out of the way, Cis," said the other. " The chief wants to get hold of you to put poor Chubby under arrest."

" Let him put him under arrest himself," said the adjutant. " I sha'n't do it. I'll bolt out of the way though somewhere."

Nevertheless that evening, though nobody wanted to help in the painful work, Berty had to go up to the colonel's presence—a dim feel upon him that 'twas not unlike slinking into the fourth form room in old days, at the head master's heels to be swished. "A fool will laugh when he's drowning," the Welsh say, and Berty kept up his reckless calmness to the last. "Well, there's nothing more for it," said the colonel, shrugging his shoulders and filling his pipe; "you must go to your room under arrest, Lieutenant New-march."

And so Berty had his dinner up there that night; and then having gathered together the younger and sillier among the cornets, a big loo was set going, and he did not go to bed at all that evening. He never thought of the position he was in—it took no hold of his mind whatever. Indeed, after the loo party had broken up, re-membering that on the day just risen there was racing somewhere near London which he must attend, he changed his clothes, about nine in the morning, and prepared to start. It was pouring rain when Berty looked out, so he finished a bottle of brandy, and hurried off to catch the train. Nobody saw him leaving barracks, pro-bably; but next day there was enough in the newspapers even, to show where he had been. Berty, it appeared, had a horse in some Hunters' Stake at one of the small races near London, and young Harlow of the Guards came specially to ride for him; but it was six to four on Mr. Newmarch's one when Berty went into the ring. Instantly he turned round, gave Jim Fagan a laying commission, and at the last moment put up that well-known thief, Mr. Chaunter, to ride, even though Freddy Harlow had already got Berty's colours on. There was groaning and hissing enough in the ring while they cantered. Only four ran, and yet betting men came and shouted out ironically, " Fifty ponies against the Captain's one," under Berty's nose. The stewards turned their backs on him when he spoke to them ; Freddy Harlow had chucked his cap and jacket right across the weighing room; and to finish all, the horse broke its back in that ditch which Mr. Chaunter was obliged to pull it into, as he couldn't stop his one in the third round. Mr. Fagan returned about twenty pounds, as the fruits of his laying commission, which had been so clumsily managed that everyone knew it; and when Berty got back at night, he found an official letter lying on his table, demanding his reasons for breaking his arrest.

Next day, everyone knew by the morning paper about Mr. Chaunter's mount and the commissions that had gone " the other way." It just wanted that to finish Berty. The Colonel was one of those antiquated disciplinarians whom the improved formulas of our day have all but extinguished; and, instead of taking a lenient view of the case, and by a mixture of firmness and forbearance, winning Berty back, said that he would not have one tarnish on the honour of his regiment. Therefore he wrote the letter to Mr. Newmarch, to Sawtry, which we heard of a few pages back, recommending that his son quitted the service at once. Charles Ellis went on the squire's behalf, to the town where the Hussars lay, and found his nephew superintending the drawing of a badger in his room after breakfast, with an armed sentry over his door. He also saw the Colonel; and, next day, Berty's papers went in, as the term is. A shabby little money lender at Ipswich got the whole of the money from Berty's commission. Most of his horses were seized for his forage bills. When he left, he hadn't a farthing to pay anybody with; and he went up to town, and took up his quarters at Strong's.

That was a nice Christmastide's work; but

Berty Newmarch didn't seem to be aware that anything particular had happened. In one or two places he had still a little credit left, and it was at this very time that he commenced negotiations for the purchase of a famous grey pearl, which was said to have tempted the chief of the house of Esterhazy not a little. It was too late for very much of that, though; and yet Berty managed to float for a while longer. It being foggy and dark in town about then, one day, remembering that it would be rather pleasanter at home, he thought he'd run down to Sawtry, and kill a few pheasants; so, on a capital shooting morning, he took the early train to Daryngworth, having with him Frank Lazurus—who owns the Café Riffe Raffe, in the Haymarket; Johnny Dale—just then under a cloud, on account of some horse poisoning affair at Ealing; Lord Scowlthorpe—whose wife had just ran away from him; and the marker of a billiard room, in which Berty was a large shareholder. They had a champagne breakfast at Daryngworth, and Berty got a team from the Black Swan, and drove his party over to Sawtry afterwards.

Traylen was cutting up food for the pheasants when his young master and these strange friends of his—very noisy already—walked up to the keeper's lodge. "Whose place is all this?" says Johnny Dale, who had not been sober for two or three days.

"Old Bob Sloman's," Berty answered, cynically. What trees there were here, to be sure! His friends couldn't help respecting him when they saw how fine an estate he ought to be heir to. Now, it was a year and more since any one at Sawtry had set eyes on the future master; and Traylen had heard that matters were going terrible bad between the squire and Master Berty. But what could he do, when the young heir told him he wanted a day's shooting in his own covers? It did look queer, though.

The keeper took them where he thought they'd do the least harm; for never had he seen such an astounding collection of "guns" as this. No doubt he sent word to the house also. But who could be vexed with Master Berty? One would think, to look at him, he was a child still— shooting at Mr. Curry's surplice, hanging out to dry behind the sexton's cottage. Brian Newmarch sent word to his son that if he stayed there ten minutes longer he'd send the village constables to turn him out. Berty only laughed, but Traylen's dilemma was the cruellest of all, When they did begin to shoot, none of them could hit anything—that was one consolation—and Johnny Dale, getting very sick of the whole affair before long, sat down in the middle of Clerken Wood, took out three cards, and began to play Scowlthorpe for a bottle of " fizz." The two very nearly came to blows ; and at last Traylen saw them all drive off to the Railway Station, to his intense relief.

Nelly Vane heard of all the trouble that Berty was in. Since he was out of the army, there was no chance of his getting shot; and she would not be sorry if all this kept him from wandering about, as he used to do, and if she could see him oftener. He had become quite a man of business now, and looked down with a sort of pity on military men. He was going to take a share in a Proprietary Chapel once ; and was almost a wine-merchant another time ; and next, half a partner in an Anglo-Parisian horse-dealing business. He ever took much interest in the drama ; and as he was frequently at that theatre where Nelly danced and acted, they became great friends again, though—on principle—he did not offer to call on her, after her behaviour. This sort of thing lasted for a few weeks. It was only Bob Sloman's forbearance that kept Berty out of gaol now, and Bob, for his own part, would have liked

to lock him up any day.　When he went behind
the scenes at the Pindaric, he used to curse and
swear to himself, at the sight of Nelly and her
young bankrupt sweetheart, laughing together
and talking low.　She was doubly civil to Bob,
now that she was so happy; and that put him in
a still greater rage.　But, when she chose, it
could not be denied that Nelly Vane had a fearfully coaxing way about her, and Bob maintained
that women had been able to make a fool of him
ever since he could walk alone.

"Drive me home, Bob," she said to him one
night, coming out of the theatre. "You've got your
phaeton and pair here—hav'n't you?"　They had
been waiting in the street, true enough, for the
last three hours, he having driven in from the
suburbs that evening.　Now it was a dark night
and very cold.　"You see, it's an open trap," he
said, nervously, dreading to lose the chance of
driving her, after all.　However, up she jumped:
"I'm going to drive," said she; and it was not
the least use his objecting.　So, taking the reins,
she rattled down the Strand, whipped round the
corners at a fearful pace, and made her team
gallop right up St. James' Street.　Bob Sloman
set out in a very savage humour.　But, before
they were at Hyde Park Corner, she made him

admire her more than ever. It was thus—in Piccadilly, at Half Moon Street, where there is a bit of a slope, the horses tried to run away. It is to be supposed they felt the breeching; anyhow off they started, like mad things. Nelly laughed; the servant was almost chucked off his seat, and as for Bob, he was within an ace of beginning to pray. A brougham and pair came spinning down Hamilton Place; the coachman just saw them, gave a shout, and pulled his horses on to their haunches. They slid a few feet on the pavement, and the pole just hit Nelly's arm below the elbow, and swung her against her financial admirer's shoulders. They were flying by Apsley House now: there Bob Sloman desperately clutched hold of the reins, in front of the girl's fingers. "Let 'em go," she muttered between her teeth. But he had quite lost command of himself, and tugged wildly across her hand; while the trap rattled on the pavement, and the successive gas lamps ran into a thread of flame as the pair shot by. "If you don't let 'em go I'll chuck the reins on the horse's backs—and you after 'em, you three months thief!"

He sank back in his seat. At Wilton Place she had the pair cantering, and, lo! and behold, made them trot down Sloane Street, like sheep.

No one notices what a girl says in a rage. "You come and breakfast with me at seven to-morrow morning, Bob," said she, opening the door with her latch key. "No, don't you trouble to get down. It's no use, Bob; there's an invalid lady upstairs, and she mustn't be disturbed—because of her nerves. Seven o'clock! Don't forget;" and she slammed the door, laughing.

Thus, she could tighten or loosen the net round her admirer just as she pleased. When he had time to think about it, he used to hate Berty Newmarch; at least, the sight of the boy made him grind his teeth. To be sure, Bob had got over such things as hating any body above his breath, for there's nobody that something can't be made out of one time or another: hence, who'd go out of one's way to be bothered with revenge, or to pay off scores? perhaps to lose a good thing by and bye. And yet 'twas more than a man could bear, to see the girl running after that young cub—aye, and actually lending him money, so 'twas said; thereby—Bob thought sarcastically—taking the bread out of honest men's mouths. He couldn't stand this for ever; and so, having a judgment against Berty for seventeen hundred pounds, he put it in Sam Pounder's, the officer's, hands, and told him where he'd most likely find his man. They had foreclosed, over the greater transactions, and had just duly notified Mr. Newmarch that they held bonds and so on for the amount of all his eldest son's life interest in the Sawtry Estates; but this thing now, was a matter of a bill, which Berty had accepted one day in a hurry on his way to catch the train, and had utterly forgotten afterwards. As it was, this evening some men were dining with Berty, and he had commanded a representation afterwards by a man he knew, who ate live rats.

Very, very late Bob Sloman strolled over to Billy Rush's sporting house, moody and troubled in spirit. He pushed through the passage, with his hat despairingly on the back of his head, not deigning to notice one or two sleek and hang-dog looking men standing about there; and down he sat in the first chair, Before long, Mr. Rush himself came from behind the bar. He was a stout, oppressed, and placid man, who walked badly. " Now, wot," he asked, " is it to be, Mr. Slowman ?"

" William," the swain said, " it'll be cold, pale, I do think." But there was plainly something very wrong.

Tommy Greenacre, the bookmaker, sat before

the fire, eating walnuts, and in his usual coarse
spirits.

" Well, Bob, you look as if somebody'd got six
to four the best of you to-night, anyhow," said
he.

But he was always at his low talk.

"She's here," whispered Mr. Rush, who had
finer feelings, " upstairs with the missus." Still,
there was no answer.

In a minute, Nelly Vane came down. Who
could gainsay her being here; for she often
dropped in to have a talk with Mrs. R.—herself
in the theatrical line at one time. Bob did but
sigh, when there were ladies present, nor could
they get him to say a word.

" You'd think Mr. Sloman wanted to swallow
those cigars whole, the way be rolls 'em about;
eh, 'Liza?" said Miss Vane to Mrs. Rush.

That made Bob grin ; but he held his tongue,
thinking who'd have the laugh by and bye. His
trials weren't over yet, however. There sat Mrs.
Rush, from time to time laughing at some joke
she and Nelly had. As if a man mightn't have
his feelings, and attend to business, too. And
yet there she was—looking just fit to be the
queen of them all. His man was put away safe
enough by this; but still he felt as if he couldn't

command himself at all. And then who should come in but his brother Ben, and old cousin Amos along with him, both looking bad. This was the famous commissioner, Ben Sloman; and rarely he did a sporting house the honour to drop in to its back parlour promiscuous in this way. He was a great man—an earldoman and seer—among the vermin bred by the action of some sun or other on the ever festering carcass of horse-racing. As for cousin Amos, he was a thoughtful little old man, who had amassed money in the West End discounting business with the rare patience and self denial of his people, but who could count, too, many a turf triumph in his day.

Tommy Greenacre was the first to speak.

"Here's Bob been preachin' his funeral oration to us gentlemen," said he. "'Asn't he been festive, Mrs. R.? Ah! if we had that young swell of Bob's here to-night—we'd have had a bottle of 'sham' stood before this, I know. Wouldn't we ladies?"

"Ah! Captain N. was a fine-hearted young man," Mrs. Rush said, looking nervously at the distinguished visitors, who were plainly in no humour for this low, vulgar conversation. Ben was contemptuously examining this Nelly Vane,

and she stared back just as haughtily. By and bye
Tommy Greenacre got up and walked off in dis-
gust with them all; and the ladies followed his
example, leaving the three relatives together.
Bob Sloman poked away at the fire like a man
who's angry with himself.

" I hate to see a man when he unman hisself,"
said Ben, witheringly.

" I want to know what's all this messing over
young N's. affairs," old Amos added, in his turn,
firmly, yet sadly. " It's not what's right, Robert,
and that I say."

" I ain't goin' into that young fellah's matters
this hour of the night," answered Bob, twitching
about as if flies were worrying him.

Ben positively laughed outright.

" Well, then," growled Bob Sloman, savagely.
" I'll tell you what's been done. I've brought
out the big gun, Mr. Amos—and he's just put
away to-night, is your young protedgee, if
you're particular about knowing."

" Did you hear that, Nell ?" said Mrs. Rush,
who, leaning out of the window, had heard the
voices ascend, when Bob Sloman got excited.
They had both heard, and if the jealous one could
have seen Nelly Vane's face then, he would have
desired no further revenge.

"Very good and right, my boy," old Amos was saying. "There'll be certain parties, we know of, glad to hear that. Oh! you silly, soft little man," he went on. But before he had said much more, Bob was knocking the chairs about, and stamping his feet. "Well," they heard him growl; "you two ain't in it at all. You looked after the big things, and who said a word? The little matter he's been took on is my own, and what are you coming here about?" He was beginning to get frightened; that was the fact.

Ben shrugged his soldiers. Such a girl as this Nelly What's-her-name—for a man, who knew something, to go right out of his mind about!

Amos Sloman shook his head regretfully. "You turn up the best man you ever had, for a bit of a seventeen hundred he never got a penny of. I had it all straight, Robert. Don't you fancy I hear nothing. And now, what d'you think of your man having a lot more of his own—aye, of his own—that other parties'll most likely have the fingering of—before this, perhaps. Eh?"

Bob turned pale. "What are you kidding about now?" he gasped.

"Kidding! you little—little foolish man," interrupted Ben, with a sneer in his turn. "D'you

think we'd have come up here after you, to-night,
for amoosment? only that Billy Ind tells me you
were going to mop up your best man, over some
bit of feminine jealousy or other."

"Ikey Moss'll get to him if he's took to Bill
Aaron's house, to-night," groaned Bob, remorse-
fully. "I shall cut down there, and see if he's
come, this minute."

"Now stop, Robert," said old Amos, softly,
seeing the better frame of mind. "You see
you've put yourself in the wrong place, through
acting silly. We hear a certain young gent's
got a certain settled property—habsolute, you
know—none o' your life hintrests, like the
Sawtry shop, worth a good six hundred per
annum. And now, what's to hinder some of our
friends bidding him a couple of 'undred above
what he's in for—this very night—for the property, and getting hold of all the stuff together?
I had it from little What's-his-name in Dook
Street this day. 'Mr. Sloman,' he says, 'I
suppose Mr. Bob's a goin' to sell young N's.
life interest right hoff,' he says. 'I see Price
and Gill's advertisement,' he says. 'But 'ave
you enquired in respect of whether he's disposed
of that little Irish property? Because my old
guvnor's been looking out for a little real, as he's

goin' to stick to absolutes, and shunt the in-
surance expenses—nothin' but doin' discounting
and absolute reversion,' he says, and a lot
more he tells me. You know, I did this chap a
bit of good, when he got kicked out of East and
East's, in Staple Inn, and I know all he tells me
is right."

Berty, it appeared, had still an absolute reversion in this property, of which he had, perhaps,
never heard—and, of course, if the young fellow
discovered that, he would make it over to the first
man who might offer him a couple of hundred
pounds for it, or get him out of the sponging
house where he might, at this very moment, be
detained for a contemptible seventeen hundred.
Their wrath might well be loosed on Bob, and he
now felt his weakness bitterly. "And now it's
my belief that he's not took yet," old Amos declared. "I've been to three places to-night, and
he hadn't been there; and we all know old Sam
Pounder's as slow as a man in boots."

"A Baron I know, that came across from Paris
purpose to see me, says he met your man at
Mabille last night, Bobby," sneered Ben, who
treated the whole affair with immense contempt.
However, Bob could not rest for an instant, till

his still valuable young client was out of danger
of being detained in durance.

It had been raining, when he got out into the
air; the lamp light sparkled on the thick ribs of
mud in the street, and on the greasy foot pavement. Bob hurried on, looking about him, and
whistling, for a Hansom cab; but for ever so far
the streets were quite deserted. There came a
woman towards him at last; he noticed her in
the great solitude, and as they approached each
other, saw that it was Nelly Vane again. There,
at that hour, by herself; what did it mean? He
laughed at the thought of her sweetheart—when
she was still far off. But when she got close to
him, and fixed her eyes on him, he stopped
and trembled, in spite of himself. She was not
ashamed one bit. " You villain!" said she,
seeing on his face an attempt at a sneer. " I
can take care of myself well enough—you know
that." She saw he was afraid. "Ah! you
villain! what have you done?" she repeated,
shaking all over with wrath.

He wished that he had some one, now, to back
him up; but there stood the two alone, on the
flags, under the muddy glare of the night; blown
by the wind and not speaking. He could not

shut his eyes and leave her, for she had worked a spell over him. He tried to laugh; but she knew what he was thinking about. "You don't care for him," he began, coaxingly.

"What!" she said, raising his hair with a look.

The street rang with a horse's hoofs; and there came a Hansom lurching by them, driven by a young marquis of that period; the cabman hanging on below the driving seat. Inside were three noisy youths bound for Knightsbridge, and some one shouted out, "Hi! Bob Sloman, jump in, and bring the lady!" But he never heard them. It was bitterly cold. "Nelly," he said, "I'm beat; don't you turn round on me, too. You know, I am desperate fond of you, Nelly."

But instead of singeing him any more with her lurid eyes, Miss Nelly hung down her head. "Well, Bob," she said, "shake hands. I ain't angry a bit."

He could have wept. "Give me your hand," said he, plunging among her fingers nervously. Still, he retained presence of mind enough to tell a lie. "Nelly, I'll get this boy right if you really want it. I'll swear to you he won't be hurt."

"Will you?" said she. But it would not do

to be too eager now. She meant to manage him by-and-bye.

Four o'clock struck, far off and close by them in the air, and Bob trembled lest it was too late to stop Sam Pounder; still, he could not leave her yet. " Let me drive you home in a cab, Nelly. It's a horrid cold night."

" No. You go on your own road this time. You know the way to my house, don't you? Let me see;" even now she could hardly endure the prospect of having to cajole him. " I'll be at home to-morrow at three. Good-night, Bob."

" Give us a kiss, Nelly." She shivered; some rain began to fall, and the wind cut her through and through. It was better not, so soon. " Not here, Bob," she whispered, with a voice like the wind on the strings of a harp. He took the hand which had no glove and kissed the back. It was as if a snail had travelled over her skin.

Thus Berty was safe for a time. Mr. Pounder had never tapped him on the shoulder, to begin with, and we see that it would not have mattered that time if he had. Nelly was plotting to keep her beloved from harm; and night and day turned over in her brain how to save him and set him up again. Before a week though, Bob Sloman had carried out the arrangements for an advance on the security of that six hundred a year; and the result was, that Berty, who we saw had become something of a business man, got his bill back and one thousand one hundred pounds in cash, for the reversion of this money which he was entitled to.

The very next day he bought that grey pearl. There was a sale of famous hunters shortly after this, and the two highest priced lots fell to Mr. Newmarch's bid. A paragraph appeared about it in the journals; but these horses never carried him across a field. His nerve was almost quite gone now. There was no hunting except in Leicestershire, he believed, and he couldn't go to the bother of setting up there again. So he stayed in town, and gave Nelly Vane the smartest brougham that had ever been seen. He gave her many diamonds too, and his respect and esteem for her increased daily. That esteem was to Berty a pleasant innovation. To drive in a carriage with a pretty woman, and sit strictly parallel to the door the whole time, was a sensation, utterly fresh and wonderful. Whenever he had time, and was at all sober, he was sure to be with Nelly Vane, and she liked to get presents from him. She couldn't help liking it; they were very pretty, and though it might be extravagant, she liked it.

Bob Sloman was more jealous and miserable than ever. He tried to persuade himself that he'd far rather they had chucked that nice bit of property to Ikey Moss, or to Ikey anybody else, and kept the young brute in quod on detainers. Yet he knew that before very long, it must all be the same with young N. again. Berty went to all the small races now. That which he had voted a bore, and declared he was sick of, when he had no money whatever, charmed him as much as formerly, now that he was well off. Still he had his old frightful luck. It used to happen to him to go down on a raw, sloppy day, to some third-rate steeplechases, where there would be three damp bookmakers, and one solitary man from Windsor perhaps, who did steward, "talent," and "upper ten" all in one—and to lose a couple of hundred, even there. He soon began to weary of it again : but then the First Flat race meeting came near. It was sure to change his luck, and he went down to it in high spirits.

It was all an ugly dream to him afterwards. The first day he lost and lost, and there was snow on the ground. He dined very late that night at the hotel by himself, and drank enough to send him unconscious to bed. Somebody drove him to the course next day; but he did not meet many fellows that he chose to talk to; and it had come to pass that Berty had quarrelled with most of his old allies. The affair when Mr. Chaunter rode, had got about too, and Berty had a queer name in these days. There used to be a time when everybody petted him, and delighted in his happy carelessness and indifference to all fortunes. But now he had grown older, sulky and hardened, and was no longer welcome among the set who knew everything. He said that it was he who had grown tired of them, and found them all out. After the numbers for the first race were run up, Berty stood by himself in the ring, and peering about in a strange listless mood, took in all the scene. The storm of voices, loosed once again, rang, roared and clattered in his ears. There were the ringmen, jostling and shouting, and waving their pencils. 'Curse them,' Berty said, helplessly. 'I know them all.' They all had his money, and had swallowed up into their maw his chances of Sawtry, and his good name, and his good spirits too. How bitter the whole thing had turned to his taste, and then he wheeled round and stared contemptuously up at the

stewards' stand. At the edge stood young Charlie
Bedford, his eyes fixed on the fray below. 'I'm
sick of seeing him,' sneered Berty, to himself;
' and of his horrid husky voice, and his bloated
nose and groggy lips. How like a nigger with
the leprosy he is. Why does he swagger, putting
on that shabby hat and cape. I remember when
he could ride too, before he took a dislike to a
crowd. And there's his pasty faced little partner
with his shirt collars up to his ears. I wish he'd
get his head over 'em some day, and cut his
throat. Will I ever go anywhere without seeing
that insufferable little Fitzpoley too, with his sky
terrier face and his crop of red hair? How white
he looks—has lost thirty shillings at hazard, I
suppose. And there's his pal, more like a long
necked condor at the Zoological, now, than ever.
Why didn't he stay behind his father's counter,
instead of taking the Queen's shilling?' To
Berty's jaundiced eyes, all his old friends had
come to look disreputable and repulsive. He
wished that he were a boy and back at Harrow
again. And while he yet stood musing, somebody came up, and said, " How d'you do, Newmarch?" It was a face Berty barely recollected,
and not one of his own set; indeed a man he
never had cared much to meet. But now it was

a change to find some one who wasn't exactly like everybody else.

"Ah! how do! Let me see, where did I see you last," he began, wearily.

The other man recollected everything about Berty, well enough. "Oh! we went down to Reading together," he said. "Knaresborough, George Ferrers, and you and I, took a carriage to ourselves—if you remember."

"Ah! yes," said Berty. 'What can this fellow want?' he asked himself. 'I wonder is he thinking that I'm a sort of fellow could get him into good society! Well, it all can't last long, any how.' And then he listened passively, while the man talked to him. He seemed to have lots to say for himself. It had the old, old jingle, about 'this one's form;' and Jimmy somebody's riding; and 'half fit;' and 'ought to have won, walking,' and so on. Berty had heard it all before, and first hand, too, he thought. And yet gradually, as he said nothing, and let the man go on, it struck him that this seemed a deep fellow enough, if what he said meant anything at all.

'Did he bet much?' Berty asked.

'No. He waited, and looked about and never put money on unless knowing something.'

"Ah! Yes, I understand," said Berty, who had heard that so often.

'But he did know just *one* thing, at this meeting; he had not bet yet nor would he, unless assured that this same thing was right.'

"Indeed !"

'Yes. It was the last race of all.' And then he took out his pencil, came close to Berty and pointed out to a horse's name. "She belongs to a sort of cousin of mine, and I've been told what they mean to do. They're certain to tell me at the last moment, and I believe 'twill be a good thing either way."

Finally, he said that if March Morning, the horse in question, were made favourite by the public, she would certainly be pulled, and one might lay as much as one liked against her. If she were *not* favourite, then they'd try to win with her; in which case it were best left alone, as she was not quite good enough to plunge on.

Then Berty went and had luncheon with this man. He had a trap there, it appeared, and a couple of other fellows stood about it whom Berty knew by sight, and didn't care for much; and it was a bad luncheon, and there was bad moselle to drink. Berty was in wretched spirits. A couple of races came off, and he hardly looked at them. He wandered back to the ring and mounted to the top of the stand and stared through his glasses at the country people in their vans and carts about the course. He wished himself away. It was bitterly cold, and he felt tired and weak. By and bye, his friend came and fastened on him again; and then the last race approached.

" *That's* right enough," said his friend, significantly. He had seen his cousin, it appeared, in the interval; and the numbers went up next, and March Morning's name was in everybody's mouth.

" She is a hot favourite, and no mistake. They only offer six to four against it. And twelve to one, bar two!" this newly found acquaintance said. " I shall lay two fifties against her, Newmarch," he added, getting strangely excited as the time drew near.

" Shall you now?" Berty answered, and he went down himself to the ring, and said, " How much March Morning, Farrer?"

" Here six to four, cap'n," was the reply.

" Pooh! I'd lay that myself."

" Well, it's a fair price; look'cer s'r, I'll take your two to one ag'in her *now*. Can't do no more," and he turned away.

Berty bit his lips feverishly. He thought he'd wait a little longer, then he repented that he hadn't laid those odds. As the time went on, they ceased betting against the favorite altogether. "They only offer outsiders, captain;" said Farrer, pushing his way back to him again. "I'll take your six to four now, sir."

"Well, put down six hundred to four hundred!"

"What's that?" cried three or four in the throng, hearing those odds. "I'll take your six to four, Mr. Newmarch;" sang out Billy Stanley, who was saluted by writers as a 'leviathan.'

Thought Berty, 'I'd like to shoot *you* for a couple of thou:' "Here, Stanley," said he, "I'll lay eleven monkeys to eight the favourite."

Down it went. There was a sensation when that was booked, and the bet Berty had made worked a change even here. As for him, he glanced over his book once, and shut it up. Then he saw his friend at his side, grown deadly pale by this time.

"Come this way," he said. "I heard what you've done. I laid a bit myself; but by Jove! not such a lot as you! They offer five to four on her now, old fellow; but my cousin's own boy is up, and he'll stop her right enough; don't you be afraid."

The two stood together; and things went round as they pleased in Berty's brain. The shouting gradually sank and ceased, and it was nearly time. Before he had a chance to think, they were off—upon the race for his life. Berty's sorely misused heart beat feebly; up in the air the fatal bell swung and clashed. Besides that, the yelling and clamour, as of hungry beasts in chorus, had flickered out, and there was a hush. Just by his side, Berty noticed two stout, common-looking men. One had mounted on some kind of stool, he saw, and had a pair of glasses. He had a queer rough brown coat on. Berty dwelt on these little things; and then the bell ceased and they were coming.

"Is ours in it, Bill," gasped the man without the glasses, clutching at the other's sleeve.

"There's—only—two—trying—my boy," his friend muttered, taking trembling gulps with his eyes through the opera-glass at the horses the while. Then Berty stretched his neck and strove to see. The knot of horses had the band of dull grass to themselves, all up to the place where he stood. To his ear their hoofs sucked in and out of the mud. And now two came away by themselves—'Mainguard' and 'March Morning.' There were none but these two in the front, and, at the distance, the boys on the pair were hard at their strife. Up sailed the lads above the crowd, their heads bent down, and a serious look upon each white face. To Berty's eyes it was a cruel sight. Berty was aware of his friend muttering at his ear, "By G—! he stopped her just in time;" when the boy on 'Mainguard' shot forward, clutching at the horse's neck, went scrambling back into his place, raised his whip, and then remained there right before Berty's eyes.

Then was to be seen the rider of 'March Morning's' terrified glance back, expecting him; amidst a roar of derision, he tried even then to stop his horse. And then it was over. 'March Morning' had won, in spite of her rider, by three lengths, and 'Mainguard,' who was to have been allowed to win, had broken down right opposite the stand.

A yell of laughter shot up here and there; a shout of derision from one knot of men to another, and then—a blank and ominous silence. Berty was still staring passively at the wounded horse, whose jockey had jumped off. The poor creature had broken the pastern of its fore leg, and was hobbling along after the rider. An immense crowd was about him, and the other jockeys coming in called to the people to get out of their way. People began to leave; there was nothing more to see, and it was growing dark. Berty heard some words said to him, but could apply no meaning to them. He felt quite calm. Everything was finished now, and looking about, he noticed that the course was emptying very fast. His things were to be fetched from the hotel, and he walked back there slowly. In the porch his friend met him. He indeed looked scared. He was awfully sorry, he said; "the boy had just stopped 'March Morning' when that other brute broke down; had Berty noticed it?"

"No," he said. "It didn't matter." As for the other man, his teeth were chattering. He declared he was ruined, and felt he had let someone else in, that was worst of all. "Don't think of that," Berty said. "I thank a fellow for telling me, just the same as if it had come off all right; 'cos I know he meant well."

He almost liked the man. Then he paid his bill, and caught the train to London in comfortable time. In the carriage there were fellows he knew, and he set himself to talk to them quite cheerily, and so to banish the horrid subject of his losses altogether. But by and bye conversation dropped; men went to sleep, while he alone

was restless, and so it all came back before long,
worse than before. At Peterborough Station he
drank a tumbler of brandy, and slept most of the
way from there on to London. Hateful London!
He wished it was a week's journey off. But there
shone the lamps in the fog, and there were the
cabs; and waking, despair completely took hold
of Berty Newmarch.

And now his day was over, and the reckoning
had come. On all sides punishments and horrors
gathered about him—yea, even already reached
out and touched him, it seemed. He had no
future to rest his mind on. From his old friends
he was going to be cut off, sure enough. He was
no longer an officer, and he had no home, and
there was no Sawtry coming to him. His brothers
he scarcely knew, and his father cursed his name.
Whichever way he turned he met the faces of
those who wanted money from him; and he was
tired of making promises and going deeper and
deeper—aye, very tired; and what was he to do
henceforth? What did it matter, after all? he'd
have one good drink. And so, late as it was, he
found a man he had quarrelled with a while ago,
in the coffee-room at Strong's. With him Berty
made friends, and swore that he should be his
guest at supper that night. But he could not

brighten up. 'One person in the world does love me,' Berty thought, when supper was over and he stood before the chimney-glass and saw his own haggard face reflected there. 'I'll go and see poor Nelly, and try if she's like all the others.'

When he mounted the stairs in the well known house, and pushed open the door, there she was sewing by a table in her drawing-room, dressed as if she waited for him, but the only light was from a lamp with a wide green shade. It fell on her fingers stringing beads, and on her cheek.

When Berty entered the house, the servant, who was Nelly's mother also, followed with glasses and brandy—such as the Captain might require. Poor Captain *in partibus!* he had not even a word to thank her with.

"What's the matter?" Nelly asked, smiling upon her darling ; yet sighing as she smiled.

He did not speak at first, but drank half the brandy off. "I'm ruined," said he, with a stupid laugh, staring intently at her. Nelly's eyes lit up with a kind of joy, and she breathed hard once or twice. "I suppose you're precious glad I'm smashed—for that's what it's come to now, Nelly Vane." He saw her laugh again, and almost clap her hands. "Oh! you ! What did I ever

do to you that you should laugh when I'm done
for," he groaned. " Oh ! yes—here ; I suppose
you're in, all the time, with those hellish Jews
that have got all my cursed property and everything else."

" Berty," said she, drawing near him with the
tenderest looks of happiness, and pity. " It's my
time to help you ? Tell me everything, my own
Berty !"

But he drew back. " Get away, you !" he said,
between his clenched teeth.   And struck her —
sending her reeling across the room.

There, by the chimney-piece she stood a second,
her hand pressed to the spot where his fist struck,
and on her face a look of curiosity and contempt.
The men she used to live amongst struck girls
and women, and was he of that sort ? There he
stood, so handsome, with his lips trembling and
his hair dropping over his forehead. Her boy
was vexed, 'twas only that ; and she was glad to
bear his blows, if need be, or his poor, miserable
words. Therefore, Nelly's wonder turned into
looks of faith and softest pity, and she came to
him as though he had not struck her at all.
" Yes, I'm glad you're done for," she went on
in her voice, which, when unconstrained, was
most sweet. " Very glad, because it's my turn

next, and I can get you round again, I think. I
want to pull you through all by myself."

She stopped to observe how he took that. .His
head had dropped, and he kept snatching at the
back of the chair near him, while waves of shame
and degradation passed over his face. But Berty
could not command his ideas. The hard drinking he had kept up had knocked away the shores
from under his mind, and he could no longer think
connectedly. He tried to say some words, and
then, finishing what remained in the bottle, he
turned his back on her and began walking up and
down. "I can help you," she said, timidly,
thinking that he attended to her. "I knew
'twould come to something of this sort. They're
trying to rob and ill-treat my poor boy. But I'll
best 'em all yet."

She smiled to herself as she said that. If he
would only have some hope and trust to her,
'twould all be right yet.

There was now a silence. He continued to
walk, twisting his hands behind his back, and
grinding the carpet with his heels. " Yes," she
heard him mutter, after a long wait, "helped by
a damned dancer—that's nearly good enough for a
Newmarch." He tossed his head impatiently,
and then went rambling on. "I know I'm done

for. And I was a gentleman always, till I had such infernal luck. Aye, I'm clean knocked out now, and they'll ask who's got my account all over the room on Monday. I hear 'em. Aye, and I paid plenty of monkeys on the lawn in my day, and no one said a word against me till that damned Jack Lister made me pull my pretty mare at Liverpool. I wish I was riding along-side of our lads again. 'Thwees about,' old Bob Sackville used to say. And I might have stayed among them and held my head up. Oh! and I'd have married Mary Gautby if that Mrs.—that fiend —hadn't come to Brailcote and told lies of me. Oh! curse her. And Mary might have known I did write. Aye, when I got Peter Melville to tell me all the spelling right, too. And I would have been steady. Yes, I would. It's all gone now. Who cares, though? Nelly, talk to me; nothing matters much, does it? Come here, my pretty girl; you are so pretty. Come here and talk to me." Thus he moaned and muttered, till she could have wept for him. Poor love! when he sat down at last she came and knelt by him. Who was that Mary Gautby? she longed to ask; but she murmured—

"Oh! Berty, don't you break your heart like that. There's some that honours you still

Who'll think the worse of you for losing your money, my sweetheart?"

Then they kissed each other silently. A loving face, he had heard, comes often between the whole world at enmity and one's own helpless self. Sweet Berty found it, to shelter there, and forget wretchedness; while she said to herself between his kisses and on her knees before him, 'He is mine now. Mine for ever.'

"You are the only friend I ever had," the poor boy kept repeating to his kneeling ballerina. "Now I'm in trouble, no one sticks to me but you."

"Yes, my ducky darling! Rest and forget 'em all."

'He must be tired,' she thought; and Berty took leave of her by and bye, having verily found some one he could trust at last.

Cool moon-light of the morning was shining on the streets, when he walked out. Up in the north, it had been bitter cold, but he felt nothing of it here. The day's work turned over and over in his brain still, and excitement sustained him. 'Would we make each other happy always?' he had asked her. She had whispered trustfully, 'I don't know.' This was the only woman he would ever ask to be his wife.

Somewhere in the King's Road, Brompton, a hansom caught him up; and worn out and dropping off to sleep, he was whirled along through the streets without thinking where he went, till the driver pulled up at Strong's.

As Berty jumped out, a man got in his way; through all his drowsiness, he recognised Sam Pounds instantly. "I'm very sorry, captain," the officer, after his kind, began. And now Berty had to force open his jaded eyes, and call back his ideas again. "I've had it a long time, Mr. Newmarch; it's a capias."

Berty paid the cabman. "You might have given me a hint, Sam," said he. "I'll never be able to put you on another winner, at Croydon, again!"

"Well, sir, I did try to see James, to tell him to let you know. But there's such a lot about for you; what's the use of procrastinatin', captain? It's one of Bob Sloman's, this is."

"Much?"

"Fourteen hundred," said the bailiff, ruefully.

Berty laughed heartily; then he reflected for an instant. "Well, you can wait half a minute, I suppose? I must see my man about the things I'll want to-night."

" No. It can't be done, sir. Well, if you'll give me your honour, Captain Newmarch, I'll stay down here."

Berty gave his word, and kept it loyally. The clocks were striking three when he drove down St. James' Street with the sheriff's officer. He was wide awake once more. And now, here was a second terrific blow given to him since the morning. Well, it didn't matter; they might do anything they pleased with him; and thereupon, all reckoning and meditation being only pain to him, he took refuge in thinking about Nelly. She was good, and patient, and loving—if there was nothing else to believe in. That no one could rob him of. Poor girl! what would she do, when she heard it? She, for one, would be sorry, and would not sleep in peace. And then Berty proved to himself how mean and heartless were all his relations, and his fair weather friends. Highly respectable people, glad enough, all of them, to lecture a fellow; but the first to desert him when his troubles came.

The host at his tawdry dungeon wished to know what he'd take. The famous Captain Newmarch was a person of consideration there at once; and a real swell, compared to the other seedy inmates. But he would drink no more that morning; he only wanted to be left alone, and to hide his misfortunes from every eye. A sort of exaltation took possession of him; he was suffering from a cruel persecution, he thought, and all the world was in league against his Nelly and himself. He could not rest. 'I will write to her,' he said; and so he sat down at his ricketty dressing table, and wrote, with shaking hand, " Dear Nelly, I'm here about a rit of that Bob Sloman's fourteen hundred which I hadn't got, so had to go with the man. Good-bye, dear Nelly; I was very fond of you. It is all up with me as they all have cut me at home, and I wouldn't take there help now. Good-bye. Yours, B. N."

" Can this go to Brompton?" he asked. 'Yes, it could go.' Half-a-crown and five shillings for the cab. Berty had plenty of half-crowns still— for one day's consumption, anyhow. He heard the door open and shut for the messenger, and then he went and looked out of his barred window. The moon had set, and there was only a scrap of brick wall to be seen, and above, the murderous outline of roofs and chimney stacks. That out there was his allowance of the world now. Was this the limit, then, of that charming land which once had spread—fair and bright, and crowded with pleasures and laughter—before him? Was this all that life spared to him? He was sick and angry at his misery. Why was he to cease enjoying himself? Till now he had disbelieved in ruin—ever convinced that there was certain happiness just beyond the thing next to him, if he only chose to push on and enjoy it. A country he had pictured to himself where there was no bother, and nothing to be feared; and where they would let him alone; and there he meant to arrive some day in safety. This to think of now! and the dull roofs and walls to look upon.

Not very many miles from that barred, narrow room, at the same moment too, George Newmarch was staring up at the same steadfast sky, expecting perhaps some pity from thence, since none was granted on earth down below.

Thus, close to each other, the two brothers were reaping a kind of reward. Offenders, both of them, against that patient and pitiless god —common-sense, who never, never forgives. How George fared, and how he was resting, is explained by and bye; but as for his remorse, he had a greater number of cunning ways of torturing himself than Berty had. For, so poor had George been hitherto that settling the greater questions in his brain was the only pastime he could afford all those years. Hence, he was a wonderful subtle thinker in his way; but for many reasons it didn't take Berty long to run through his stock of thoughts; he never had gone to the root of things; it was a stupendous exertion to him to reflect at all, and even the simplest processes of the mind quickly fatigued him beyond endurance. So the rebels slept.

CHAPTER XIV.

THE morning after that, Berty's first waking sensation was some half-remembered pain or other. He was vaguely unhappy that his sleep could last no longer; and, when all his senses smarted with the return of sensation, his wounds, as it were opening afresh, and he saw the dirty wall paper and sniffed the musty air in the room, he knew that there was no reprieve. It was not in a dream then, that he had come to this place; ah! no. He was shut in still, and there was no chance of the sun waking him, and bringing bright views under his windows, nor of the cheery noise of trumpets beginning the " dress" for stables, in his ears, like long ago. To have the misery of the day before, just as present after the night's sleep—which generally wipes away all yesterday's sorrows—was very hard to Berty's mind. He hated to have a trouble always slapp-

ing him in the face; to him, hanging would
have been nothing much, if they would but allow
him to go about as he liked up to the very day
he was to be hanged.

He had never dressed in such a place as this;
and the squalor of it sickened him. He seemed
years older when he looked at his face in the
glass. How long was it since he had slept at
that hotel after the first day's racing up there?
Only a few hours, indeed; could that be possible? ' Did they eat anything in this place?'
Berty thought to himself. After that he lay
helplessly in bed for a long time. At last he
dressed and went down stairs. There was
nothing clean or safe to eat, except some dry
bread and tea; and, after nibbling at that, Berty
sat himself in a corner at the window, as far
from the other people as he could get, with a
novel before him. He would never leave this
prison, and he cursed everyone belonging to him.
The law might be that he should die here, in
this place; what a place! A lanky street boy
came and stood under the window, and grinned
up at him; but Berty did not feel his jeers one
bit; he supposed it was part of being kept here,
and as the hours went on, his head began to
throb and a sort of fever took possession of him.

He would not live long, he thought; his head was heavy, and he tried to rest it at times on the window sill. The door kept opening and shutting, and people came to see their friends or clients, and went away; but he watched for no one. It was two o'clock then, and these people were going to dine apparently. A man came once or twice and spoke to him, but Berty scarcely heard him.

There used to be so much unlocking of doors; he wondered what the process was. It was getting dark, and his thoughts rambled off to all sorts of queer channels.

There were the keys going again below! Then footsteps on the stairs for the twentieth time.

"Mr. Newmarch," said the man of the house, "wanted."

Berty slowly turned round. In the doorway stood Nelly Vane, and behind her a couple of men. It was half dark; he only saw her sweet round face. Why had she come to such a horrid place? She was too good for company like this, he thought; and then he was doubly sorry that he was a prisoner here.

"It's all right," whispered Nelly, as he came slowly towards her, just glancing at the other people inside the room. "We've got the what

you call 'em from the old sheriff; and there's no
detainers yet." He was listening reverentially
to all that, and meantime, the attorney Nelly
had with her was getting out some papers, and
Berty's fellow prisoners pricked up their ears.

"Mr. Bertram Edmund Grandison Newmarch," the proprietor began, "I hold in my
hand an order for your release for So-and-so,
duly signed by So-and-so." Berty somehow did
not hear him very well.

Nelly was so happy that, whether the other
fellows there saw or not, she could not help
squeezing her Berty's hand. Though he hated
those other poor wretches and despised them, he
forgot that they were by, and stood gazing at her
as if they were alone.

"Have you any things to pack, dearest—Mr.
Newmarch?" said Nelly.

"Can I go, then?" he asked.

"All paid, sir. 'Ere, bring the gen'lman's
things down stairs, you!" screamed the proprietor, to the dirty servant. "Thank you, sir;
good day, sir."

Berty turned his back on the place; and Nelly,
laughing with delight, tripped down the stairs
to the cab after him. It was all right now. He
was safe out in the street, and yet he could

hardly speak or think. " Drive 'away, for God's sake ! " he whispered, dropping back in the cab.

As for Nelly, she leant across and kissed him, as if he were a baby. " I hav'n't a right to, I know," she said; " but I do love you so! How hot your pretty, pretty head is !"

" It will be better soon," he muttered, pressing her hand.

They were just turning the corner of Chancery Lane, then. The noise, and the bright shops, and the change of faces and people in the Strand, revived him. " Thank God ! out of that cursed place," he said at last, with a sigh of unutterable relief; and then he sat up and looked at her. " And now, how did you manage all those thieves, and get me out? for I can't believe it hardly."

" Yes, I'll tell you it all; but it's a long story. Why, how serious ill you do look, pet! Don't plague yourself talking, now; lie back here and rest."

He allowed her to press his head against her sealskin jacket, and then closed his eyes and rested on her shoulder. How the horrid cab did jolt, she thought, looking down at him. If she could, she would have gladly rocked her sweet pet in her arms tenderly, like a baby. It wrung her heart to see the change which the shock of the last few hours had made in him—the dark shade under his beautiful smooth eyelids, and the twitching about his lips! He would die, she believed, just when he thought much of her at last. But Berty was still capable of much offending. He sighed, and sighed a little more, and then shook off his dejection and sat up by her. "When did you get my note?" he asked.

"This morning, some time about five. Lord! when I did get your note, Berty, I never slept— no, never. I didn't know what to do, dear, at first. And then, about nine, Tilly Roberts comes round, just to learn me my part, because we was to have a rehearsal to-day, and I said, ' Look, Tilly, I don't know whether I'm dead or alive.' And she says, ' Lord! Nelly, you do look white.' And I never had time to get the brougham out, or anything. You don't mind my not bringing it for you, dear? but that man's so cheeky if you hurry him with his horses; and so I just set off in a hansom straight to—to Bob Sloman. Well, you know how he is about me."

She blushed in real earnest for the second time, and Berty mildly looked at her. " Well?" he said, still weary and puzzled.

She bit her lips. "Well, dear, there was the

fellow, in the middle of reading his paper, smoking a cigar. And he began, very down in the mouth at first; and so I did pitch into him. Ah! Berty, you've never seen me in a rage; but I've had lots of practice, and it's the only way with some of 'em. And then I told him he was a rogue. Well, d'you know, that put him in good humour, the brute, and he began to laugh, and said you should stay there 'till you got thin,' he said. So I could have killed him, my darling; I wish I could. And he kept telling me how— how—all sorts of things, the villain. Well, just then," she went on excitedly, "who should come in but old Amos. You know him—him they call old Bull's Eye—and he was down on Bob at once. Bless me! how he did give it him, and told him if you stopped there, there'd be fifty detainers, and I don't know what all, and that Bob would never get a halfpenny of this fourteen hundred. So, I said at last, 'Look here, Mr. Amos, you're a gentleman'—(though that was a lie, God forgive me)—'and I offer,' I says, 'two hundred for this bill; and I'll pay it in an hour if we get out.'"

"And did he take that?"

"No; Bob wouldn't have it a bit at first. But I could see 'twasn't the bill he cared about" she turned her face away again. "Well, I must tell you, Berty. Old Amos, he says on that, 'You come back with the money,' he says, 'and we'll see if he'll take it or not.' So off I went, and I found Paddy Sago, our manager, and he begins pitching into me for cutting rehearsals. But I got round him, and got him to give me a cheque at last, and you know I had a little at the bank, and I drew that, and then cut home, and just took all my furs and diamonds, and things— except this I've on—to little Meyers, in the Brompton Road, and I just told him how it was; and he gave me ninety on them; but it don't matter. And so, back I went to Bob Sloman, and—got the bill, and—"

"Well?" said Berty again.

Nelly was pale now. "After more talking the villain gives me this as well," said she, in an eager tone, pulling out a bundle of crumpled bills. "Won't that help you to get back your property, my darling?"

They were at Nelly's door by this.

"Give them to me," gasped Berty; and, with the papers shaking in his hand, he followed her up-stairs.

"I've had some dinner got ready for you, darling, if you'll stop," she said.

"Aye, but let me see these first. Here, clear these books away."

He spread the bundle of papers open on the table. There they lay—bills of exchange, promissory notes, memoranda of agreements, warrants of attorneys, dishonoured cheques—all the varieties of documents that had born his name of late years. The signatures of half the discounters in London were dotted about them too, and " no orders," " not provided for," " no effects " pinned at the corners of nearly everyone. There were bills for three, five, seven hundred, odd sums of that sort; but it took Berty little time to see that there was not more than three thousand pounds before him there. " How did Bob Sloman get these ?" he asked dejectedly. " Half of them ain't his. Ah! Nelly, a cart load of things like that wouldn't get me back Sawtry." She dropped into a chair, and hid her face in her hands. "Don't cry, Nelly," he said, going to her. " You've saved me, I know ; and we'll never part again. I'd rather have your love than all the estates in England."

But she refused to look at him. " Oh! the villain," Nelly cried, " he swore to me that them was everything you'd ever put your name to in your life. Oh! what have I done—what have I done ?"

CHAPTER XV.

"Rufamne illam virginem, cæsiam, sparso ore, aduncto naso ?
Non possum pater."—CLITIPHO.

FRANK KERSEYTOR sat in his tub the morning after
that.   It was four o'clock in the afternoon, and
the good and wise man had just risen to breakfast.   The tub was of warm water, and Frank
lay before the fire therein, drinking tea from a
great cup, and languidly perusing the closely-
printed pages of a small volume.   In fact, he was
reading "Ruff's Guide." The fire-light glistened
on each little drop of water, spread over seventeen stone of Frank, and the placid smile of the
student suffused his brutal though tranquil countenance.   Four or five parrots' cages, with
parrots, were hung about.   To these, Frank from
time to time addressed observations, suggested
by the contents of his book. Breakfast was ready

on the table. It was a very snug room on the whole; and, as the owner couldn't possibly expect to be in England for more than six weeks longer, everything had been provided there on the most durable and expensive scale. He had been asking his birds some questions, when there was a knock at the door, and Frank crying to ' come in,' Berty Newmarch opened it, smiling languidly as soon as he saw Frank in his bath. Frank had thought it was ' his washing coming home,' he said. ' So Berty had been down to What-you-call-um Spring Meeting. Frank had heard he lost his money there. Would he have a branny an soda? Frank would get up in a minute, on receipt of those towels, and on Berty putting his little head in a bag, for a bit.' Berty went to the window and stared moodily into the street, until Frank, violently drying and clothing himself, asked what was wrong. ' It would only be another old kite at three months, he supposed. Had Berty given old Bob Sloman a dinner lately? There was nothing like liquoring them up well.' Berty gently expressed a wish that he could be as cheery as Frank. " Cheery, my little boy!" said Frank. " I'll tell you. I was at Johnny Dale's mother's funeral yesterday afternoon. Johnny went from motives of respect, he said, and declared it was the only dead one he never made anything out of in his life. And I tell you we drove home with the undertaker's people, and stopped up at a house that the fellows in the black business use, till about three. I learnt a famous song—going to sing it at Lady Wallsend's to-morrow night."

"Frank," said Berty, throwing himself on the sofa, "you'd stick by me, wouldn't you?"

"Why certainly, little chubby Newmarch. Are you going to fight my eldest brother in the morning, or what?"

"I'm going to be married to-morrow, Frank. We've got the license and given notice, old boy."

There was a pause. Frank, now all draped in an orange satin suit, stood before the fire reflecting, and nodding his head ominously, from time to time. "Is it square or what?" he asked, now snuffling and sticking his chin in the air more decidedly than usual.

Berty merely frowned.

"I wish you hadn't come and told me," continued the other. "I've seen so many fellows do it, and they're always sold. Tell us all about it, little boy."

"I'll trust to your honour, to keep it quiet, Frank," Berty said gloomily, and then he related what he meant to do, how matchless an angel the woman was whom he intended to make his wife, and that nothing could ever alter his resolve.

"And which of the women is it?" Frank Kerseytor asked, speaking through his nose.

"Nelly Vane is her name," Berty answered reverentially, not noticing the sneer.

"Nelly Vane—Nelly Vane? Why she's married to me. I shall bring an action. Why, Bob Sloman 'll break your little head, too. Nelly Vane! Red-haired woman you mean—got two great sons, privates in the blues? Why you little fool, you ain't going to do that? Just look here, little boy, you talk sensibly. I won't allow it, you know, and that's flat."

Berty jumped up very pale. Now Frank nobody could fell with one blow, because he was so big and heavy; besides, he had seated himself in a great easy chair after his speech, and was calmly eating *foie gras.* Then he, of old, had a license to say anything to anybody.

"I didn't expect this from you, Frank," Berty said, chokingly.

"Why there's plenty," said the cynic, "better than that. I'll tell you a dozen prettier women. Don't you go jumping about the room. You sit there and take your branny an soda, and

let me eat my Strasbourg pie. These Foreign
Office fellows are shocking smugglers; but it's a
good thing to have a brother one of 'em. I'll
stick by you, of course, if it's done now. But
how the deuce d'you think your people 'll ever
pay your bills if you bring a wife out of a penny
gaff to do the lady of the manor at—what-its-
name where you live ?"

If that were all there was little to deter him,
Berty thought. He was glad he had provoked
this. How sick he was of such talk; it was part
of his old life to hear it, and things like it.
Now, he was going to have done with them
finally, and to win his Nelly's faith and tender-
ness in their place.

" You won't frighten me that way," he said,
with a laugh. " There's no one at Sawtry I care
much about."

" Well, you've got some people anyhow. Not
that they should bully you—of course; for after
all, as the old story says, your father never asked
your advice when he was going to get married—
don't see why you should ask his. What your
mother say, though? Let's see—Lady Adelaide
Newmarch—is she your mother, or grandmother?
I remember, gave me small book, at Somerthorpe,
when I was down there, and the Bishop confirmed

the new church, or licensed it for dancing, or
something last year. You ought to think of all
that."

" Kerseytor, I'm going to be married to-
morrow morning, and I want you to be there,
and to do one or two things for me. Will you, or
not ?"

" Do it all for you, if you like, little Stick-in-
the-mud—choral service, or anything. Give me
the tea, like a good boy. Look at those parrots
there ! I have got a broad-church parrot and a
dissenting parrot, and a ritualistic parrot. Would
you like to hear 'em perform ?"

But Berty interrupted him. He was hit hard,
he said, and Frank was the only man that he could
trust to, now, of all his friends. Would he desert
him too. No, Frank would not. " Cut this girl,
Chubby ; that's my advice. And go abroad for six
months ; and then come back, and marry an heiress,"
he added. " There's nothing to prevent you coming
round, if you choose. Nature, my boy—while
ordaining that there should be younger sons—um
—mercifully redressed the balance, by, you see,
also creating the heiress, after her kind, to set
him on his legs again, poor beggar. Let's see,
you're an eldest son, but you've lost all your
quids—eh? So one looks on you almost as

one of us. Now, you ain't a very ugly little
brute, and there's lots of girls would buy you—
you just give me the commission, and I'll get
you something with a lot of tin, and we'll pay off
the Jews, and buy the favourite for the Derby,
and pull him, and make a hundred thousand
pounds, my boy!"

But Berty had come out from all things of that
sort. He shook his head, amused at Frank's
characteristic plot for restoring him to his old
standing in the false and selfish world. "I've
made my mind up," he just said once or twice
more. "Frank, I'm tired of it all; and I've
found some one worth all the heiresses in the
world put together. There are some things
better than a hundred thousand pounds."

'Marrying a doubtful person from a superior
sort of penny gaff,' thought the other, 'that's
one of the better things, is it? I know the form.
They're all the same, when they once kick their
legs over the traces!' So, he let Berty talk on
after that, and strove no more to put truth before
his eyes. 'He would come down, if Berty really
wanted him,' he said. 'Of course he was not
to say a word. He was going to do such a jolly
thing himself the week after next.' 'What was
that?' 'He was going to India. It was such a

nice place. Berty ought to come out with him. They would take a couple of good thorough-bred horses with them, and would win all the fellows' money out there. It was as easy as shelling peas. One wanted a big animal, capable of staying, and galloping through the sand—that was all.'

Then, in the intervals of breakfasting, dressing, and singing sundry choruses, Frank promised to be at Berty's lodgings, somewhere close to Armageddon Villas, by ten o'clock the next day; and from thence they would go, with Nelly and her mother and sister, to the Registrar of the district, to whom due notice had been given. And would Berty persuade the sister that Frank was a married man, and hated liberties? Was she 'better than a hundred thousand pounds, too?' because Frank did not recollect having ever seen her about at any of the well-known places of evening amusement.

Then, after a little more of the same sort, they shook hands, not very cordially, and Berty walked away. While the flavour of Kerseytor's raillery was still fresh to him, he almost felt dejected and nervous at the prospect of what he was going to do. But before long, he fell to thinking of what his darling had done for him when he was in trouble and deserted. It was a bold, generous

sort of deed that he was going to do in return ;
and—if they were not past caring about it one way
or the other—his governor, and mother, would be
sure to welcome his Nelly, and get fond of her by
and bye.   A cold twinge, to be sure, came across
him for an instant, when he seemed to see poor
Nelly's mother sitting by the graceful and
melancholy Lady Adelaide Newmarch, under the
eye of each grim canvass Newmarch and St.
Lys hung on the dining-room walls at Sawtry—
perchance, too, drinking from her finger glass,
or calling Simmonds, the butler, 'sir.'   But
what mattered those fancies?   Was not his
Nelly one of nature's Norman families—or something to this effect?   All the people at Sawtry,
or anywhere else, ought to kneel down to her.
Berty had little reading in this well worn subject, or he might have dilated further in the
same strain.   At last he had found that pearl
of great price, a faithful woman, one who was
to be trusted—who loved him.   He would not
give up his Nelly—not if the whole peerage put
together came and asked him.   And then he
again reckoned up how many hours there were
till they would be man and wife for ever.   Berty
and his true love had settled that it would be
wiser for him to keep out of the way for a few

days; but still, he thought he might just run down for an hour to Bill Somebody's—where he had spent many an evening in old days—and have a turn with the gloves, and see a few rats killed—just to brace his nerves. There, it happened that he fell in with one or two men he knew, and was persuaded by them to dine somewhere; after which, they kept going about, and Berty never remembered exactly how that night was spent. Accordingly, Frank Kerseytor was the first to wake him on his wedding morning. It was a quiet little two-storeyed house where Berty had taken lodgings, and the good people there looked on him with awe and wonderment, as a mythical young swell, whom they never could be certain of not offending. There was a brougham waiting at the door for Captain Newmarch already, and Frank, descending from his hansom with an imperial presence, impressed those householders still further. And then he had kept the cab waiting for him, instead of disputing about the fare, and taking refuge in doors as some did.

It was past ten o'clock, and Berty slept still—his head thrown back and his mouth half open. His was a heavy, senseless sleep, as if he had been struck down and left there in a stupor. 'How old and shattered he looks,' thought

Frank. ' I've half a mind to leave him there—
and go and marry the girl myself, or give the
cabby a fiver to do it. Can't one get the little
idiot out of it, somehow?'

But then, he had rather a curiosity to see this
marvellous performance to the end. A stupendous piece of folly, such as this, is not to be met
with every day; it interested him; and, though
his sentiments were so noble, it must not be supposed that Frank loved good for its own sake.
"Get up!" says he, shaking Berty. "The
bishop's downstairs, waiting; and the reporters,
and everything."

Berty opened his eyes, and smiled on him.
For a moment, perhaps, he listened again for the
trumpets to sound for ' stables' outside. But,
quickly, he jumped out of bed, and into his bath.
" Tell me, if it's near ten?" he asked gently.

Frank pitied him. " Oh! I wish 'twas thir-
teen," said he. " I suppose any time will do up
to twelve: now that you've really staked the
money, and mean fighting."

Before many minutes the bridegroom and his
friend were on their way to Armageddon Villas.
Berty was silent enough still. " I've written out
one or two things I want you to see to, in this,"
he said, giving Frank a thick letter. " D'you

know, there was nobody I cared to ask to do anything for me, but yourself. There's some notes and
one or two things to pay, but not much, because
—I havn't got any money, Frank. But I'll pay
everybody by and bye. And put in a good word
for me, anywhere you can—will you, like a good
fellow? You have seen her, Frank, hav'n't you?"

"Me? oh! yes, often."

"But you don't know what an angel she is.
You *can't* know! Why, she sold everything she
had, to get me out of quod two days ago."

And then Frank noticed that Berty had not yet
got over the effects of the night before. "I wonder
what they'll keep house on for the future, then,"
he thought to himself. But he merely nodded
his head and looked out of window, more and
more curious about it all.

One of the younger Miss Vanes opened the
door for them : but to be sure, her name wasn't
Miss Vane at all. This one was so plain that she
kept to the rightful surname, and, indeed, was in
service at Denmark Hill. There was another
sister in the parlour, and she, too, was clumsy to
look at, and accustomed to wait on the beautiful
Nelly, and to be ordered about by her. Besides
the ugly and humble sisters, there was Nelly's
brother, a young man in the cabinet-making

trade, and he, it is to be supposed, looked on
the bridegroom and his friend with suspicion and
contempt; at all events, he never relaxed a
certain gloomy reserve of manner until the breakfast came. As for Nelly's mother, she had been
sitting upstairs for the last hour, dressed out in
silks and with her gloves on. And, thought Frank,
' Now, I've often heard that people wore rings
outside their gloves, but I never saw it before.'

However, he was introduced in due form ; and
when they had all examined him, they respected
him a good deal more than Berty, to whom they
were beginning to get used ; having almost learnt
to treat him familiarly. Then no doubt they all
knew the story of Nelly's taking him out of
prison with her own money. His imposing friend,
never seen before, was, on the contrary, still one
of the fabulous ones; and so big, and with such
grand manners.

But they might well be dressed out, and
anxious, and hurried that day. Was it not their
bread-winner who was going to be made a wife ?
And then who could tell what she might not be
able to do for them when she was married to a
real young gentleman. And now Nelly herself
appeared, very prettily dressed, and having
on a grand lace shawl which became her to
perfection, and which indeed had been lent

to her for this eventful day by Mrs. Ann Montgomery, who lived close by, and had lately been brought out, as an actress, on the stage. The idea of borrowing that shocking person's finery for so solemn an occasion had horrified Nelly's mother. But Nelly knew everybody, and by this time could borrow things *from* impropriety without being *of* it. So she wore the lace shawl, and looked as happy and quiet as a Sabbath school teacher, about to be rewarded with marriage at the end of a short story. If Frank had been capable of emotion he would have shewn it then. The way Nelly spoke, and her air of grace and sweetness, put those relatives of hers out of his head altogether. Nelly was beautiful on that day; her skin was of that dead white which people attempt to imitate, and her dark eyes being set in a pale face, had even more than fair play. She looked twice as clever as she was, and she held her head and walked somewhat indeed, like an empress.

To Frank it was hardly possible that this could be the same Nelly Vane whom he used to think so little of; it must have been the paint she wore behind the foot-lights that had spoilt her hitherto. And now he could better understand Berty's infatuation. And then she was clever, no doubt; and then the boy here hadn't yet

learned that a pretty face is only bitterness afterwards—to Dead Sea apples, Frank may perhaps
have likened it; probably he put it more roughly.

When Nelly was ready, they drove to the
Registrar's. It is easy to be married. In fact,
the very same evening that Berty drove home
with his darling frcm the sponging house, he
went with Nelly and her mother to the district
superintendent and got the license. It is rather
a pleasant thing to be asked for a license, and
so the superintendent gave it to them, late as it
was. Nelly wrote her name as best she could;
it was not a pretty name—Sarah Ann Lukin
—and then Mrs. Lukin had signified consent,
her child being under age. After that one clear
day must intervene; nothing more was required.

Therefore it took only about three minutes
to make Berty Newmarch and Sarah Ann—as
above—husband and wife. Frank was one of
the witnesses, and a young man who hardly
deigned to take his fine meerschaum pipe out of
his mouth, another. Then the securely married
pair walked out into the street again. There the
winter's sun was shining brightly to welcome
them, and a knot of small boys gathered round
the brougham which carried Berty and his bride
back again. Frank gravely handed Mrs. Lukin
and the humble sister into the other carriage,

which at once followed the happy couple.   If
possible, the elder lady was more grim and unap-
proachable on the return journey than she had
been before.   Perhaps she was looking on Mr.
Kerseytor with an eye to her second daughter's
peace of mind.   The poor girl, though, was really
wondering at the great difference which steady
washing that morning had made in her mamma's
face.   Frank was a little oppressed by the dread-
fulnesss of those people.   He couldn't shake
off a feeling—as if he had just been married
among them himself—and as if it were all over
now and repented of, and he were taking his
unpresentable bride back with him to show the
world.   And yet, murdering one's relations, in
certain cases, is still unrecognised by the law !
" Had he ever been on a visit to Mr. Newmarch's
estates ?" Mrs. Lukin asked.

" Yes ; I've been there," said Frank, collecting his ideas with an effort.   " It's a nice place
—lots of dogs, and hens, and cats, and birds,
and pigs, and things to eat; and then, within
five minutes' walk of a railway station, and
eligible sea bathing, and that sort of thing."

Miss Lukin said, " Lord !" or " Lor !" rather ;
thinking he was chaffing them.

"They entertain in a princely way, I presume ?"
said the mother.

"Yes; I always went," said Frank. "You paid for nothing, and they gave you two suits of clothes if you stayed over a month."

But it was poor work, mystifying them; and the awful woman might, at any moment, detect him, and begin beating somebody.

They sat down to breakfast the instant they got back. It, perhaps, had been a supper somewhere a few nights before; and Frank was sure he had seen most of it in the pastry-cook's window when walking away from that neighbourhood recently. He never had felt less hungry. There was plenty of champagne, though, and a man to hand it about. Berty was thinking of nothing but his bride; and Nelly and he kept looking at each other and talking in whispers, at their own end of the table. Mrs. L. was in terror lest all the best things should be used up and wasted, and the son had begun at once on the champagne. He was determined that the fun should not flag, and hence was soon chaffing the waiter at a merry rate. The man had a certain awe of Frank, and tried to keep up appearances for a while; but by and bye he answered back, and Mr. L. insisted on his drinking glass for glass with him.

'What was his opinion of these strikes which were just coming on?' Frank asked wearily, on

the chance, indeed, of interrupting the noise
they were making.

Berty heard that, and looked up reproachfully
at his friend.

"Trays unions?" said Mr. Matthew Lukin.
"What you think's going to win the Derby, old
fellah? That's more in my line. Jeames—John
Thomas; bring the sparkling wine, I say."

"You ain't drinking anything all this time,
though," said Frank, meekly. "And you're not
enjoying your meals, I'm afraid, Miss Lukin."

"Maryhann eats very 'earty, thank you, sir,"
answered the mother for her. She did not like
that Mat should slaughter the champagne.
"Mat!" she called out, nodding towards the
bridegroom, "propose 'is 'ealth."

"What 'iz?" said Mat, with a loud laugh,
waiving his glass contemptuously towards Frank.

"'Ers, mamma—'ers first," suggested Mary
Anne.

"Them both, stoopid," whispered the youngest
sister.

"'Ere, fill the ladies' glasses, John," the son
called out. "What'll your beverage be, Mrs.
L.?"

"Ah! Matthew, stout's my drink, and well
you knows it; but go on, waiter; go on," said
Berty Newmarch's mother-in-law, with a coy

glance at the man who was replenishing her glass.

Then Mat got up, after rattling the table with his fist. He wanted to make a joke. " Unaccustomed as I am to public speaking," he began ; then he burst out laughing. " 'Ear, 'ear," whispered his ally, the waiter. " Tell us what to say, old fellah," said Mat to him ; and then commenced laughing gaily again. It was very wretched work for one just entering the family to have to sit out.

Frank watched them curiously. Then Berty rose to go with his wife. He seemed impatient to be rid of his relations. Probably Nelly persuaded him that she abhorred the scene just as much as he did. In a few minutes they had driven away. Thought Frank—' He didn't even tell me where he was going.' Mr. Mat was shouting to him to come back and return thanks for the ladies. " Call me a hansom," said Frank to the waiter, who instantly got sober at the prospect of a shilling. And as soon as he was on his way, Frank took out Berty's letter. " Now let's see what he wants of me. I should think to make his adieus at the corner, principally. Well, he's another—clean gone, if ever a man was. Poor little Chubby Newmarch ! !"

END OF VOL. II.

T. C. NEWBY, 30, Welbeck Street, Cavendish Square, London.

www.ingramcontent.com/pod-product-compliance
Lightning Source LLC
Chambersburg PA
CBHW060529030726
47498CB00004B/1131